PRAISE FOR *THE VILLAGE HEALER'S BOOK OF CURES*

"A stunning achievement in historical fiction. *The Village Healer's Book of Cures* is by turns a work of luminous beauty and a harrowingly dark exploration of the perilous role cunning women played in a society rife with suspicion. Mary Fawcett is an unforgettable heroine, and Roberts's nimble prose enchants with its honesty. An exquisite, wise, and ambitious debut."

—**Paulette Kennedy, author of *The Witch of Tin Mountain***

"A firecracker of a debut, packed with well-researched historical details, a tense mystery, and a few twists I never saw coming. Mary—a strong, independent woman trapped in a gender-centric panic—is the perfect character to take the reader on a perilous journey . . . one that could almost happen today."

—**Olivia Hawker, bestselling author of *The Fire and the Ore***

THE VILLAGE HEALER'S BOOK OF CURES

THE VILLAGE HEALER'S BOOK OF CURES

JENNIFER SHERMAN ROBERTS

LAKE UNION
PUBLISHING

Text copyright © 2023 by Jennifer Sherman Roberts
All rights reserved.

Published by Lake Union Publishing, Seattle

www.apub.com

Amazon, the Amazon logo, and Lake Union Publishing are trademarks of Amazon.com, Inc., or its affiliates.

ISBN-13: 9781662511769 (paperback)
ISBN-13: 9781662511752 (digital)

Cover design by Cassie Gonzales
Cover image: © Polina Bottalova / Alamy; © RachenStocker / Shutterstock;
© X-Poser / Shutterstock

Printed in the United States of America

To Tim, my sun and moon, and to Lucy and Miriam,
the brightest stars in my firmament

I have—
Together with my practice—made familiar
To me and to my aid the blest infusions
That dwell in vegetives, in metals, stones;
And can speak of the disturbances
That nature works, and of her cures; which doth give me
A more content in course of true delight
Than to be thirsty after tottering honour

—From *Pericles*, William
Shakespeare

CHAPTER 1

The way how to distill a pig, good for those that are weak
and faint and yet not sick

*Take a pig of twelve days old or thereabouts being scalded
and washed, and take the four quarters and the feet
thereof and wash them in a pint of white wine, one after
another, and let them soak a little in the wine . . .*

August 1646

She could still see the pig when she closed her eyes, still hear its pained,
high-pitched squealing when she clapped her hands over her ears. He
was splayed on the rough wood foundation of the gallows, sitting squat
like a man on his haunches, his hind legs covered in a filthy pair of
child's breeches. A blue coat stretched from his back to the ends of his
hooves, pulling his forelegs into a shallow triangle. Around his neck
hung a scroll delineating his crimes.

The pig belonged to Mr. Grandley. He had been a good pig,
Grandley told the judge, docile as pigs go and fattening up nicely—
until the night the witches came. Grandley had heard the pig squealing,
witnessed him dancing a jig and then running off to the woods to join

the invisible witches in their unholy Sabbath. The next night, when Mr. and Mrs. Smith's youngest babe was found dead, his little neck snapped, Grandley knew it was his pig to blame.

Grandley did not balk at offering up his hog to be punished for the murder. It would cost him dearly, but justice had to be served. He went to the magistrate with the pig on a leash.

The trial of Grandley's pig was all the village of Bicknacre had talked about for weeks, even eclipsing whispers of the king's surrender to the Scottish army some months earlier. Young Mrs. Smith told the assembled crowd about leaving her newborn son in his cradle, the dog protecting him, while she went to the back of the house for some wood for the fire and a chat with her neighbor, then testified that she came inside to find her precious babe awash in a pool of blood, the dog nowhere to be found, the smells of pig and sulfur permeating the room.

Mary had paid little attention to the trial at first. She had her doubts about the pig's guilt, having seen the Smiths' dog viciously harassing sheep just one week earlier. The dog had been fierce, unhinged. Maybe rabid. But Mr. Grandley was adamant about the witches, and the townspeople were convinced. Mary was dismayed by the whole affair. None of it made sense to her. She had lived in Bicknacre her whole life and been a healer, a cunning woman, as the villagers called her, for years. Her skill mostly involved cures for the body, but she had other remedies, too: lavender, for example, calmed the uneasy mind, and borage often soothed a broken heart. She had seen strange and wonderful things arise from her healing and her charms, but never had she witnessed anything that stretched the limits of her credulity as this had.

Some of the townsfolk in Bicknacre, those with a more skeptical bent, had objected—the pig could not have run from Grandley's pen to the Smiths' cottage with enough time to kill the baby, they argued, and thus the pig should be acquitted of all charges. Others pointed out that another of Grandley's pigs had been killed, and the piglets standing nearby were stained with blood. Had they colluded? It was all too suspicious. They had best be safe and put the piglets on trial, too.

Due to their tender age, however, the piglets were granted clemency.

In the end, Grandley's pig was convicted of the murder of young John Smith, aged one month, and given the sentence of death on the gallows, the same gallows Mary now walked away from, though her heart ached. She knew she could alleviate some of the pig's pain with a simple touch. But her neighbors encircled the poor animal—neighbors who, she knew, whispered about her, stared at her suspiciously even as she cured their illnesses. She could not draw attention to herself or her young brother, Tom, could not risk their wrath and disdain. So instead, she set out on the long path to her little cottage on the outskirts of town, self-recrimination echoing through her head. She'd seen such terrible fear in the eyes of some of her neighbors—and a sick kind of joy in a few others—and it terrified her. The sensible part of her, the Mary who worked her fingers to the bone and did what needed to be done to keep Tom safe and secure, convinced her not to make a fuss for a pig destined for the slaughter.

Nevertheless, when she saw the poor creature sprawled on the gallows floor, jeered at and pelted with rotten vegetables, squealing in fear and pain, it was all she could do to keep walking, head down, minding her own business.

Most days, it wasn't the sore arms from stirring, or the headache from the acrid smells, or even the blistered fingers from plucking leaves that made Mary want to quit her herbs and her cookery. No, it was her aching heart as she felt the misery of those she healed.

That was how she did it so well, the secret behind the efficacy of her cures. Some of the village folks attributed her skill to the book of recipes she had inherited from the women in her family, each one adding and refining the recipes in turn—generations of her foremothers who had long been the subject of whispers and sidelong glances for their ability to alleviate the troubles of others.

Mary knew she owed much to the women who'd come before her, especially her own mother. She had precious memories of her mother reading the recipes to her, walking her through each step—how to bruise the rosemary leaves for a poultice good for cuts, or how to gently boil white wine and marshmallow for a sore throat. Mary could not remember her mother ever making the recipes for her neighbors, however. When she'd asked why, her mother stiffened and ground out an unintelligible curse. "When I was a younger woman, I did. But I refuse to accept scorn and suspicion as payment for my help."

The book held powerful recipes and knowledge, but it soon became clear that Mary brought something extra to her cures. From an early age, she had instinctively known what small acts made people and animals feel better. She would seek out the runt of the pigs' and sheep's litters and comfort them, coo at and calm them, pet, stroke, and cuddle the weakest of the creatures. With her attention, they thrived and, after a time, often rivaled their healthier brethren in weight and disposition.

With people, too, Mary could ease the pain of the ill or grief stricken when all hope was lost. She could think herself into the body of the sufferer, feel what humors were out of balance or what foul miasma had infused the blood. Before she made a preventive plague water for Mrs. Davies, Mary would remember the young mother's grief at the death of little Benjamin Davies, only three years old when he died from the kink, the whooping cough that racked his small body. And while she puzzled over how to heal young Peter Harrison's pustules, she imagined the embarrassment he felt when village youths ridiculed the pimples that lit his face on fire—then she cooked the potion that would relieve his pain and restore his dignity.

Some called it magic, and sometimes she even wondered if it was true, but that word didn't quite fit. She just felt what others felt and tried to heal them. It was her calling, but it was also her burden: to spend her days caring for her neighbors, curing their ills and soothing their hurts. She longed to have the time and space to explore her gift, to unfold its potential. Her mind burned with the fire of possibility, only to be quenched by the cold reality of her responsibilities. She feared she was turning into a bore and a drudge.

There was too much to do. She still needed to beat together the pigeon dung with the yolks of six eggs for Mr. Park's glaucoma, and the distilled plague water had been ready to bottle for quite some time. Plus, she had promised her teacher and friend. Agnes Shepherd, that she would deliver a balm for Mrs. Chamberlen's sore back along with a cordial for her cough.

She sighed and pushed a stray piece of hair behind her ear. She heaved the heavy iron pot onto the fire and went back to plucking leaves off the stems of yarrow branches.

"May I help you with that?"

A tall figure blocked the door. He was obscured by the shadows, but Mary recognized his high, thin voice immediately. She finished settling the pot onto the flames before turning around to greet her visitor.

"Good morning, Simon. How do you do?"

Tom, sitting on the floor of the kitchen, barely glanced up.

"Well enough, I thank you," Simon replied with a quick glance and a blush before staring at his feet.

She swallowed a sigh of impatience. Most of the time, she considered Simon's visits a welcome interruption to the mundane labor of her days. And when she was honest with herself, she admitted that she simply liked being around a man again. Her bed had been cold in the five years since her husband had died, and she wondered if Simon was the kind of man who could fill it.

Today, however, she was busy.

"Is there something I can help you with?" she asked pointedly.

"Oh, yes." Simon reached into the pocket of his jacket. He pulled out a small folded piece of paper.

"A note from my sister." He passed it to her. "Verity is not feeling well."

As Mary unfolded the note, Simon bent down to speak with Tom.

"What have you there, young man?" he asked, pointing to the blocks Tom had used to erect intricate buildings complete with tunnels and turrets.

Tom thought for a moment, and an impish look settled on his face. "Hedgehogs."

"Young Tom, those are not hedgehogs." A note of reprimand entered Simon's voice. "They are blocks. See, they have four sides and are made of wood."

"They are hedgehogs," Tom countered.

"Do you know what a hedgehog is, Tom?"

"Yes."

"Then you know that a hedgehog is a small animal with prickles."

"Yes."

"Then you know that these are blocks and not hedgehogs."

"No. They are blocky hedgehogs."

Mary suppressed a chuckle at the belligerent look on Tom's face. Simon sighed and offered a hand to Tom, which he ignored as he scrambled to stand on his own, a complicated choreography of hands and elbows and the corner edge of the table to accommodate his clubfoot.

Tom would accept help from no hand but Mary's.

Tom left the house and was greeted by the large black crow that lived in the oak tree just outside their front door. The bird had settled there after she and Tom had saved him from a group of older boys—his wing had been bent, and the boys were taunting him and throwing rocks and sticks at him while he furiously tried to hop away. Mary and Tom had bandaged his wing and tended to him until he was capable of flight. And though he did fly away, he never failed to return. Tom named him Greedyguts for his voracious appetite.

Through the open door, Mary could see the crow playing with Tom, hopping ahead, letting Tom come within inches of catching him, and then flying to the nearby tree. It was one of his favorite pastimes, second only to a useful sort of game they'd taught him to play in which he'd carry little household items back and forth between Mary and Tom—but only provided he was rewarded with a berry at each turn.

She remembered the note from Simon's sister.

To Mistress Fawcett, she read, *I beg of you a cure for the pain caused by my monthly time. I cannot bear the pain in my stomach. Yrs., etc. Verity Martin.*

Mary went to the shelves holding her medicines and located the right cordial, a mixture of herbs and wine with powdered ginger and fennel that would give young Verity relief from her monthly pains.

She'd mixed it while she herself felt the great dull ache in her own belly that occasionally sharpened into a breathtaking stab of pain when she was in her courses. Her cures were more efficacious when blended at this time, as though her own pain were one of the ingredients.

Mary turned back to Simon. He stared at the bottles lining the walls of Mary's kitchen.

"Have you heard?" he asked with a note of eagerness. "There's a new arrival in town."

She would need to write new instructions for Verity, she recalled—the ginger she'd used in this batch seemed much weaker than it had in the past.

Simon followed her, walking to the other side of the table to hold her attention. "His name is Matthew Hopkins."

Mary sat to write her note and gave him a blank look. The name sounded familiar, but she needed to focus on her work.

Simon sighed. "The new person in town," he repeated, a hint of annoyance in his voice. "And you'll never guess what he is!"

"Is that so?"

"He is a witchfinder!"

Mary froze. No wonder the name sounded familiar. She had heard stories in the last couple of years of a self-styled "Witchfinder General," a man who'd made it his mission to eradicate witchery from Essex. In Chelmsford alone, he was responsible for the execution of almost twenty souls. He claimed they'd had intimate relations with the devil, sold their souls to various imps and familiars, and wreaked havoc on their neighbors' crops and herds.

The village had seen a few witchfinders before. They tended to be unimpressive men, mostly just listening to the complaints of the villagers, tormenting one or two lonely old women, and pocketing some coins on their way out of town. But Matthew Hopkins was different. He claimed that Parliament had specifically selected him to ferret out witches, and from the rumors she'd heard, he did his job with great zeal and religious fervor. His relationship with Parliament gave him a certain gravitas as he went about his terrible work. The Parliament's power was growing, and even out in Bicknacre they heard rumors of more war and strife in London. They were living in terrible times, and though the rhythms of work and worry and the rituals of birth and death and marriage persevered in Bicknacre, Mary feared that the unthinkable banishment of the king could lead to a purging of all the old ways.

Simon's voice rose in awe. "He is a very clever man, said to be an expert in the signs of the maleficium and the habits of witches and the various creatures—the cats and birds and vermin—they use as familiars."

"Hmmm," she replied. She rose from the table and crossed the room to close the door on Tom and Greedyguts—she'd rather her brother not hear these rumors. "And has he had success?"

"Oh, he has indeed. The village of Ipswich has even raised a tax just to have him visit. Imagine the devilish evil he could purge from our own countryside!"

Mary ignored the icy prickles of fear that skittered down her spine at Simon's enthusiasm for witchfinding.

"Imagine," she replied. She held out the small bottle. "Please give this to your sister."

"What's in it?" he asked, looking at the vial with some curiosity.

"It's a simple cordial," she said vaguely. She was sure Verity would not want her brother to know about her monthly cycle. "She writes that she is feeling lethargic. This will raise her spirits."

Simon reached for the vial. As he took the bottle, he allowed his fingers to linger on hers and then clasped her hand in his. She was surprised how bony his hand felt.

"Mary," Simon whispered.

"Simon, I have work to do. I must deliver medicine to Mrs. Chamberlen. I haven't time for—"

Greedyguts's caws got louder as the door opened. "Why are you holding my sister's hand?" Tom stood at the door staring at them, hands on hips, outraged.

Simon sputtered and blushed. "It's nothing, young Tom. I was . . . merely holding the bottle. It was about to slip."

"Why did you keep looking at her, then?" Tom now stomped his foot.

Simon turned toward him. "Children should not ask such questions of their elders. It is impertinent."

Tom merely cocked his head. "Why should I be a pert'nent?" he asked. "You are the one staring at my sister."

Simon turned toward her again, and his eyes softened.

"Mary, I thank you and my sister thanks you for your help. We will add the cost of this cordial to our payment next week." Simon smiled at Mary and exited the small house.

As soon as Simon walked through the door to the yard, he startled, and Mary heard a riot of noise from the large bush to the side of her cottage. She smiled to herself. Greedyguts was cawing at Simon, furious at his intrusion.

"That bird is a fierce protector," she said quietly.

Simon squared his shoulders and attempted a calm, measured pace as the raucous crow followed him down the path. He surreptitiously kept an eye on the dark shadow darting about overhead. Truth be told, Mary couldn't blame Simon for his skittishness. There was something uncanny about the bird, an intelligence about his one dark, piercing eye. When Greedyguts stared at a person, they felt stripped bare, brought to account. She'd seen it before, when the bird followed Tom to the village and watched over him with his one eye cocked to the side, threatening but still protective. And his cawing could wake the dead.

Greedyguts continued his shrill calls as Simon walked away. Mary gathered together a few bundles and called to Tom to get ready. She had her deliveries to make, and her friend, Mrs. Woods, had offered to watch her brother. Tom walked with her as she left the house and went down the path, his limp somehow more pronounced. He stopped and bent down to pat Greedyguts on the head and give him some seeds.

"Good bird," he said softly. "Good bird."

CHAPTER 2

A medicine for those that have lost their speech, either by sickness, fear, or otherwise

Take a primrose root, scrape it clean, then take a slice of the inner part of it, of a good thickness, and put it under the party's tongue, then anoint the noddle of his head, the nape of his neck and about his ears, and jaws, with the ointment for the palsy . . .

The path to Chamberlen Manor wound through common fields and sheep pastures and past ancient oaks she had known since she was a girl. She loved this walk, loved taking off her shoes and feeling the soft grass between her toes. Whenever she was freed from chores, she came here, relishing the chance to study life above and below. She'd wander the hedgerows and lie in the long grass, wondering what made the sky blue and the clouds white, admiring the grace of the damselfly and the speed of the hummingbird. Then she'd dig into the dirt below, counting the worms and marveling at the cunning armor of the wood louse.

The Chamberlens were wealthy beyond what Mary could imagine, rich enough to maintain a manor house in Bicknacre and a house in London, with servants. She slowed as she approached Chamberlen

Manor and allowed herself to admire it anew. The mottled-gray stone of the building gleamed in the afternoon light, and a well-manicured lawn set off its stately elegance. The manor calmed Mary, assured her that there was order and beauty in the dreariness of the workaday world.

Mary went around the house directly to the kitchen. She breathed in the scents of bread and freshly roasted duck. Her stomach growled. It had been some time since she and Tom had eaten anything other than porridge and salad gleaned from her garden.

She found the cook, Mrs. Thomas, deeply involved in carving radishes into intricate little roses. Mary stood, transfixed, watching the cook's nimble hands deftly transform vegetable into flower. It was a practical kind of magic.

Mrs. Thomas looked up from her handiwork and smiled broadly. She motioned Mary to come farther into the kitchen.

"Why, Mary, welcome! Thank you for bringing the mistress her medicines."

Mary set the medicines on the pocked wood of the table, but Mrs. Thomas picked them back up and handed them to her. "Mrs. Chamberlen would like to speak with you this time. She is in her chamber." Her eyes grew concerned. "She does not leave it much anymore, poor lamb. Betsy will show you the way."

Usually Mary communicated with Mrs. Chamberlen by note and the payment came later, delivered to her cottage by a kitchen maid or stable hand. She had only spoken with the woman a few times. Mrs. Chamberlen had to be cautious in her communications with Mary and Agnes—her husband would sneer at her reliance on a mere cunning woman rather than the London doctors and apothecaries he preferred.

Mary followed Betsy out of the kitchen and through a labyrinthine passage of halls and stairs to Mrs. Chamberlen's rooms. An intricate tapestry dominated the small sitting area, the rich threads intertwining to depict a unicorn gleaming in the moonlight, its head resting on the bosom of a virgin. Behind the dyad a knight stood ready to plunge a spear into the unicorn's flank, and above them all hovered a glowing phoenix, caught in the moment of its resurrection from the ashes of its own death. Mary thought it a strange piece, but she didn't have experience with these sorts of rich and glorious things. She slowed her pace, transfixed by the tapestry's glowing colors and fine details. Betsy urged her along, motioning her into Mrs. Chamberlen's rooms and clearing away an untouched breakfast tray.

"The mistress is lying down in the chamber beyond that next door," Betsy whispered. "She is in a tender mood today."

Mary knocked gently on the door and announced herself.

"Enter."

Mary could barely hear the feeble voice.

Thick curtains darkened the room, but Mary could still make out a figure reclined on several feather mattresses stacked together, looking like a prisoner guarded by the four towering posts of the bed. Mrs. Chamberlen lay propped up by several pillows, but her head lolled to the side until Mary came closer and she mustered enough energy to sit up and look at her visitor.

Mary smothered a gasp. Gone was the elegant woman whose stateliness Mary had long admired. She had often thought of Mrs. Chamberlen as her polar opposite. Where Mary was small and rounded, Mrs. Chamberlen was tall, thin, and elegant. Where Mary had thick, dark locks that fought to curl out of pins and caps, Mrs. Chamberlen had obedient blond hair that stayed in place. And where Mary walked with hurry and purpose, Mrs. Chamberlen had the grace of a woman with no worries to rush her along.

The woman in front of Mary now, however, was pale as death, with dark smudges staining the skin below her eyes and an alarmingly thin face. Mary had seen many people at death's door. She knew the look.

"Is that you, Mary Fawcett?" The lady's voice shook.

"Mrs. Chamberlen, I've brought the salve for your back and an extra cordial for your cough." Mary tried to keep the shock from her voice.

Mrs. Chamberlen nodded at the table near her bed. "You can set them over there," she managed to whisper.

Mary went to place the small leather pouch containing the cordial and salve on the table, but as she approached the bed, she grew even more shocked at the other woman's pallor. She took a deep breath.

"Madam," she said gently, "you don't look well."

Mrs. Chamberlen turned her head slowly. "No, Mary, I'm quite sick indeed."

Mary took her limp hand without asking. The sickbed was no place to defer to social strictures. This woman needed human touch.

Mrs. Chamberlen squeezed Mary's hand. "You are well versed in medicinals. Your concoctions have always brought me relief, more so than even Agnes Shepherd's. You have a great gift. I need to call on your expertise. Do you see the bottle on that writing desk by the window?"

Mary nodded. The thin hand in her grasp shook ever so delicately.

"Smell it."

Mary looked up in some confusion.

"Just do it," she commanded, a note of desperation in her voice. "Please!"

Mary walked over to the desk, on which perched a glass bottle with no markings. As she picked up the bottle, she saw it sat on a note carelessly folded in half. Shifting her body so that Mrs. Chamberlen wouldn't see, she surreptitiously flipped open the rough paper.

The writing was childish, poorly formed. *Give this to her daily,* the note read. *It will do the job well. If she does not . . .*

"Mary?" Mrs. Chamberlen called out in a plaintive voice. "Did you find it?"

Mary hurriedly folded the note and turned toward the bed with the bottle, giving a little tug at the stopper. She sniffed at the lip, gave Mrs. Chamberlen a look of horror, and sniffed again. It had a sharp scent, like grass that had been cut and left to rot. She had smelled it before—some called it Christmas rose, but her recipes called it hellebore. It eased gout and forced purgation. But it was to be used very carefully—in excess, it was dangerous, even deadly.

13

"You cannot continue to ingest this liquor, madam," Mary said. "This may kill you."

Mrs. Chamberlen simply shrugged. "My husband says I must take it, that it will help me to conceive a child. And since that is all we women are good for in this world, it is my duty."

"If you conceive, this could kill the babe. Will you take that risk?"

Mary would not learn the answer. A loud scream pierced the air, and Mrs. Chamberlen's eyes went wide with surprise.

Mary dropped the bottle and ran to the door to find Betsy, her eyes wild. She grabbed Mary's arm and tugged her into the hallway.

"Mrs. Chamberlen cannot know!" she panted.

Mary grabbed the woman's shoulders and looked her directly in the eye. "Breathe," she ordered. "Calm down. What's happened?"

Betsy gasped for air and only just managed to whisper, "It's Mr. Chamberlen. Mrs. Fawcett, he's dead."

Mary had seen dead men before. She had helped her neighbors prepare their fathers, brothers, and husbands for burial.

But she had never seen a murdered man before.

And she had no doubt that was what lay before her.

A massive carved oak bed dominated the room, and in the middle lay the lifeless corpse of Henry Chamberlen, naked, covered only in a linen sheet. His neatly trimmed beard was matted and rank from vomit. There was no purpling or bruising, and Mary might have thought he was merely unconscious if it weren't for the unnatural bend of his arms and legs and the glassy eyes staring into oblivion.

Mary forced herself over to the bed and felt for a pulse, knowing she would find none but compelled to check.

Nothing.

The bile rose in her throat. She knew death, but this was something more. This was evil.

She turned to Betsy. "Send someone for the constable. Now."

Mary stayed in the kitchen until Mr. Franklin, the constable, arrived. She was unsure whether her testimony would be needed. She thought she'd wait to see if Betsy fetched her and was surprised when Mr. Franklin himself walked into the kitchen.

"Mrs. Fawcett, you have a great understanding of medicinals and potions, do you not?"

Mary nodded. "I do, sir."

"And poisons?"

Mary's heart stilled. Such an admission could be dangerous, especially with a witchfinder in town.

"Sir, I do not teach myself how to use poisons, only how to purge them and to avoid using good medicines in poisonous ways."

Mr. Franklin sighed. "I understand. But I know nothing of either medicine or poison. Will you do me the favor of examining him?"

Mary and Mrs. Thomas exchanged nervous glances.

"Certainly, sir."

Mr. Franklin led Mary into Mr. Chamberlen's bedroom. It was decorated in rich reds and golds, opulent and decadent. Much like the man himself, Mary thought.

Mr. Franklin handed her a piece of paper. "The servants found this note. The handwriting matches Mr. Chamberlen's."

Mary took the proffered note with trembling hands. How strange to read the writing of a man who'd been alive only hours before.

I have lived a sinful life, and my misdeeds overwhelm me, the note read. *God will never accept me into His bosom on my death, so I choose to end my suffering now.*

Mr. Franklin took the letter back with a grimace. "From what I have heard of the man, this is not far from the truth."

Mary, too, knew something of Mr. Chamberlen and his misdeeds. He was breathtakingly handsome—when he walked through town, every eye followed him, and on the few times he attended church, the reverend struggled to keep the congregation's attention on the sermon. But it wasn't just his looks or his wealth that made him stand apart. He had a charisma that Mary had never encountered before, and though her experience of the world was small, she felt sure this strange magnetism was unique. And Mary also knew that Chamberlen used his charm to get whatever he wanted—his reputation for catting around was legendary.

Mustering her courage, Mary approached the bed and peeled back the coverlet. She hoped the constable could not see her blush when she saw Mr. Chamberlen's nakedness, but what she saw eclipsed any maidenly modesty.

The dead man's abdomen was a canvas of scars, scratches, and inked designs. Some were white and deep, indicating they'd been carved into his skin long ago. Others were more recent—reddish and light pink—and some lines looked like they had recently been applied. The marks were clearly intentional, as they seemed to form strange symbols and glyphs.

"Not all of those marks are new," the constable whispered. "Some look like they've been there a long while."

Fascinated in spite of herself, Mary bent forward to get a better look at the symbols limned out on Mr. Chamberlen's abdomen. At precise angles around his navel, combinations of strange symbols made up circles, triangles, and arrows. It looked like an ancient foreign language, the structure apparent but the meaning just out of her grasp. Drawn to the bizarre symbols, she would have liked to examine them further, but she was acutely aware of the constable watching her.

Mary shifted her attention to Chamberlen's hands. They were covered in a green, gelatinous substance starting to harden.

"Betsy," she called out. "Would you get me some soap and water?"

Mary cleaned Chamberlen's hands while Mr. Franklin looked on with interest. She spied a series of fierce rashes and pointed them out to the constable. Mary could not say who had killed Mr. Chamberlen, but she could say what had: the same poison he had been giving Mrs. Chamberlen. The signs—and the smell of rotted grass—all pointed to it.

And further: the rashes on his hands showed he had handled it before ingesting.

Mary heard a ruckus. As the constable hurried to the door, she worked on cleaning the corpse's finger joints. With a sort of pop, Chamberlen's hand opened and, to Mary's shock, a small object fell out.

She was about to call Mr. Franklin over to view her discovery when she saw Simon at the door with two men she didn't recognize. The first was tall and wide, a great brute of a man with a bored look on his face. Mary couldn't fathom how a person could seem detached in the midst of such a scene.

The second man, though, looked entirely different—his eyes burned with intensity as they took in every detail in the room and finally settled on her. He was a slight man but for an exaggerated paunch at his belly. He dressed formally and seemed well groomed, if a little sweaty. She'd have passed him on the street without notice—except for those feverish eyes.

Mary felt an overwhelming urge to run, and out of some deep instinct, she put the token in her pocket.

"What are you gentlemen doing here?" the constable demanded.

Simon blushed. "Mrs. Thomas told us what happened. I wanted to leave you to it, but . . . Well, this is Matthew Hopkins, the new witchfinder in town." He pointed to the man with the keen stare. "I was bringing him to see Mr. Chamberlen at his request. And this is Mr. Stearne, his assistant."

Matthew Hopkins drew himself up tall. "I was called to purge Bicknacre of witchcraft, so it was essential I meet the most powerful man in town. I am no ordinary witchfinder. I am the Witchfinder General, and by the authority of Parliament, I demand to know what has happened here so that I may determine whether witchcraft was in some way involved."

Hopkins pushed himself past the constable. "Is this the body of Mr. Chamberlen?"

"I don't see any other corpses here," Mary replied.

Hopkins's head swiveled her way, and he looked her up and down, leisurely, with a leer that made her clench her jaw tight. "Simon, who is this wench?"

Mr. Franklin replied instead. "This is Mary Fawcett, and she's a well-respected friend and neighbor in this town. I'd advise you to watch your mouth."

Hopkins stared a few moments but gave a dismissive snort and moved toward the bed. He pushed Mary out of the way.

"Is this where he was discovered? Was he naked when he was found? Was that window closed? Were there any unfamiliar people or strange animals seen in the house this day? Any portents or omens? Foul smells, like sulfur or shit?"

The constable tried to answer Hopkins's questions, which kept coming. Hopkins asked about Mr. Chamberlen's habits and whether he had any pets that had been behaving strangely. He even asked if anybody had seen any dolls in the room or if there had been reports of him pissing milk or blood. Mary knew, even if the constable didn't, that the questions all pertained to the dark arts.

Despite all his probing questions, however, Hopkins did not bother to actually examine the corpse.

Mary lost patience waiting for the questioning to end. She gathered her cloak. "Mr. Franklin, I believe Mr. Chamberlen was poisoned with hellebore. I know not whether it was by his hand or another's. He has clearly been vomiting, and the distinctive burns on his hands arise from contact with the plant. And now, since Mr. Hopkins is here, I believe it is time for me to leave."

Hopkins turned to her as she exited the room. In an oily voice, he commanded, "Do not go far, my dear. Do not go far."

Mary turned, trying to hide her trembling. "You have no authority over me."

Hopkins sneered and licked his lips. "We shall see."

CHAPTER 3

A special good drink for those that be given to melancholy
and weeping

*Take a quart of claret wine, put it into an earthen pip-
kin, add thereto half a pound of sugar, and so set it
upon a very soft fire, and when it doth boil, and is clean
skimmed, put thereto a quart of rosemary flowers, being
clean picked, and half an ounce of cinnamon and so let
them simmer softly together for the space of an hour, then
take it off, and when it is cold, put it into a glass altogether, and drink thereof, with a little claret wine after
meat, and when you go to bed. Note that if you do make
it of dried flowers, a pint will serve, to a quart of wine.*

Mary's return home took longer than expected, but she didn't think
Mrs. Woods would mind given the events of the day. She needed time
to think without work and worry and Tom pulling on her skirts.

She couldn't rid herself of visions of the dead man that kept pop-
ping into her head—his unseeing eyes, the unnatural cold that bit into
her own hand as she held his—but her mind also kept returning to the
problem of Mrs. Chamberlen. Mary marveled that the woman was

ready to perish by her husband's now-dead hand. She knew that bearing an heir mattered more to the rich than to regular folks like her. But at what cost? The poison had left Mrs. Chamberlen bereft of vitality, near to death. It was clear she was being poisoned. Had she believed that ingesting the poison would help her conceive a child? Or had her husband's lies robbed her of the will to live?

If that were so, Mary was stunned that the woman would risk death to have a child. But wasn't that what all mothers did? With each pregnancy, each childbirth, women risked their lives. Death hung over the birthing chamber like a storm cloud, set to rain down destruction on mother and babe. And even when both survived the hours of pain and fear, the specter of disease lingered. This she knew all too painfully. That horrible fact had destroyed her own dreams of being a mother, her marriage—and almost Mary herself.

She and her husband, Jack, had grown up together. Their mothers were dear friends, and it was just assumed that their children would marry. Neither Mary nor Jack was surprised to find themselves, at the tender age of seventeen, yoked to the other. It had been a good marriage. When her parents died, struck down by a devastating influenza that none of Mary's cures could defeat, Jack welcomed baby Tom into their home with open arms. Jack worked with his father raising sheep and selling the wool. He was every bit as attentive and funny a husband as he'd been a friend. They were content, and when, a year later, Mary gave birth to a baby girl, they were overjoyed.

But their good fortune did not hold.

At only a few days old, the babe stopped nursing and her tiny body trembled and became hot to the touch. Her breathing grew irregular, and her skin took on a bluish cast. Mary and Agnes tried every recipe they could in a desperate bid to return her to health. They took the freshest butter and infused it with mallet leaves, chamomile, and feverfew, then spread it from the roots of the baby's hair to the balls of her feet. They made a broth with agrimony and Roman wormwood and spooned it into her tiny, unresponsive mouth. They followed that drink with wine and oil boiled with Saint-John's-wort and then infused it with Venice turpentine, almond oil, dittander, gentian, tormentil, and *Calamus aromaticus.*

None of it worked.

After six weeks, though the baby breathed, she failed to respond to Mary's touch.

On the fiftieth day of their daughter's life, Mary and Jack buried Elizabeth Agnes Fawcett in the little churchyard next to her grandparents.

Through sobs that racked her body, and despite eyes tinder dry from weeping, Mary bruised elderberries and boiled them in cow's milk. She used the poultice to soothe her breasts, which ached with the milk her daughter could no longer drink.

Jack, who had stood by helplessly as Mary and Agnes worked feverishly to save the baby's life, grew despondent and resentful. He disappeared for hours at a time, and Mary heard tales of his carousing in town, keeping company with Bridget Jenkins, the butcher's daughter.

The day she witnessed his tryst with Bridget, Jack confessed and fell into Mary's arms.

She forgave him, but he seemed unable to forgive himself. He poured himself into helping his father, working out his demons in the honest, hard labor of tending to the flocks, shearing the sheep, mending the fences and buildings. Anything to forget his sins. He died only a few weeks later, exhausted by the long days of sheep slaughter at Martinmas, after falling off a mossy roof he was helping his father repair.

In the course of three months, Mary had lost her daughter and her husband. She'd walked through her days devastated, numb, lifeless. If it hadn't been for her baby brother, Tom, such a sweet and tender soul, she would have been sorely tempted to follow Jack and little Elizabeth Agnes to the grave. Grief did unthinkable things to a person.

No, she shouldn't judge Mrs. Chamberlen, but she must do something to help the woman. She was not yet beyond hope. The poison had left Mrs. Chamberlen frail, but something had glimmered in her eyes when she'd talked about the possibility of a child—a shimmer of life, of promise—that made Mary think she might survive. She would have to make a visit again soon.

Mary knew well the vital importance of that glimmer of purpose because Agnes had given it to her during her darkest days.

Mary had never believed the tales the villagers spread about Agnes. They said she was strange and vengeful, and whispered that her cures were unreliable, that they seemed to work only for small children and people Agnes particularly liked. Rumors circulated of a man who'd refused to sell Agnes herring out of spite—he'd died of a fearsome spasm the next week. And the townspeople blamed her when the only crops that withered that summer belonged to the Candlers, who had filed a complaint about Agnes's chickens escaping into their fields.

But Mary refused to listen to the rumors. A woman who lived alone, supporting herself with her own skills, whose parents had even taught her to read and write: such a woman was bound to be the subject of speculation. Certainly Agnes could be cantankerous, even rude, but her heart was gold, and something about her—a toughness, a strength of mind—reminded Mary of her own mother. When Jack died, it was Agnes Shepherd who coaxed her away from the corner of the kitchen, the corner where her baby had died, where Mary had curled herself into a tiny ball. It was Agnes who stayed with her when she was too heartsick to care for Tom. And, eventually, through sheer cussed stubbornness, it was Agnes who convinced Mary to take up her healing again, working together. She tried to convince Mary that she needed a partner, that she was getting old and tired. But Mary knew that Agnes—tough, pigheaded Agnes—would work until the day she died.

Mary poured her grief into her profession, and the work saved her. It set Mary's mind ablaze. As she cured her neighbors, she wrote down every method she tried, tracked every subtle change of ingredient or application, made notes on the pertinent details of each of her patients. Would a potion work better if she distilled *Carduus benedictus* before adding it to her plague water? Why was it that one poor soul suffering from the bloody flux fared better drinking rose water rather than pigeon blood boiled in wine, when the same treatment threw another into fits?

During this time, she learned an incredible amount, both from Agnes and from her own studies, but she yearned to learn more and to make a mark in the world.

Coming out of her reverie with a start, Mary wondered whether she still had the medicine she had intended to give Mrs. Chamberlen. If so, she would have an excellent reason to return and check on the woman. She reached into her apron for the leather pouch. She sighed—the bottles were gone. She would need to find another reason to return to Chamberlen Manor. But as she pulled back her hand, her fingers brushed something cold and metallic. She dug around a bit more and found the strange token that had fallen from Mr. Chamberlen's cold fist. She vaguely remembered slipping it into her pocket when Simon and Hopkins appeared.

Mary pinched the thick metal token between her fingers and studied it in the light. On one side there was a strange symbol—it almost looked like a small man squatting, but instead of eyes on the circle that represented his face, there was a single dot. It looked very much like the symbols she had seen in an old astrology chart, but she could not place it. The symbol on the other side of the token, however, was unfamiliar to her and fantastical: a bird with a long beak with drops falling from its chest into the mouths of three baby birds, their necks reaching up so realistically Mary could almost feel their hunger.

Mary wondered what she should do with the token. She knew she should give it back, but she feared the questions that would follow. Why had she taken the token? Why hadn't she said anything to the constable?

Why had she felt the need to steal the object away, to possess it? Mary asked herself. She didn't wonder for long. She knew the answer lay in that same deep hunger she brought to her healing work: the drive to know, the thrill of solving a deep and mysterious puzzle. Agnes had no patience for these sorts of questions. What worked, worked, she said, and it was arrogant to question the wisdom of the women who'd come before them, who'd compiled these treatments and charms. But Mary couldn't help but think about her foremothers who discovered these cures. Surely they felt this same driving ambition to know, to discover? The same impulse that led her to pocket the medallion?

Mary was so fascinated by the token that she failed to notice the man approaching her on the path until he was nearly in front of her. She quickly tucked it in her apron and felt into her bag for her knife when she realized with relief that she recognized him. It was Robert Sudbury, a man some five or so years her elder, who had moved to Bicknacre almost a year before. He was tall, and his gait was steady and sure on the uneven rocks. He was dressed simply, but his clothing was elegant and enhanced his dark curls and eyes. He was a handsome man, if one ignored the most startling thing about him: a ghastly red burn streaked across his face like a comet across the night sky.

Mary smiled. He did not reciprocate.

"Mistress Fawcett, how do you do?" Sudbury avoided her eyes.

She was surprised he knew her name.

"I am well, thank you." She felt a sort of thrill shoot through her. She could not help feeling deeply curious about the man standing in front of her.

His arrival had been the most intriguing thing to happen in Bicknacre in years. Not only had he taken residence in one of the town's most expensive houses, he had fine furniture and dishes delivered, together with mysterious equipment—casks and flasks and boxes and boxes of books. Packages arrived for him day and night.

Despite his disfigurement, Sudbury was still attractive enough—his obvious wealth more than making up for the scar—that the women of Bicknacre watched keenly for any opportunity to introduce themselves. But Robert Sudbury kept to himself, interacting with the villagers only as necessary. And the longer Sudbury stayed in town, the less desirous the townsfolk were of befriending him. After a short time, rumors began to swirl and got wilder by the day. Sudbury had been a scholar in Cambridge, the townsfolk whispered, but he had moved to Bicknacre because of the horrible accident that caused his scar. He was dabbling in some sort of dark magic, said others. The scar blazing across his face helped the rumors along, as some said it was the mark of the devil himself.

Mary smiled again, politely, and stepped aside to let him pass, but Sudbury slowed his pace as he approached.

They stood awkwardly for a few moments, Mary playing with the frayed threads on the cuff of her dress and Sudbury staring into the distance.

Mary shifted her feet. "I'm just returning from Mrs. Chamberlen's house," she said. "She was in need of a salve to ease her sore back." Mary blushed at her babbling. She didn't want to gossip about Chamberlen's death, so why did she bring up her visit?

Sudbury nodded and finally looked at her. "May I accompany you?" he asked.

She hesitated because she had been relishing her solitude. Still, she was curious about Sudbury, about the strange smoke and smells that issued from the chimney of his house. Some of those smells were familiar, especially the foul ones, as when she added pigeon dung to her eye ointment or urine to her treatment for the kink. Some she recognized but did not use herself, like sulfur. And then there were smells she hadn't encountered before. These especially sharpened her curiosity. She wanted to know if he did work like hers, and what she might learn from him.

>Jennifer Sherman Roberts

"My apologies, Mrs. Fawcett," Sudbury said as he noticed her hesitation. A chilly note entered his voice. "I can see you would rather not have my company." He turned to leave.

"You mistake me." Mary laid a hand on his arm to stop him. Sudbury froze.

He muttered something under his breath that Mary couldn't hear, and they turned down the path together. He cleared his throat. "I hear you have great skill with medicines."

"I have some practice, yes."

Sudbury nodded. "The people in the village say you are a sort of cunning woman. That you have a gift. They marvel at it."

Something in Sudbury's voice struck Mary as odd. It did not sound like praise but rather like a warning.

Mary hesitated. "Since I was a girl, I've wanted to help those in pain or distress. Mrs. Shepherd taught me how."

Sudbury glanced at her as they continued walking along the path. "And you do so with your recipes?"

Mary wondered at his interest. "Yes, usually. I am not good at charms, but I have a book of healing recipes handed down from my mother and her mother and grandmother before that—though they had to ask men to transcribe for them, so I've learned to trust my own experience in addition to what's written on the page. I've added to my collection over the years, both Mrs. Shepherd's recipes and my own."

Sudbury hesitated. "In some ways," he said, "your work and mine are very similar."

Mary's steps faltered at hearing her own thoughts echoed in his words. "How so?"

"I am sure you've heard rumors about me in the village. You must know that I'm interested in alchemy. In my art, we often use recipes of a sort to further our knowledge."

Mary knew of alchemy, of course. She didn't know what alchemists did, exactly, but she heard rumors of dark magic and natural

>26

philosophers who played with the secrets of nature. It was a murky, mysterious business.

"Are you also working on medicines?" she asked.

Sudbury shook his head. "I have been experimenting with academic . . . well, recipes, I suppose you could call them. Some are salutary and practical, but most are based on manuscripts I have discovered in my travels. They involve much distilling and cookery. It can be dangerous."

Mary nodded her head and gave him an uncertain smile. What an odd conversation, she thought. And yet it was gratifying, too. No suspicion darkened Sudbury's face, as it usually did with the village folk when she discussed her remedies at any length. Mary had long ago learned that while people were happy to benefit from her treatments, few wanted to delve too deeply into why they worked. Knowledge of such things was dangerous. The secrets of nature were far too close to the secrets of God Himself, a point Reverend Osborne frequently made from the pulpit since Sudbury's arrival in Bicknacre.

They stopped walking. Eager to break the awkward silence, Mary blurted out, "Is that how you got your burn?"

Barely realizing she was doing so, Mary reached out to touch the pitted scar that began on Sudbury's cheek and sprawled down his neck. "I know of an ointment made from the sap of aspen bark that would provide you relief."

As Mary's fingers grazed the mottled red of Sudbury's skin, a powerful sense of fear and anger and a white-hot burning sensation ran from Sudbury's cheek up her hand into her arm. She gasped and stepped back.

Sudbury jerked away, and his hand rose automatically to cover his cheek. A veil of mistrust dropped over his face. Gone was his look of open curiosity, replaced by pain and suspicion.

"I . . . I am sorry, sir," Mary said, her voice shaking. Never had she felt the suffering of another with such ferocity and immediacy. It usually took a moment or two for her to understand and feel the cause of another's pain, and this waiting period gave her a chance to adjust.

The connection with Sudbury, however, had happened straightaway, and she wasn't sure she liked it.

And what had possessed her to touch his face like that? She must be careful. He seemed a dangerous man to know.

"I must go now," he said. Mary thought she could hear a tremor in his voice. "I can't leave, however, without giving you the warning I came to convey."

She'd been right about the warning she had heard in his voice. Mary shivered. Sudbury noticed and his eyes grew even more pained.

"There's no threat, at least not from me. There's a new arrival in town. His name is Matthew Hopkins."

"I know of him."

"Yes, gossip travels quickly in Bicknacre. You've heard that he's a witchfinder, then?"

Mary nodded her head. The rest of her body was frozen in fear.

"The man's a fool and a fraud, but you need to be careful around him. He has more power and influence than most in his profession. Hopkins claims Parliament directed him to purge the country of the scourge of witchcraft, but that is a lie. He has nothing to do with Parliament, and they want nothing to do with him. He enters a village or town and uncovers their resentments and petty squabbles. Then he finds some poor, beleaguered souls to take the blame for all of the village's hard feelings. He has them arrested and thrown in prison, and then he questions them for days, tortures them until they confess to crimes they never committed, just to have their freedom. But not all walk free. Many are hanged."

"Sir, I will not believe that the people of Bicknacre would follow such a man, much less that they would suspect me of anything," Mary said, trying to keep her voice from shaking. "I've lived here all my life and have treated their illnesses and aided in their births and deaths."

She tried to sound certain of her fellow townsfolk, yet she couldn't help but wonder about those who'd been hanged for witchcraft in other villages, villages just like Bicknacre. Had they felt secure in their neighbors' support? Or had they also felt a sliver of uncertainty? She remembered Grandley's pig stretched out on the gallows, the villagers giddy with the drama. She remembered the near savagery with which they viewed the animal's punishment. Could she be so sure of her neighbors' friendship and goodness after all? Was there a chance they could turn on her, hold her in suspicion and condemn her as they had the pig?

Sudbury looked at her intently before answering. "It has happened before. You and Agnes Shepherd are exactly the type Hopkins targets—women who have no men to stand for them. Old maids, maidens, and widows. And cunning folk. Especially cunning folk. Too often these women find themselves dangling from a rope."

Sudbury paused and continued. "I, too, need to take precautions. I'm a student of natural philosophy, and those who uncover the secrets of nature are always under suspicion."

Mary was startled when Sudbury once again gave voice to her previous thoughts. Whether it was their shared bank of knowledge, the frightening events of the last few hours, or something about the man himself, Mary felt a pull to confide in him, to show him the token and ask if he knew anything about the symbols engraved on it.

Her hand moved to the pocket where she had hidden the token, but something stopped her, some intuition that the token was unclean and dangerous—that sharing it with Sudbury might make her feel better but would put him, or anyone else who saw it, in danger.

Sudbury noticed when she jerked her hand away from her pocket and gave her a questioning look.

"Well, sir, I thank you for your warning," Mary said in a small voice.

Sudbury murmured goodbye as he walked away, his hand once again covering his scar.

CHAPTER 4

A medicine, to cleanse the brain of corrupt matter, and to help those that have a stinking air at their noses, and to cleanse the lungs of such gross humors, as are distilled down from the putrefied head

Take a good quantity of rosemary leaves, and chew them lightly in your mouth, that the air may ascend into your head, and as you do this hold down your head and void the humors, out of your mouth, as they do fall . . .

Tom wriggled on the pew next to Mary and scowled at her warning glance. In truth, Reverend Osborne's sermons, filled with admonitions against moral laxity and the sin of covetousness, made her want to fidget as well. But she supposed it was better than the sermons in which he made mention of witchcraft while staring straight at her. He'd never been comfortable with her healing gifts, though his wife came to Mary's door often enough to purchase a salve for her nether parts. The salve had the happy effect of making Mrs. Osborne feel lusty, Mary thought with a tiny smile. Yes, Reverend Osborne should appreciate her efforts.

Mary surreptitiously stretched her neck from one side to the other, trying not to attract notice. The tension of the last few days had manifested in bunched muscles and headaches she could not abate with even her best cures. And she could see that tension mirrored in the faces of her neighbors. The death of Henry Chamberlen hung over all of them. It had been impossible to keep the details of his death—and the suspicion of poisoning—a secret.

Mrs. Morgan, sitting in the pew behind Mary, jumped as Mary's neck popped loudly from her stretching. Mary turned carefully with a look of apology to Mrs. Morgan and then peered around the church. As the rector droned on, she admired the light streaming in, the golden glow of morning touched with green from the trees visible through the windows. She was grateful that some zealot in years past, goaded on by anti-popish hostility, had destroyed the stained glass. She felt it only natural that God be worshipped within view of His own creation: the light, the sky, and her beloved trees and plants.

As Mary turned her attention back to Reverend Osborne, her gaze locked on the one person she wanted to see the least: Bridget Jenkins, the woman Jack had tupped while Mary mourned their lost baby. Bridget boldly stared back, her mouth twisted in disdain. Reverend Osborne's lesson on covetousness might be beneficial for Bridget, Mary thought, a sour taste in her mouth—especially the coveting of other women's husbands.

None of that was solely Bridget Jenkins's fault, Agnes had scolded her—it took two to join paunches, after all—and Mary eventually came to accept that. Even so, she couldn't help but remember that terrible day whenever she saw Bridget. The day she knew she had lost her husband.

She and Tom had been walking past the church when she noticed a man tucked into an alcove of the cemetery, bundled in a coat with his hat pulled down to cover his face. He was a large man, but somehow he'd made himself small, had dressed to blend in and render himself almost invisible.

She recognized him as her own Jack, but he'd not yet seen her. Why wasn't he at home? More importantly, why was he skulking around the graveyard?

"Mary, I tired!" Tom had whimpered.

Putting her fingers against her lips, she motioned for Tom to remain silent. "Tom, I'm going to take you into the church, and I want you to wait for me there. If you're good, I promise you some candied apple."

Mary settled him into a pew and then doubled back and hid behind one of the larger tombstones. With her senses trained on Jack's movements, she almost missed the small, feminine figure with her head covered in a cloth, making her way across the other side of the cemetery. By the time she noticed, Jack had stood up to greet the woman.

And what a greeting it was.

Jack reached his hand out and led her to a copse of trees some hundred yards away. He bent his head toward her and kissed her hungrily, his hands grabbing her shoulders and pushing her up against an oak. Mary could see the woman's hands clawing at his back.

Her stomach heaved, and she feared she would void her guts right there.

After a few moments, Mary moved to another tombstone, trying to soften her tread as much as possible. She crouched only a few yards from them and could hear their soft murmurs and moans. Jack moved the square of linen that covered the woman's head, and Mary caught a glimpse of bright, golden hair and knew that it was Bridget Jenkins.

A shriek sounded from the church, then Tom's giddy shout: "Mary, Mary, I see'd a mouse!"

The couple hurried to disentangle.

Mary's heart sank as she heard the church door open and Tom's uneven footsteps approach.

"Mary, I see'd a *baby* mouse!" Tom's face was eager and aglow with discovery.

As Jack turned slowly, Mary could see the growing horror in his gaze. He hurried toward her, apologies already pouring from his mouth. She turned to walk away but not before glancing at Bridget.

The other woman stood alone, her arms outstretched, yearning in her eyes and a small, keening cry on her lips.

For a moment, Mary felt sorry for her, but that pity was short lived as Bridget's eyes turned cold and she spat out, "Mary Fawcett, you bitch!"

A rustle of the congregation brought Mary back to the present. She noticed whispers and the discreet turning of heads toward the lectern side of the church. Tom grabbed her hand and pointed at the men who'd just sat down.

It was Matthew Hopkins and Jonathan Stearne. They seemed not to care that they caused a disruption, seating themselves noisily with smirks on their faces. Stearne wiped his nose on his sleeve, and Hopkins elbowed him sharply. Then Hopkins caught sight of Mary and winked.

The rest of the service passed in a haze. She said her prayers as fervently as she could, considering that her attention remained fixed, against her will, on Stearne and Hopkins.

After Reverend Osborne gave the final benediction, the villagers gathered in the church courtyard, eager to gossip about Chamberlen's death and the new arrivals in town. Mary tugged Tom's arm and guided him to the side of the small crowd, hoping to slip away unnoticed. She'd almost made it to the end of the path when she heard her name called. "Mrs. Fawcett, can you spare a moment?"

Simon walked quickly toward her, an uncertain smile on his face.

"I thought I should check on you after the ghastly events at Chamberlen Manor. Are you well?"

Mary nodded. "Indeed." She followed Tom, who had run ahead down the path that led home, hoping Simon would take the hint and leave. Instead, he quickened his pace to keep up with her.

"Mr. Hopkins thinks it was murder, despite that note they found by Chamberlen's body, and he thinks the murderer was a practitioner of the dark arts, did you know? He asked the constable many questions, and he said many elements of Chamberlen's death mirrored cases of witchcraft throughout Essex. And did you see Mr. Hopkins in church?" Simon's face had the gleeful look of a boy given a treat. "He is an imposing man, to be sure, a man to be feared by the wicked. Why, in Chelmsford alone, he freed the town of nineteen of the devil's handmaidens."

Simon reached out and grabbed Mary's elbow, stopping her. His eyes were eager. "Hopkins says his assistant is a dull fellow, and he needs somebody more clever, for he means to solve the mystery of Henry Chamberlen's death. He wants a man who knows the village, who can tell when strange and unnatural events are afoot. He's already asked Mr. Grandley about his pig. And are you ready for a surprise, Mary?"

Mary nodded her head reluctantly.

"He's chosen me to be his aide, and I believe my father will release me from my duties long enough to be of some help."

Mary gave a false smile and picked up her pace. Some distance ahead, Tom looked back and scowled.

"Master Hopkins says we'll begin by listing any of the peculiar things that have happened in the village. There's Grandley's pig, of course, but can you think of anything else? I told him of the wheat blight last summer, and that pestilence that killed Mr. Leaver's cows. And do you think he would find it odd that Mr. and Mrs. Bailey's child was born with a cleft lip right after Mrs. Bailey accused Mrs. Tompkins of selling spoiled eggs?"

Mary stopped and fixed Simon with the stern look she usually reserved for her little brother.

Simon had the grace to blush.

"Yes, well," he replied. "No woman would be interested in all that, I suppose." He shook his head a little and puffed up his chest, cloaking himself with his former bluster. "Probably for the best. Such things are better left to the men."

The next day, Mary put aside all thoughts of the witchfinder. She gave her day over to work rather than worry. She still needed to find slugs for an ointment to treat the rash on Mrs. Birkenshaw's chest, and the distilled plague water sat ready to be bottled—it was always popular, and her reserves had gotten worrisomely low. She would have to go see Agnes for some more pennyroyal and *Carduus benedictus*.

The work soothed her like nothing else. It was what she was born to do.

Mary would always remember the first time Agnes had taken her on one of her calls, to a woman who suffered a loosening of the bowels. The woman lay listless, drained of all vitality, and more than a little embarrassed by the stink issuing from her guts. Agnes had shown Mary how to prepare a recipe for an enema. She took red leaves of a young oak and boiled them in water and white wine. After distilling the liquid, she had taken a few spoonfuls and put it in an aleberry, explaining that the red leaves would work sympathetically to attract the blood, while the aleberry would treat the underlying imbalance of phlegm.

Before Mary administered the enema, however, she laid her hands on the woman's abdomen, talked with the woman about the discomfort, the painful swelling, and the guilt she felt about not helping her husband care for their children. Mary felt the woman's shame, the embarrassment, the confusion, and she imagined herself helping the woman drain those emotions out of her guts. By the time Mary and Agnes left the woman's cottage, she could sit up for the first time in weeks, and her complexion had turned from deathly pale to rosy cheeked.

Mary had been taken aback by the intensity of the cure—and more than a little exhausted. Agnes, on the other hand, was almost giddy in her enthusiasm for Mary's talents. Mary had the power to touch the pain of others, Agnes said, and that was the real cure—all Agnes had taught her to do was to put that sympathy in a bottle. Mary was the better healer, Agnes insisted, and had the greater natural skill. Mary demurred, but Agnes told her matter-of-factly, "You needn't worry I'll be jealous of your skill. Healing brings relief for the sufferer, but there's a price that must be paid, and sometimes it's the healer who pays it."

How did she do these things she did? Where did the gift come from? And how could she nurture it, develop it? Someday, she promised herself. Someday she would have the time and freedom to answer these questions. Her gift was precious, and she would not squander it.

Mary sensed something was wrong as soon as she entered Agnes's cottage. Normally Agnes kept it tidy and in order, the hearth swept and the air sweet with lavender. The cottage was too small for the many supplies and equipment Agnes needed for her work, but she always stored the glass bottles of cordials and ground medicines dusted and meticulously ordered on the shelves. Sometimes when she got lost in her work, the blankets on Agnes's straw mattress lay in an untidy heap and her morning bowl of porridge sat on the table, forgotten and cold. "I was too busy with the cordials!" Agnes would protest when Mary insisted she finish her breakfast. But most days the cottage was organized, scrubbed, and redolent with herbs.

When Mary knocked, Agnes hadn't greeted her with the usual cheerful, "Hullo, what do you want?" Instead Mary waited through a long silence, followed by the sound of Agnes limping across the floor. When Agnes opened the door, Mary was shocked to see her hunched over, clutching her stomach, and grimacing in pain. Her gray hair, usually pulled into a tidy bun, hung lank and greasy on her bosom.

"Oh, Mary, praise God it's you," she said, looking relieved. "I think the eels I ate were rotten. My guts have been voiding all day."

Dirty bowls and cups littered the table, and Agnes had left the glass bottles out, unstoppered, some even tipped over and spilling out. The reek of vomit permeated the room, not quite covered by the smoldering sage in the corner. Mary tried to hide her shock. Agnes had always been the epitome of health and vitality. Any weakness she suffered from she treated with her own medicine quickly and efficiently. The villagers joked that foul humors could never plague Agnes, that instead of bile, phlegm, and blood, she was made of gristle, piss, and vinegar.

Mary immediately sent Tom to the yard to play and settled Agnes in bed. She busied herself making bone broth to strengthen Agnes's blood and help her fight whatever foul contagion occupied her body.

The dim firelight did little to illuminate the small cottage, but Mary knew exactly what she needed and where to find it. She'd spent so much time in Agnes's home in the last few years, she could have made her way around it with her eyes closed. Mary found water in the wooden cistern to pour over the chicken bones Agnes had dried earlier that month. She added some rosemary and thyme and set the soup to boil over the fire.

Mary helped Agnes sit up and rearranged the soft wool blanket over her shoulders. She shared some village gossip with her, and eventually Mary worked the conversation around to the topic of Matthew Hopkins.

"Agnes, this stranger in town, this Hopkins . . ." She paused and gripped Agnes's hand. "Things have already changed because he is here. People are telling stories, horrible fictions. Just yesterday I heard Mr. Clark complain that his sight began to dim after you gave him that cordial for his gout, and the children in the village square are saying they saw you speaking with the geese in Joan Smith's yard. And now that Mr. Chamberlen has died . . ."

Agnes sat up straight. "Henry Chamberlen died?"

"Yes, three days ago. Hadn't you heard?"

"No, I've been stuck here with this sickness. What killed him?"

Mary hesitated for only a moment before telling Agnes everything that had happened at Chamberlen Manor. If she couldn't trust her oldest friend, whom could she trust?

Mary had expected Agnes to be shocked and appalled, but instead the older woman just gazed at her hands and began picking at the blanket in her lap. When she finally looked up, she looked strangely pleased.

"Agnes?"

"What a bastard he was. Well, how is Mrs. Chamberlen?" Mary thought it strange that she didn't have more to say about the death of the richest and most powerful man in the county.

"I don't know, but when I saw her, she looked close to death."

Agnes did look surprised at this.

"What was wrong with her?"

"Chamberlen had been giving her hellebore. He told her it would help her conceive a child."

"That monster!" Agnes attempted to get out of bed in her anger, but her energy was sapped.

"I agree, but, Agnes, given all this, you must be more careful now that a witchfinder is in town. Matthew Hopkins is a dangerous man. Do you know Robert Sudbury?"

"That strange man who moved into the old Akins house? The standoffish one?"

"Yes. He warned me against Hopkins, said he was worse than other witchfinders—more influential and dangerous. And that he had a history of accusing cunning women of maleficium."

Agnes tilted her head and gave Mary a curious look. "You know Sudbury well enough that he would issue warnings to you? Take you under his wing?"

Mary blushed, recalling her fascination with the man and his work. "No. I encountered him in the field north of town, and he said he'd been wanting to warn us to be careful. Hopkins is to be feared."

Agnes dismissed Mary's concerns with a light wave of her hand.

"Me, afraid of Hopkins? Why would I be afraid of that toad?"

"You've met him?" Mary asked, surprised. She could smell the broth now, a good sign that it was strong and robust. She went to fetch it while Agnes went on.

"A couple of days ago. He came to introduce himself and poke around here. Said he was looking for witches. I told him that Bicknacre is a fine town of fine people, that if he wanted to stir up hatred and sow division, he'd have to look elsewhere. The poker I held in my hand seemed to convince him more than my words."

Mary urged Agnes to take Hopkins's threat seriously. "You've heard the stories, Agnes. Witches aren't discovered, but rather created in the minds of the people. Even in the best of people and the best of places. We're only one step from the animals when we're weak or afraid. And women like us are the first they look to. You must listen to me." As she repeated Sudbury's warnings, they seemed even more ominous. "I can do most of the work that needs to be done in the village. You must stop your cookery—all of it. Especially the potions."

Agnes gained a sudden strength and sat up straighter. She pushed the bowl of broth away.

"Mary, how could I possibly do that? I've worked too long and too hard, sacrificed too much for the knowledge I've gained, to just quit." Mary wondered at her fierceness, but then her face relaxed and Agnes sneered a little. "Hopkins has come to the wrong village. He may try to stir up trouble, but he'll have no luck here in Bicknacre, at least not with you and me. We know too much—who has coveted his neighbor's wife, who has stolen chickens from his neighbors' yards. Yes, we know too much, and that makes us powerful."

Agnes looked almost frenzied. Mary suspected it was from fever and lack of food, so she decided to try another tack. "What about your health? I've been too busy to help lately. What if you make yourself sick with too much work?"

Agnes glanced at Mary and quickly looked away. "I'm sure to feel better soon, and I . . . I have had help lately."

Mary thought she sounded rather casual about this important news—for so long it had been only the two of them.

"You have? Who?"

Agnes hesitated. "Bridget Jenkins came to my cottage wanting to learn more about herbals."

"Bridget Jenkins? You've been teaching Bridget?" Mary felt her gut clench with betrayal. She took a deep breath. Bridget's dalliance with Jack was years ago, and Mary knew that it was unkind to object to Agnes's decision and unreasonable to feel jealous. Agnes needed the help, and Mary was too busy. Just because she knew Bridget to be a selfish, mean-spirited slattern didn't mean Agnes couldn't like her, teach her, and mentor her as she had Mary.

Mary couldn't help but wonder, however, exactly what Agnes was teaching Bridget. A few times Agnes had tried to introduce Mary to recipes that could harm rather than heal, but Mary had objected. Some would say that the abortifacients Agnes administered were evil, but Mary didn't agree, especially when she saw girls like Maggie Wrenshaw, only fifteen years old, who'd been violated and died in childbirth, or Alice Hayes, who discovered after her husband passed away that she was with child—a seventh, with six starving children still at home. But Agnes had tried to teach her other recipes, like salves to cause massive boils, a posset to cause all the hair on the body to fall out, even a cordial that could cause a sleep so deep it mimicked death. There was demand for these concoctions in Bicknacre, but Mary could not bring herself to provide them. No, she had been given her gift to heal, not harm. But she had no doubt that Bridget Jenkins would feel no such compunction.

"We haven't gotten very far," Agnes continued. "She can follow the recipes with few mistakes, but she can't seem to understand that they aren't miracles or potions, that they have reason and sense to them. And she lacks your ability, Mary, the way you understand the pain and suffering of others. You and I have spent years learning our craft and honing our skills—but we were also born healers. Bridget was not."

Agnes gave Mary a stern look. "But you must not judge her harshly for her past. She surpasses us both in one way—she never assumes she knows what's ailing the sick and suffering. She always lets them tell their own story without interfering with her own ideas. Anyway," Agnes continued, "I feel much better now, Mary. Thank you for all you've done. You should leave now." She added kindly, "I know you have much work to do."

Mary hesitated. "There is one more thing."

She reached into her pocket and pulled out the token. "I found this in Chamberlen's hand when I was inspecting his body. Do you know anything about it?"

Agnes took the token and traced out the picture of the bird feeding her fledglings. "Well, that's a pelican in her piety, isn't it?"

The confusion must have shown on Mary's face. Agnes pointed out the features of the symbol.

"She is a symbol of the sacrificial blood of Christ. You see it sometimes in the old churches. See, she's piercing her own breast to feed her children with her blood." Agnes turned the medallion over. "But this symbol is odd. I haven't seen it before."

"But why would Chamberlen have been holding it?"

Agnes gave Mary a piercing look. "Perhaps the better question is why you've been holding on to it? Have you mentioned this to the constable?"

Mary blushed. "I have not. Honestly, Agnes, I have no idea why I took it, and afterward I was afraid to say what I had done. Hopkins already looked at me with suspicion—I didn't want to give him anything more to hold against me."

Agnes nodded. "That was wise. Mary, do you see that small rug? Lift it up."

Mary walked over to the woven rug and moved it aside to see an iron hoop.

"Pull on it," Agnes said.

Mary lifted the ring and a small door popped open. Inside lay Agnes's book of recipes.

"What's this doing here?"

"I'm not worried about Hopkins, but I'm also not a fool. I didn't want him taking my book for any reason, even a ridiculous one. As you know, my grandmother had to bribe men to write down her cures, and my poor mother, barely able to write herself, added to it with great difficulty. It's far too precious for the likes of Matthew Hopkins. Bring it to me."

Mary lifted the pile of papers—it could hardly be called a book. A dozen or so threads held the cover on, and a leather thong kept the bulk of the pages together.

Agnes caressed the collection of pages lovingly and untied the strip of leather. She flipped over the cover and, with nimble fingers, separated the leather book board to reveal a pocket.

"How did you do that?" Mary asked with surprise.

"This has been my hiding spot for years. I took the book apart and put it together again—look closely and you'll see that the stitching covers a slit I cut in the pages. If you want, you can hide the token here until you decide what to do with it."

"But you might get in trouble if somebody finds it."

"Don't be silly. Who would suspect something so strange would be hidden in an old woman's recipes?"

Mary nodded, slipped the token inside, and replaced the book in its hiding place.

"Agnes, you're a dear friend. What would I do without you?"

Agnes's face, pale from her illness, turned a mottled red. "You would be lost—how else would you find pennyroyal at this time of year?"

Mary chuckled, gave Agnes a tight squeeze, and readied to leave the warm cabin. Before she left, she bent down to kiss Agnes on the cheek. "Promise me you will be careful."

CHAPTER 5

To deliver a woman of a dead child

*Take leek blades and scald them in hot water and bind
them to her navel and she shall be delivered. Take them
soon away, or they will cause her to cast all in her belly.*

For a few days, Mary hoped she'd have no reason to meet the witchfinder
again. She didn't encounter him on her next trip into town, and he didn't
attend church the following Sunday. She heard stories about him snooping
around, eavesdropping, asking uncomfortable questions that resurrected old
quarrels. And she'd heard that Simon had become a sort of aide-de-camp for
him, providing background on his friends and neighbors.

She couldn't help studying the face of every person she passed to see
if they looked at her any differently, if their eyes shifted or their smiles faltered. As intently as she studied her neighbors, however, she couldn't determine whether she was in danger. Did the villagers glance at her furtively,
or did she imagine it? Did the children run away from her, or were they
just eager to play with the puppies newly delivered by the Smiths' bitch?

This was the power of Hopkins and his ilk, she thought to herself:
to make people fear the unknown, to prompt neighbor to doubt neighbor, friend to look askance at friend.

In the end, it was Tom who encountered Hopkins first.

Mary had just left her house to visit Agnes, whom she had not seen for several days. Lost in her thoughts, Mary let Tom scurry ahead on the path, but she startled to attention when she realized she no longer heard the distinctive sound of his shuffling steps ahead of her. She called his name and started hurrying down the path when, to her great relief, she heard Tom's high voice ringing out around the next bend. Her relief was short lived. She heard a lower voice, a man's voice, responding.

Panic gripped her, and Mary broke into a run. As she turned a corner, she saw Tom, skipping back toward her with Greedyguts beside him, followed by Simon and Matthew Hopkins. Hopkins was glowering fiercely at the crow.

Something about the look in Hopkins's eyes made Mary freeze. "Tom, come over here this instant!" she said sharply.

Tom looked up and gave her a bright smile.

"Mary," he called. "Mary, this man says he knows how to blow bubbles without a straw and will teach me how!"

"Tom! Here. Now," she commanded.

Tom ran to her side. Mary noticed Hopkins's scowl as he took in Tom's lopsided gait. When he saw her watching, he quickly pasted a smile on his face. She found his smile more terrifying than his scowl.

"This is your brother?" Hopkins's eyes narrowed into slits when he smiled. "A delightful young man. He is very intelligent. You must be proud."

"Yes," Mary replied. For a brief moment she felt embarrassed by her terse response, but then Hopkins walked to her, a glint in his eye, and placed his hand on her arm.

Mary glared at him and tried to tug her arm free. Hopkins's grip tightened. His eyes bored into her, and he licked his lips. She could hear Simon begin to object, but his voice seemed to come from very far away. Mary had started to panic when she felt a rush of air and caught sight of a blur of black flying toward Hopkins's face.

Greedyguts.

The crow hovered, beating his wings on Hopkins's head, forcing him to raise his arms to protect himself. When Hopkins let go of Mary, Greedyguts flew within a few inches of their heads and then veered off for the nearest tree.

From the shadows nearby, Mary heard a laugh.

"What a good bird. And, sir, if you ever touch Mary Fawcett again, you will answer to me."

Robert Sudbury emerged from the shadows. Hopkins looked up, and his face twisted.

His arm was still poised over his head to prevent a further attack. At Sudbury's sneer and pointed glance, Hopkins moved his arm back to his side and muttered a word that caused Mary to put her hands over Tom's ears.

Tom looked back and forth at the two men, fear and excitement in his eyes as he sensed the tension between Sudbury and Hopkins. Simon, too, appeared shocked.

"Ah, it is a familiar monster. Hello, Sudbury," said Hopkins.

Sudbury ignored him and instead walked to Mary's side. "Mrs. Shepherd has asked that I fetch her cordials from you, Mrs. Fawcett." He told the lie loudly enough for Hopkins to hear.

"Mrs. Fawcett has some business with us first," Hopkins said. "There are questions that need answering, my dear."

"I shall stay," Sudbury said without hesitation.

Mary grimaced. "Wait here while I settle Tom," she replied, and walked him back to the cottage.

"Mary, I don't like that man at all," Tom confided in a whisper when they were out of earshot. "I wouldn't even want to see him blow bubbles." He paused. "Why am I scared, Mary?" he asked, a perplexed look on his dear face. "Nothing happened to me."

"You are scared because that man has bad intentions."

"What is a 'tention?"

"It means that those men do not plan to treat Mrs. Shepherd nicely."

Tom spun around and headed in the opposite direction. "Then I am going to hit and kick and punch them," he declared.

Mary grabbed Tom by the collar and got on her knees to look him in the eye.

"Tom, that is not how we treat people. And it wouldn't be safe for you."

"But they will be mean to Mrs. Shepherd! We must protect her!"

"Mrs. Shepherd is perfectly capable of protecting herself. And regardless, we do not use our fists to hurt when we can use words to heal. When we do, we become as brutish as those we fight." Mary paused. "But truth be told, I'd like to hit and kick and punch Mr. Hopkins, too."

"I don't like Mr. Hopkins," he repeated. "Mr. Sudbury looks like a bad man with that ugly scar, but he is not, I don't think. Simon Martin is okay, I s'pose, but that other man scares me."

"He scares me a little, too," Mary said. "But, Tom, I want you to be a brave boy and stay here."

Tom reluctantly agreed to remain in the cottage, but before he let Mary go outside, he walked to the fire and grabbed a knife. He handed it to her silently, solemnly.

Mary kissed Tom's head and walked up the path to where the men awaited her. The tension was so thick she could cut it with the blade her little brother had given her. Hopkins sat next to a nervous-looking Simon on a log in her garden. Sudbury stood as far from them as he could.

Mary wasted no time on pleasantries. "What do you want?" she asked Hopkins.

Simon looked away as Hopkins spoke. "Mistress Fawcett, you are acquainted with Mr. Martin's sister, Verity Martin?"

Mary nodded.

"Are you aware that your . . . friend . . . Mrs. Shepherd, has given Verity potions and cordials?"

"Yes. As have I."

"And what were these potions and cordials used for?"

Mary hesitated. "That is between Verity, Mrs. Shepherd, and me."

Hopkins cocked one eyebrow. "Well, you are very noble, Mrs. Fawcett. I wonder what can be so unspeakable that you can't tell us what you and Agnes Shepherd gave her?"

Mary stood a little straighter and turned to Simon, a question in her eyes. Simon blushed.

"Perhaps you can inform Mrs. Fawcett of your sister's claims," Hopkins said to Simon. The calm in his voice was at odds with his heightened color. Matthew Hopkins made it clear that he brooked no dissent, especially from a woman.

"Verity is not well," Simon stammered. "She has been feverish, and subject to . . . to strange fits. She trembles and wails and sweats. It's as though she is possessed."

Mary stared, fear gripping her. In her last note, Verity had complained only of discomfort from her monthly pains. "Simon, I can assure you that she told me nothing of this. She sounds gravely ill. Would you like me to come take a look at her?"

Hopkins stepped forward. In a commanding voice, he said, "You shall do no such thing, Mary Fawcett. You will stay away from that young woman, or you'll face the consequences!"

"Under whose authority?" Mary asked, indignant.

"Under the authority of Witchfinder General Matthew Hopkins," he replied, his chest puffed out.

Sudbury laughed, and Hopkins turned toward him, his face contorted in fury. He started to say something, but Simon interrupted him. "Mary, I'd be grateful if you could see my sister. But first I must ask you a question." He paused. "Did Mrs. Shepherd or . . . or you . . . give my sister medicines that would help her to lose a product of the womb?"

Mary was shocked. Under normal circumstances she would say nothing, but a cunning woman could hang for helping a woman end a pregnancy, especially if it had advanced to the quickening. She refused to die for a crime she did not commit.

"A baby? No, sir, I did not," she said with great authority. "Your sister's note asked me for a cordial to help with the pains of her monthly courses. That is all."

Simon gave Hopkins a triumphant look. "I was right, it wasn't Mary!"

"Hmm, then it was Mrs. Shepherd who helped her shed the evil she carried," Hopkins replied. "We shall have to see what Verity says to that!"

Mary glared back. "And what has Verity already said?"

Hopkins crossed his arms. "Miss Martin says either you or Mrs. Shepherd, or both, gave her a cordial that would cause her to abort the thing she carried in her womb."

Robert sucked in his breath.

"What 'thing' did she carry in her womb?" Mary demanded, struck by Hopkins's choice of words. "And why do you call it a 'thing'?"

"Verity Martin confessed that the devil visited her at night some months ago and spilled his seed between her legs, getting her with his spawn."

Mary gasped.

"Further, she said you and Mrs. Shepherd claim special knowledge of a cordial that would cause her to expel the devil's get. Mrs. Shepherd became adept at its creation because she herself had taken it many times after lying with the devil at the witches' Sabbath. Further, within an hour of Miss Martin taking the cordial, a hairy beast burst from her and flew up the chimney." Hopkins stared at her closely. "She says she may have seen you there as well, Mrs. Fawcett, with a familiar that accompanied Mrs. Shepherd to that unholy ceremony—a crow with the tail of a mouse hidden beneath its feathers."

Mary looked away from Hopkins. Sudbury stared at her, unblinking, whereas Simon's eyes begged her to plead her innocence.

Mary pulled herself up to her full height and returned Hopkins's stare. He looked away. She said, slowly and precisely, "I have never attended a witches' Sabbath and I have never given Verity Martin anything but medicinal plague water and a cordial for her monthly pains."

Simon gave a loud sigh of relief.

Hopkins shrugged. "It matters little, I suppose. No one could object to the disposal of the devil's get." Then he raised his hand to the sky and said, as though pronouncing for an invisible audience, "I wonder, though, what of others? Have you given such medicines to others?"

She had been afraid of that question. She and Agnes had agreed they would not broadcast their knowledge of which herbs could cause a miscarriage. Mary didn't know if or when Agnes had used them. She herself only had cause to turn to those jars of herbs after a visit from a young woman—almost a child herself—who, face veiled in shame, mumbled something about her uncle, how he had forced himself on her for years, and how after she got her courses he got her with child. Stomach clenched in rage and revulsion, Mary had given the poor girl what she needed. She remembered John Martin, Simon and Verity's short-tempered and violent father, and thought that if Agnes had given those herbs to Verity, it could have been for a similar reason.

Simon looked at her with sadness. "Is it true, Mary? Have you mixed those herbs for others?"

Mary would not utter a word.

Hopkins turned and looked at Simon, triumph in his eyes, and gave a high, girlish giggle.

"Mr. Martin, I recommend that you be careful with the company you keep," he warned. "No woman's cunt is worth a hanging."

Mary felt rather than saw Robert move toward Hopkins, fists clenched, but he wasn't fast enough. The punch Simon landed in Hopkins's face took Mary's breath away with its force. Before Hopkins's words had even started to make sense to her, he lay sprawled in the mud and pine needles.

After a shocked moment, Hopkins sat up and massaged his jaw. Simon stood over him, threatening to deliver another blow. Mary pulled him away.

Hopkins stood, his feet shuffling on the slippery path, whimpering and trembling. He pointed at Simon. "You will regret that, Martin," he whined. "You have attacked a representative of Parliament." Then he spat on the ground and stalked away.

Simon gave her a look of apology.

"That was well done, Mr. Martin." Robert's voice broke the silence. "You may be a better man than I thought."

Simon glared at Robert, the heat of the violence animating him. Mary thought Simon would hit Robert, too, and she suspected Simon would come out the worse in that fight. She stepped between the men.

Simon took a deep breath. "I apologize for that man's degrading language, Mary. I hope you can forgive me for leading him to your cottage. But you will keep your promise, won't you? You'll come to visit Verity and make her better? My sister needs you."

Robert frowned as Mary nodded her consent. "Yes, I'll see her as soon as I can."

The fear felt like a lead weight in Mary's belly. She wanted to flee this horrid mess, to retreat to her cottage and find solace in her work, to ignore the judgment and suspicion that had plagued the town since Hopkins's arrival. She feared what would happen if the whispers about her healing skills were twisted by Hopkins's vile speculations. Would her neighbors believe she was a witch, in league with the devil? And if they did, what would Hopkins do with her? She'd heard rumors of the terrible tests suspected witches were put through, that women were tortured until they confessed. But far worse: What would happen to Tom if she were taken away? Would he be suspected of witchcraft as well?

She sensed she should stay close to home, make no trouble with her neighbors, remain quiet and follow the unwritten rules of the village. But Verity needed her help, and she had made a promise.

Mary fetched Tom from the house to resume their trip to Agnes's cottage. Sudbury asked to accompany them, and though normally she would have preferred the time for her own thoughts, she was still on edge from the encounter with Hopkins.

Tom, too, had yet to recover, but he was mostly excited about the news that Simon—dull, stuffy Simon—had punched Hopkins in the nose, and he chattered on about it until Mary directed him to run ahead.

Sudbury watched him for a bit. "He's a fine lad."

Mary nodded. "He is indeed."

"You take care of him by yourself?"

"Yes, almost since he was born."

"And you had no children from your husband?" he asked. Mary saw something like sorrow, like sympathy, in his eyes.

Mary fought back tears and stood taller. "I did. We had a babe. She lived less than two months."

A tear slipped down her cheek. Sudbury surprised her by reaching out and gently brushing it away. "I am sorry to hear it. I'm sure you were a fine mother." She stared at him, mesmerized by the gentleness in his face and the rough calluses softly scraping her skin.

"Mary!" Tom's voice rang out from around a bend in the trail.

Sudbury jerked away and held his hands behind his back.

"My apologies, Mrs. Fawcett, I didn't mean to come here to make you cry. I came to talk about Mrs. Shepherd."

"Mary!" Tom cried out again.

"Yes, of course," she replied. "Let me see what Tom needs, and then we can talk."

Mary walked quickly ahead, relieved to have a few moments to collect herself.

Tom had caught his sleeve on the snag of a log, causing a little rip. He expected a scolding and was happily surprised when instead his sister kissed the scrape on his elbow and bade him to sit in a little glade off the trail and look for toadstools.

Mary returned to Sudbury, who sat on a small mossy log. He waved for her to join him.

He did not meet her eyes. "Mr. Hopkins doesn't like you," Mary said. "And I have the feeling he hasn't liked you for some time."

"Hopkins and I have met before."

"Before you came to Bicknacre?"

Robert sighed. "I should tell you the whole story." He seemed deep in thought, slipping into a sort of reverie before he began. "I grew up in London. I had a nurse who was like a mother to me. She was there when my parents were not. She sat with me when I was sick, consoled me when the other children shunned me. Hugged me when I cried. I had no brothers or sisters, so when I went to Cambridge, she had no reason to stay on. My parents set her up in the town where she grew up—Chelmsford—with a place to live and a small stipend."

Robert began examining a small mark on his hand.

"I didn't see her for another year, not until I was on break from Cambridge and returned home for a visit. She couldn't easily read or write, and while I sent her letters, she could not respond. I visited her that spring, and she seemed happy. Not thriving, exactly, but she had enough to eat and stay warm, and to keep her beloved pets. And despite an ongoing argument she had with the local butcher, who overcharged her and refused to make it good, she enjoyed her neighbors. We had a nice visit. The next time I saw her, she was hanging from the gallows."

Mary gasped.

Robert buried his head in his hands. Without thinking, Mary reached out to caress his hair, the urge to comfort him overwhelming. But wary of a repeat of the blistering heat she'd sensed when she'd touched his scar on their first meeting, she only brushed a dark curl that swept his forehead. Sudbury lifted his head and gave her a pleading look—pleading for what, she didn't know. For trust? Sympathy?

"Go on," she whispered.

Robert gave a shuddering sigh. "While I was in my second year at St. Benet's, Matthew Hopkins came to Chelmsford. He claimed, as he does now, that Parliament had sent him, but in fact some locals had paid him to rid the town of witches. He stayed in town for only a few weeks, and yet it was long enough to uncover petty jealousies and long-buried suspicions. He determined that a recent spate of miscarriages and the blight in the wheat crop were caused by malicious spells. He targeted the weakest people in town, those without many friends or family and those who caused trouble with their neighbors. The butcher pointed him to my old nurse.

"From what I can piece together, he took her to the castle in Colchester where other suspected witches were being held. He kept her awake for several days, starving her of food and company and shaming her with physical examinations. She broke, finally, and confessed to being a witch and causing the death of the chandler's baby."

Mary shuddered. Sudbury took her hand and looked her in the eyes.

"It wasn't true, of course. My nurse was no witch. She was the kindest, warmest, and most loving woman I knew."

Robert looked away. "I had no idea of any of this while I was in Cambridge, of course. I learned of it from the local priest. He, too, refused to believe that my nurse could be guilty of witchery, and he hoped I could persuade Hopkins and the townspeople to see reason. But it was winter, and the roads were difficult to navigate. I got to town the day she was scheduled to hang. By the time I arrived, she had been dangling from the rope for twenty minutes, left there as an example to other supposed witches in the town."

Robert gave Mary a piercing look. "This is what I want you to know, Mrs. Fawcett. In order to afford heat and some little luxuries, she had started helping people: finding lost baubles, making potions for the people in the village—nothing like the work you and Mrs. Shepherd do, just little cordials for clear skin or for good health."

Mary and Robert sat quietly for several long moments before Mary said, softly, "Your nurse was a sort of cunning woman then. Just like Agnes. Just like me."

Robert looked up, a mixture of anger, sadness, and pity on the unscarred half of his face. "Hopkins accused her of using devilish poisons to torture the villagers. He's been doing this for some time, this witchfinding. Beware that man, Mrs. Fawcett. He brings pain and death."

"And what can I do to save Mrs. Shepherd?" Mary asked. She tried to swallow her fear. "And myself?"

"Just what I told you before. You must both stay quiet and preferably at home, at least while Hopkins is in Bicknacre. Get along with your neighbors. And you must stop your cookery."

"I've asked that of Agnes already, and she has refused. She's not one for staying quiet, and many in town rely on our help."

"It may save your lives," Robert said. "I overheard Hopkins say something to Stearne, but I want to confirm it with you, to see if it is true . . ." He hesitated.

"Yes?" Mary prompted him.

Robert looked away. "The first time we spoke, you had been visiting the Chamberlens. Hopkins says that Mrs. Chamberlen is very ill, and that you had been bringing her your medicines."

Mary gasped. "Does he dare accuse me of poisoning her?"

"Mary, can you tell me what was wrong with Mrs. Chamberlen? What were her complaints?"

"Why does that matter?" Mary asked, suspicious of his motives.

"It may help me discover why Hopkins is so interested in you."

Mary watched Robert's face for several long moments, wondering if she could trust him. But the need to confide in somebody about her worries overruled her caution.

And she told him that she smelled hellebore in the cordial Mrs. Chamberlen imbibed and that Mrs. Chamberlen said her husband had given it to her to help her conceive a babe. Robert looked startled and asked more questions about the cordial—its color and consistency, the size of the bottle, whether it had a label of any kind, any markings.

He grabbed a stick in a sort of frenzy and drew some markings in the dirt. One symbol looked like a stick figure of a man with a huge head and one eye.

Mary gasped, and Sudbury looked up. "Yes?" he asked with an intense glimmer in his eye.

"Not on the bottle, no," Mary replied. She hesitated, then continued on. "But I did see similar markings. There were symbols like that carved into Mr. Chamberlen's abdomen, and some were drawn in ink." It was only a small lie, she consoled herself. So what if the symbol was on the medallion instead of Chamberlen's abdomen? Lord knew there had been enough symbols limned out on his flesh.

"What about a bird? A phoenix, maybe, or a pelican?"

Mary nodded, but she still didn't want to tell anybody but Agnes about the token she'd taken from Chamberlen's rigid hand.

Robert stood up suddenly and walked a few feet away, shoulders slumped.

After a few moments, Mary went to him and touched his shoulder. "Mr. Sudbury?"

He turned to her, his eyes communicating such pain and fear it took her breath away. "Not again," he muttered. He looked as though he were in a trance.

She began to remove her hand from his shoulder when he quickly covered it with his own, pinning it in place.

Mary was startled by this sudden move. He shook his head as though dismissing whatever dark thoughts possessed him and instead gazed at her intently. Whether it was the swirling fear in her gut or some inexplicable pull toward the man himself, Mary wondered what his kiss would feel like.

Mary closed her eyes in expectation of a soft exhalation of breath, the tender feeling of lip on lip, but it never came.

Instead, she heard Greedyguts's frenzied caws and her little brother's terrified screams.

CHAPTER 6

A recipe for puppy water

Take one young fat puppy and put him into a flat still, quartered, guts and all ye skin upon him, then put in a quart of new buttermilk, two quarts of white wine, four lemons purely pared and then sliced . . .

Sudbury rushed up the path ahead of Mary only to pull up short. He blocked whatever lay ahead, so she maneuvered around him, desperate to get to Tom.

She stopped dead in her tracks as Tom threw himself in her arms, wailing.

On an ancient yew tree just a few feet off the path hung a dog, swaying from the lowest branch with a noose around its neck and its tongue lolling from the side of its mouth.

Mary hugged Tom closer to her as she turned to watch Sudbury approach the gruesome sight. His mouth set in a grimace, he took a cloth from his pocket and wiped blood from the poor animal's abdomen.

He turned to the side and retched.

"Sir, what is it?" Tom's voice was small and afraid. "It looks like a dog. Is it a dog?"

"I'm afraid so," Sudbury said. "You two should go home. I will stay and give this poor creature a proper burial."

Mary nodded and thanked Sudbury. She picked Tom up to carry him to safety, but after a few steps, he wriggled free.

Mary watched in horror as he ran back toward the mutilated dog. "Tom!" she yelled. "What are you doing? Come here at once!"

But Tom continued toward the yew tree and kneeled in front of the dog. He placed his hand on the dog's head, right behind its ears, and gave it several loving pats as he intoned the Lord's Prayer.

Sudbury lowered his head and joined in the prayer.

"I am sure you were a very good dog," Tom said as he gave the corpse one last pat.

He walked back to Mary and took her hand. "We can go now."

Mary nodded and led him away, trying to appear calm. But as Tom had intoned the Lord's Prayer, she had caught sight of the dog's stomach, cleaned of blood by Robert, and she saw the horrifying images—symbols she'd seen once before etched on the abdomen of Henry Chamberlen.

Mary debated whether to continue on to Agnes's cottage. Her stomach clenched when she thought back on the events of the last few hours. Tom was too young to be exposed to such threats and awful sights. But she worried about Agnes and how she fared, so she and Tom hurried on.

Standing at the front door, she was glad they had come—simply being in Agnes's home, sitting with her friend, would calm her.

Agnes's garden was coming along nicely—she took in the tall, elegant peas climbing up willow tresses, cheerful green leaves belying the comically ugly parsnips below, the blushing pink of a partly exposed turnip. Mary breathed deep of the rosemary and lavender scents tinged with onion. These treasures and perfumes made all the hard work—planting and weeding, harvesting and mixing, crushing and cooking—worth the trouble and effort.

Agnes answered the door, looking markedly healthier. After hugging Tom, she sent him off to pick apples and invited Mary inside.

Mary lost no time telling Agnes all that had occurred that day, eager to unburden herself. Agnes sat quietly for some time before responding.

"Well, Hopkins may be right—there is evil afoot in Bicknacre."

Mary was shocked. "You really believe there are witches here?"

Agnes shook her head. "No, I believe the evil is Hopkins himself. He cannot be allowed to treat you like that. And who's to say he wasn't the one to mangle that poor dog, to make it look like we have maleficium in our town?"

Mary hadn't thought of that possibility.

Agnes put her hands on her knees and grunted as she stood. "Well, Mary, we cannot let him get away with this. If he tries anything else, I have a potion that will turn his guts into jelly. It will be painful, and it might take him several days to die, but it will be for the best."

Mary was stunned. How could Agnes suggest such a thing—and so cavalierly?

"You jest."

Agnes stoked the fire and looked over her shoulder, surprised. "If it comes to that, what choice do we have? Sometimes we must do terrible things to protect the ones we love."

Mary took a deep breath. This was not the Agnes she knew, the tender healer who'd helped her during the most painful periods of her life, who'd taught her how to ease the aches and suffering of their friends and neighbors. The Agnes who poked at the flames in front of her was willing to kill a man, to torment him, to make him suffer an agonizing death.

She could not believe that Agnes—her confidante, counselor, teacher, and friend—could do such a thing. Instead, she thought, this was what fear and suspicion, and Hopkins, had created.

Mary had just finished telling Mrs. Allen about a treatment for her aching back—rose water and amber mixed in an eggshell with white wine—when she heard her brother calling. It was market day, and they were surrounded by the sights and smells of commerce: dairymen selling their eggs and milk, fishmongers their cockles and cod. To the side of the market cross, the blacksmith's son hawked small nails and candleholders, and all around them farmers herded sheep and pigs—even the occasional cow—intended for the slaughter. With all the busyness and cacophony, she almost didn't hear Tom. She had left him with some of the other boys making a game of pouring water from a puddle in the grass onto a little berm made of sticks. He stood a bit apart from the other children, as he so often did. He had fashioned little people and animals out of mud balls and twigs and put them in a boat floating in a mud puddle nearby.

"Mary," Tom called out. "Mary, look! I've made Noah and Noah's wife and Noah's sons and all the animals!"

Mrs. Allen began to chuckle, and Mary looked over to admire his work.

"Such a fine young boy. Such a pity about his foot," Mrs. Allen said.

Mary had grown tired of the subtle barbs the townsfolk aimed at her and her brother. "At least his foot does not end up in his mouth," Mary said without thinking, regretting it at once. She should know better—Mrs. Allen was popular with her neighbors, and Sudbury had advised her to get along with all and sundry.

Mrs. Allen harrumphed and was about to reply when Matthew Hopkins, who had been examining the boy's biblical diorama, interrupted.

"Young man," Hopkins intoned as he peered at the crowd nearby. "Who taught you to make such poppets? And where did you learn about such symbols?"

Mary's body rocked with terror and fury—she knew exactly what Hopkins insinuated. Tom's little stick-and-mud people were nothing like poppets, the cloth dolls witches were said to use to inflict illness or pain on their victims.

Mary stepped closer to the boy's creations and her heart sank. Tom had carved a circle with a dot in the middle. He must have seen it on the mutilated corpse of the hanging dog. Strange how something so simple could look so dangerous.

Mary wanted to run away with Tom, to run from this oily man and his smug accusations. But she knew that to do so would lead only to more suspicion and rumors.

"If you have a question for my brother," she said in a voice loud enough for the crowd to hear, "you would be better served to speak with me first."

Hopkins stepped forward to address her but was interrupted.

Little George Perkins, only a year or two older than Tom, had run up to Hopkins and was pulling on his sleeve. "Is it true," he asked, "what they say about Mrs. Shepherd? That you took her to the jail? Is she a witch?"

Mary went cold. Her feet felt frozen to the path, as though taking even one step would cause her to collapse and crack into a million shards of ice.

Hopkins stared at her, smiling, and then he looked at George. Mary's hands itched to slap the self-satisfied look off Hopkins's face. "Young Master Perkins, is it? My fine young man, we must not make assumptions. We must put Mrs. Shepherd to the usual tests and examine the witnesses."

"But what tests are those?" George asked.

The crowd drew closer, and each person leaned in to hear.

"First we shall interview the townspeople," Hopkins declared. "Any man, woman, or child who has pertinent evidence shall be given a chance to present it."

Mary stifled a groan. By nature, Agnes was brusque, arrogant. She scolded those who questioned her, and had a fierce temper. Her skills and willingness to help her neighbors had won her acceptance in the community, but it was grudging. She had no real enemies, but she had made few true friends who would stand for her.

Mr. Smith, who had argued with Agnes about the placement of a fence between their properties, nodded and looked at Jane Gunter, whose daughter miscarried around last Martinmas, just weeks after Agnes had given her a caudle to help with her morning sickness.

"She's not from here," a voice called from the back. "Don't know anything about her from before Richard brought her around."

It was true. Agnes's past was a mystery to most. There were many things even Mary didn't know. Mary knew Agnes had married Richard Shepherd, a Bicknacre man who'd brought her home well over two decades prior, but nobody knew who her people were or where she came from. Richard had simply returned to town after a sojourn in another city, Agnes in tow. When the villagers discovered she could read and write, they indulged in ever more gossip and speculation: surely she'd been rich, they whispered, to have such skills. Many had tried to pry information from Agnes about her former life, but she remained stubbornly mute on the subject. She and Richard had lived quietly in the village for almost two years when Agnes's stomach began to swell, much to the villagers' surprise. They had thought her too old to bear a child, and many assumed she would lose it quickly. But Agnes treated herself with her own medicines, and Grace was born healthy.

The townspeople whispered about Grace, though. She was "touched," they said—by the angels or the demons, nobody knew. Grace had no voice, could not utter a word, but she had eyes that could see to a person's very soul and an insight that drew her to good and generous people and bade her shun those with evil intentions. As Grace grew up with her smiles and giggles and her refusal to say a word, rumors circulated that she was a changeling or the product of Agnes's coupling with a fairy.

And then Grace died of smallpox when she was only thirteen years old. Agnes mourned Grace's death so long and with such grief that some whispered she'd been driven to madness.

Hopkins's voice pierced Mary's reverie. "During the interviews, we shall keep Mrs. Shepherd at the jail for observation." He turned to Jane Gunter and explained in an unctuous, overly intimate tone, "You see, a witch's familiars will often visit in the night—we shall be on hand if such an event occurs."

Tom ran to Mary. "What is a familiar?" he whispered.

Mary shushed him, but Hopkins overheard.

Tom's question put an unholy gleam in Hopkins's eyes. "Ah, young Tom, an excellent question! A familiar is a witch's companion, compelled by her dark arts to serve her. It's usually a small animal, a cat or rat or mouse. Sometimes it's a bird, like a crow." He gave Mary a pointed look and then turned back to the crowd, which stood enthralled with his rhetorical flair. "And sometimes it's an unnatural combination thereof. The witch imbues the creature with her very soul, and then the creature has no choice but to carry out her will. They're often plain animals of the dark, but they can also be strange creatures, impossible to mistake." He bent down and said softly, so that the crowd had to strain to hear, "One witch I uncovered in Chelmsford had a familiar that looked like a mouse but with tusks and a man's beard!"

The crowd gasped. Hopkins smiled in delight, relishing the attention. He was a masterful orator.

He straightened, and again his voice rang out strong and clear. "We shall also do a thorough examination of Agnes Shepherd to see if she bears any of the marks of a witch. Often what looks like a mole or a boil is a teat used to suckle the devil himself." He stared at Mary for a moment or two. "If after that we determine Mrs. Shepherd is, indeed, guilty of maleficium, we shall seek out any of her companions. Witches often gather together at night, at witches' Sabbaths in the forest."

Mary's heart pounded as several people in the crowd turned to look at her.

"And how long will Mrs. Shepherd be imprisoned?" asked Bridget Jenkins. The question was for Hopkins, but Bridget stared straight at Mary.

"She'll be held in the jail until the assizes in Chelmsford."

The assize judge would not arrive in Chelmsford for another two weeks. It could have been worse—he usually only came through every three or four months. But Agnes Shepherd would likely suffer greatly in the two weeks she waited.

Hopkins's voice got louder. "And if we do, indeed, discover that there have been witches' Sabbaths in the forests of Bicknacre, we shall ferret out every witch, every case of maleficium, of evil magic, and see who was responsible for the death of Henry Chamberlen." His voice rose to a fevered pitch, and he broke into a hysterical giggle. Then his face took on a look of unholy glee. "The devil's handmaidens shall answer to our higher justice!"

Mary could keep still no longer. Heedless of the crowd's hostile stares, she grabbed Tom's hand and led him away.

"Mary?" Tom asked in a plaintive voice. "Why did you make me leave? I was going to tell that man that Mrs. Shepherd doesn't have any pets, no dogs or cats, unless you count Greedyguts."

"That would not help Mrs. Shepherd, Tom," Mary replied in a stern voice. "Please do not talk about Greedyguts to anyone, at least for a while."

"Yes, Mary." Tom worried his lower lip and stopped her. "Mary?"

"Yes."

"Now may I punch Mr. Hopkins in the nose?"

"No, Tom, you may not. But I want you to know that I very much understand the desire."

As soon as they were out of sight of the peering eyes in the market, Mary led Tom to Sudbury's house. She needed help, she admitted to herself, and he was the only person in town not under Hopkins's sway. Her heart beat wildly with fear as panic set in. She knocked on the door with shaking hands.

While she waited, Mary examined the house. It was finely constructed and one of the largest in Bicknacre. The former occupants, a family with six children, had built it for hosting company and often had large dinner parties. Mary couldn't imagine why Sudbury needed all that room. White smoke issued from the chimney, and she detected a faint scent of sulfur in the air. Inside, she heard what sounded like pots and pans clanging together.

Mary knocked again. And again. She knew Sudbury was inside, and she refused to simply go away.

"Who is it?" he said finally, an aggressive tone in his voice.

"Mary Fawcett," she replied. "And Tom."

Silence, and then she heard two or three locks being worked. The door opened to reveal an exhausted-looking Sudbury, even paler than usual. His eyes were red and swollen, as though he'd been up all night.

"Good afternoon, Mrs. Fawcett," he said. He ran a hand through his hair and fidgeted with a glass bottle he held in his other hand.

"Good afternoon—"

Before she could finish her sentence, Tom hopped in front of her.

"Sir, may I see your house?"

Mary put a restraining hand on Tom's shoulder. She didn't want Sudbury to think she had put Tom up to this, though she had to admit she, too, was eager to come inside, not just from curiosity, but because every minute that she stayed outside his door she risked one of the townspeople seeing her. She felt betrayed by her neighbors' suspicions and had an overwhelming need to hide from them.

Sudbury sighed and rubbed his eyes. He gave a reluctant chuckle and ruffled Tom's hair, then ushered them in.

As soon as Mary ventured inside, she saw why Sudbury had chosen this house. The interior was unlike anything she'd ever seen. The sitting room to the side was almost empty, but the dining area was filled with books and cookery implements. A makeshift oven had been built in the corner, embedded in the fireplace. It looked like a kitchen and library combined. She had imagined Sudbury's home would be rather messy and cluttered, a bachelor's abode. Instead she found it tidy and well kept. Stacks of books and papers sat on every surface—more books than she'd ever seen—and countless cooking vessels. A subtle but acrid smell of smoke hung in the air.

It felt like heaven.

Sudbury watched Mary as she walked over to the glass vessels neatly laid out on the table and gently ran her hand down the graceful neck of one particularly beautiful piece.

"What does this do?" she whispered with curiosity and a bit of reverence.

"That's an alembic. We use it for distillation."

Mary moved over to another vessel. "And this?"

"That's a retort, for heating liquids."

Mary could scarcely tear herself away from the fascinating containers. She wanted to know what they could do, and what she could possibly do with them in her own work.

"And this?" She pointed to a tall vessel with a circular mouth and two thin arms.

"That's called a pelican, and it, too, is for distilling."

Mary swallowed. Could these strange pieces of glass and earthenware have any connection to the medallion she'd taken from Chamberlen's corpse?

Sudbury gave a little cough. "Have you come merely to inventory my equipment, then?"

Mary blushed.

Sudbury walked to the little table by the fire and fumbled with some cups. "Would you like some wine?" Mary nodded. He bent down to whisper loudly to Tom, "I have some cake, if you would like."

Tom's eyes lit up. "Yes, please, sir!" he said quickly.

It was strange to see Sudbury do something as workaday as fixing refreshments. From the inelegant way he did so, Mary guessed he didn't have frequent visitors.

After a few awkward moments, Sudbury set Tom up at the table with a large square of rosemary cake. He handed Mary a cup of wine and led her to the other side of the room.

Sudbury again ran his fingers through his hair, glanced anxiously at the pots burbling on the stove, and sighed. "While I'm delighted to see you, I have some experiments in a critical stage. May I ask what brings you here today?"

This Sudbury was colder, more distant than the man she'd previously met. But she had more important things to worry about. "Have you heard anything about Mrs. Shepherd?"

Sudbury's head snapped back and he gave Mary his full attention. "No."

"She's been taken to the jail by Matthew Hopkins."

Sudbury swore loudly. Tom looked over at them with wide eyes, and Sudbury apologized.

"When?"

"Yesterday, I think. I learned about it just now."

Sudbury set down his wine. "Good. Hopkins has not had her for long, so she may not have confessed yet."

Mary gaped. "She has nothing to confess! She's innocent!"

"Well, of course she is," Sudbury replied irritably. "That hardly matters." He sighed and took a deep breath. In a gentler tone he said, "With what they put the accused through, it's no wonder these poor women and men confess. He will have kept her up all night, badgering her with stories and innuendo, and he and Stearne will take turns keeping her awake many nights more if we don't intervene. In time she'll confess to anything out of fear, pain, and exhaustion."

Mary stood quietly for a few moments, trying to absorb all that Sudbury told her.

"She is not strong," Mary said. "She's been ill. Will she make it to the assizes?"

Robert looked down at the floor. "It depends on what Hopkins wants from her."

The room that imprisoned Agnes reminded Mary of the cellar where her parents stored potatoes and onions: dark and fearsome, moisture hanging in the air and coating every surface.

At least Agnes had a candle and a thin mattress in the corner—even though the tang of sweat and rot told Mary that the straw hadn't been changed in some time.

Mary had known Geoffrey, the jailer, her whole life. He had always been big, always been cruel. He grunted as he motioned to where Agnes lay and closed the metal door with a bang.

Only a thin blanket covered Agnes, and even from across the room, Mary could see her shivering. She tried but failed to raise her head as Mary approached the bed. Already she had lost weight from her previously plump frame, and her cheeks looked sunken, her lips flaking from lack of water. Her skin was sallow, and she had dark circles under her eyes. Mary couldn't know for sure which of these symptoms to attribute to her previous sickness and which to attribute to Hopkins, but she had a grim suspicion that a good deal was from the latter. A mighty rage gripped her. She dare not complain to Geoffrey for fear of being kept from Agnes in the future—she was shocked they'd let her visit even this once. She would do whatever it took to get Agnes out of this fetid pit.

Agnes coughed, and Mary heard the wet rattle of phlegm that she hadn't the force to expel. She needed heat and dryness to counteract the cold humors that dominated her body, but Mary saw no way to provide a fire. She reached under Agnes's back and helped her sit up, hoping that a shift in position would help her cough up some of the vile pus in her lungs.

Agnes groaned, but the cough interrupted her protest. Mary slipped behind her and rested Agnes's weight on her chest, struggling not to gag at the stench of urine and sick that assailed her. When Agnes was settled, Mary gently touched her cheek and sensed her anger and fear, her derision for Hopkins and Stearne, and—crowding out the others—her worry for Mary and Tom. And then Mary felt nothing but Agnes's exhaustion.

"My dear," Agnes said weakly, "you should not have come."

"Nonsense," Mary replied. "You need somebody to take care of you."

Agnes leaned her head back under Mary's chin. She took a deep breath and shifted more of her weight onto Mary as Mary ran her fingers through the older woman's tangled hair.

"You should not visit me," she said. Her voice was clearer, but it shook. "They will accuse you, too."

Mary tutted. "Do not fret about such things. Here, I'm going to lay you down for a moment." Mary reached under her skirts and found the little bag filled with medicines she'd smuggled in. She pulled out a bottle with a thick cordial and a little spoon and fed some to Agnes.

"Ahhh, aqua mirabilis," she said with relief. "I have taught you well. I don't suppose you've brought any syrup of violets with you? That always helps my cough."

Mary smiled. "Right here," she said, reaching into her bag. "And I have brought some bread, as well."

Agnes took the bread eagerly but yelped when she began chewing. She saw Mary's concerned face and patted her hand. "Not to worry," she said. "It is but a little sore. Hopkins tried to get a confession by pulling on my tongue with a pair of hot tongs, but that son of a whore got nothing from me."

Mary shook with rage, but Agnes stayed eerily calm. "He is evil, Agnes. Just evil. I will bring some salve next time I visit."

Agnes smiled her thanks.

Mary continued combing Agnes's hair with her fingers for a few minutes before asking, in a quiet voice, "What else have they done to you?"

Agnes tensed.

"They came to get me in the middle of the night. It was Hopkins and that assistant of his, Stearne, and Simon Martin with them at the end of it."

"Simon!" Mary exclaimed.

"Yes, and thank God he was there, or I shudder to think of the treatment I would have had. He made them stop. They charged me with witchcraft. I asked on what evidence, and they said on the testimony of Verity Martin. She said Greedyguts was my familiar and had tortured her, claimed the devil whispered in her ear that I gave her herbs to miscarry his spawn and that I killed Henry Chamberlen. But you should not be here with me. Mary, you must promise me you will be careful! If not for me, at least for Tom!"

Mary promised.

Agnes, somewhat placated, continued. "Verity still claims I made her sick. They tore up my cottage looking for a poppet, said I used it to make Verity vomit and cough up pins. They accused me of consorting with the devil, of having relations with him and getting with his child. Mary—" She broke off. "Hopkins even said Grace herself was the devil's get."

Mary put her arm around Agnes's shoulder. "Grace was God's own angel."

Agnes shuddered. "After accounting my supposed sins, they brought me here to see if I would be visited by the devil. I will say no more about what happened that night."

When Agnes had finished, Mary sat quietly. "I suppose that's why they allowed me to visit you," she said. "It wasn't out of kindness or compassion. If they prove you're a witch, I'm guilty by association."

Agnes nodded, and a tear rolled down her face, leaving a glistening trail in the dried mucus and dirt on her cheek.

Mary had never seen Agnes shed a tear.

Mary stood up. She knew what she had to do. "I will visit Verity Martin, and I will not let her father stop me. I must convince her to recant. In the meantime, do what you can to stay well and do not utter a word—not a word!—until I return."

Agnes reached out a shaking hand. Her grasp was weak, and Mary was startled by the heat emanating from her skin. She prayed Agnes didn't have a fever. She had two enemies now: Matthew Hopkins and the sickness that consumed Agnes.

She would have to act fast to defeat either.

CHAPTER 7

The admirable oil the virtues whereof are these. It maketh sound and healeth all wounds in short time, the sinnows being cut, it is good for any burning with fire, it easeth the passion of the stomach. It provoketh urine, it alayeth the pain of the bladder and lower parts of the belly and thighs, it is good for the morning in children for gouts and deafness

Take eight wine pints of old oil, two like pints of good white wine, eight handfuls of the buds of Saint-John's-wort, bruise it in a mortar and put them all in a glass stopped very close . . .

Mary could scarcely sleep that night, overwhelmed by anxiety about confronting Verity in the morning. She had only just drifted off when she felt Tom's small hand shaking her awake.

"Mary?" Tom's voice shook. "Why is the roof moving?"

Mary struggled awake, blinking at Tom as she grasped the strangeness of his question. She sat bolt upright. Tom had moved from his usual spot on the bed and perched at the bottom. He pointed up at the ceiling of the cottage.

"Listen, Mary, listen."

Mary pulled him close and they sat, waiting. She was starting to think Tom had just heard rats scurrying about in the thatch when, out of the darkness, came a thumping on the roof, followed by the faint sounds of ripping and tearing.

Mary set Tom on the side of the bed closest to the wall and gave him a poker that had been sitting by the fire.

"If anybody tries to hurt you, poke them in the foot or crotch," she instructed.

Tom nodded, his eyes huge.

Mary pulled a blanket around herself and grabbed her longest and sharpest knife, the one she used for cutting the heads off chickens. She crept along the cold wood floorboards. She knew which were the squeakiest, but she couldn't open the door without making noise, so instead she tugged it open with all her might and charged out into the darkness. Her knife glinted in the light of the moon.

"Who are you and what do you want?" she shrieked.

Whatever was on the roof started scrambling and then, with a muffled curse, fell to the ground. Mary raised her knife high over her head, holding it with both hands, ready to plunge it into the heart of whomever had violated her home and threatened her and Tom. Mary had never felt so in danger—or so powerful. The combination of the moon, the darkness, and the fierce need to protect her brother made her wild, primal. Only the urgent plea and raspy whimper of the invader stayed her hand. She took a deep breath and carefully stepped toward the prone body. She kicked it and quickly stepped away. She heard a yelp, and then the intruder turned toward her.

It was Simon.

He rolled over onto his side and held up his arms, partly for protection and partly in supplication.

"Mary, please, please do not hurt me—I mean no harm!"

Mary dropped the knife to the ground. "Simon, you ridiculous whelp! What are you doing here? Are you alone?"

"Yes, Mary, yes, I'm alone."

Mary heard footsteps on the path. She looked at Simon accusingly, but he shook his head in confusion. As a dark figure appeared, Mary bent to retrieve the knife and Simon picked up a nearby stick. They tensed, suddenly on the same side, ready to do battle with the unknown assailant.

The figure came into sight. Robert Sudbury.

Seeing Mary and Simon wielding their weapons, Sudbury raised his hands in front of his face.

"Do not attack! I heard the shouts and came to help."

With a sigh, Mary dropped her knife again and motioned for the two men to come into the cottage. Simon entered first, and just as Mary followed, she heard a muffled cry and a curse.

Tom stood just inside the door, poker in hand and looking fierce while Simon hopped on one foot.

"The little brat poked my foot!" he cried.

"Well, you shouldn't have scared my sister," Tom said, puffing out his chest. "You're lucky I didn't poke you there!" He pointed at Simon's crotch and Simon blanched.

Mary went to get a chair for Simon. Robert ruffled Tom's hair and whispered, "Well done."

Mary left the two men to glare at each other as she took Tom back to her bed and sang to him until he fell back asleep. Then she stormed into the little sitting area next to the fire.

"You first, but talk softly." Mary pointed at Simon as she plopped down in her chair. "If you awaken my brother again, I will use that poker on you myself." The well of her patience had run dry. "Explain. What were you doing on my roof?"

Simon at least had the decency to blush.

"I was gathering thatch."

Robert gave a snort of disgust while Mary sat in confusion.

"I would have thought you could afford your own, Simon. But if you needed thatch, I would have gladly given you some. During the day, of course."

Simon reddened and looked down at the floor.

"He doesn't need the thatch," Sudbury said, his voice dripping scorn. "At least not for his roof. He's trying to prove you're a witch."

Simon's head snapped up.

"That is false!" he cried. "It's just the opposite!"

Mary shushed Simon with a scowl. "Quiet!"

"Ignorant people, unschooled in logic, resort to this trick," Sudbury explained. Simon's fists clenched at the insult. Robert gave a mirthless laugh and continued. "They take thatch from a suspected witch and burn it. If one of her so-called victims recovers, they proclaim they've found their witch."

Simon sighed and turned his face toward the ceiling, avoiding Mary's eyes. "I thought I could get some of the thatch from your cottage and burn it with Hopkins himself present as a witness. When Verity didn't recover from her ailments, it would prove you're not a witch. I didn't want to tell you yet for fear of providing false hope."

"So instead you terrified her and little Tom by thumping around on their roof in the middle of the night?" Robert asked, icily. Even Mary cringed at the derision in Robert's voice.

Simon stiffened. "I didn't mean to. I got on the eaves without making too much noise, but the thatch there was woven too well and wouldn't come out. I had to go up farther on the roof."

Robert snorted again.

Simon surged up from his chair. "At least I'm trying to help them," he cried. "Not just brewing up devilish potions like you!"

Robert clenched his fists and stood. The men's faces were mere inches from each other. Mary was fascinated by the contrast between Simon's smooth, boyish cheek and Sudbury's pitted and scarred one.

When Robert raised his fist Mary hurried to insert herself between the two.

"Stop it!" she whispered with a hiss. "Stop it right now! You'll wake Tom."

Simon gave her a hurt look. He straightened and, in as imperious a voice as he could muster, said, "Mrs. Fawcett, I'm sorry for any fright or inconvenience I may have caused you. It will not happen again. Good night."

He walked out of the cottage without turning around.

Mary let out the breath she'd been holding and sat down.

Robert sat, too, and rubbed his temples.

"He's a well-meaning man," she said.

"He is an arseworm."

"A well-meaning arseworm, then."

They smiled at each other and sat quietly.

Mary gave voice to a thought that had been nagging her. "Robert, how is it that you were so close at hand to hear the shouting? And why are you clothed for the day?"

Despite the weak light of the fire and the mottled texture of Robert's scars, she could tell that he blushed.

"I've been keeping watch on your cottage," he admitted.

Mary didn't know whether to be annoyed or pleased.

"How long?" she asked.

"Ever since Hopkins darkened your door and threatened you." He gave her a piercing look. "Does it bother you? If so, I will stop."

Mary thought. "No," she said finally. "But I'm sure that it's cold and uncomfortable out there on the path. You may come in, from time to time, for a drink and some food."

Robert gave Mary a cautious, almost shy smile.

Gone was the standoffish scholar she'd encountered at his home. Encouraged by his smile, she ventured to ask, "Sir, when did you start your experimentation? What made you decide to explore alchemy?"

Robert laughed a little, and Mary bristled.

"I apologize, I wasn't laughing at you. The opposite, in fact. It occurred to me that you're the only woman I've ever met who, sitting with me—alone—in the dark, would ask about my experiments." He gave her a look filled with admiration, not scorn.

Mary chuckled. "And yet you haven't answered."

Robert smiled and settled deeper into his chair. He told her stories of his teachers and other students meeting to discuss the laws of nature. They didn't practice magic, he insisted, despite what others might think. Rather, they labored to understand the laws governing matter itself, the chemical properties of the lead and salts and iron they handled. Could these materials be transmuted into other substances by exposure to fire? By combination or refining? Could they be transformed into medicines or precious metals?

Mary shifted to the edge of her seat and listened intently as Robert told her of his theories and his successes and failures in proving them.

Then Robert stopped midsentence and a look of self-consciousness crossed his face. "But I've been going on too long."

Mary began to disagree, but he shook his head. "No, that's enough from me. I want to know about your work as well. What started you on your path?"

Mary hesitated. She had never discussed these things with anybody but Agnes.

She began slowly. "I think I was born with something, some sort of ability to heal. I've heard that my grandmother had it, and my mother, too—though she refused to heal anybody outside her own family. She'd grown wary of outsiders and the accusations they could make. I inherited the recipes, but I find it's not enough for me to simply use them. I want to know why they work, and how."

They stayed up the rest of the night talking quietly, careful not to awaken Tom, discussing their work. Mary called it cookery, Robert, experimentation, but they both saw the similarities in what they did.

Mary valued efficiency, the best way to cure or ease the discomfort of the people she treated, while Robert looked for novelty, working to purify raw material and then transform the substance itself into something altogether more valuable. While their aims were different, they shared a common desire to fully understand the principles guiding their work.

Is this what it's like to be a man? Mary wondered. Free to expand her mind with new thoughts and theories and possibilities? A lightness of spirit came over her as they continued their conversation. Her mind buzzed as she felt inspired and enlightened by the new ideas floating around in her brain. She had never before experienced this kind of giddiness in her thoughts, even with Agnes. While the women discussed the recipes and sometimes reported back on *how* the recipes worked, they had never analyzed, theorized, or argued over *why* they worked. Why did pus—made up of cold and wet humors—issue forth from a patient who was hot to the touch and whose skin flamed red? Why did the shell of a snail help with pustules when they were dominated by the same phlegmatic humor? She burned to know not only the answers but the right questions to ask.

Mary knew that her cookery had nothing to do with the dark arts, but that didn't mean her cures weren't magical. Magic didn't always come from the devil—she had learned the distinction between the magical and the miraculous could easily shift and blur. And sometimes what people thought was magic could be explained if one only knew the workings of nature: how the humors operated, for example, or how foul miasmas could penetrate the body to cause sickness.

When Mary noticed that the darkness had lightened into a rosy pink, she stood to usher Robert out. She didn't want Tom to awaken to find Robert there, and she had to get at least a little sleep before going to see Verity.

"You should go now," she said.

"Yes, I suppose so," he said. He stood but made no move to leave. "I . . . I have enjoyed our conversation. Very much."

"As have I." Mary looked down at her hands. "I've never spoken with anybody like this before. It's not easy to find a man who will discuss such things with a woman. Thank you."

"It's not easy to find *anyone* to talk about such things with. I haven't had a conversation like this since I left Cambridge. I hope we can continue our conversation some other day."

Mary looked up to see Robert watching her intently. She imagined what it would be like to trace the scar that marked out the geography of his face like a stream cutting through the land, to feel the depth and texture of his healed burns.

Almost without thinking, she raised her hand. Robert leaned forward, in a sort of daze, but as her hand neared his cheek, he snapped to attention and took a step back.

With her hand still hovering in the space between them, Robert abruptly turned on his heel and exited the cottage without looking back.

CHAPTER 8

A receipt for the cure of the falling sickness

Take 3 ounces of dead men's skull which you may have at the apothecary's, 4 ounces of mistletoe of the oak, 4 ounces of red coral, 4 ounces of wood betony, let all these be wiped dry and clean, then dry them and beat them to fine powder and mix them together . . .

The events of the night before seemed like a fever dream as Mary went about her morning ablutions. Fears crowded her mind as she pondered the gravity of her situation: rumors that she practiced maleficium were pervasive enough that Simon felt compelled to go to great lengths to prove her innocence. And even if he did, she knew that some would still suspect she had a hand in Chamberlen's murder, and her association with Agnes also made her a suspected witch. She focused on her tasks and tried to push away the fear—and the tempting memories of a brilliant man with a scarred cheek.

She worked on a cordial for Agnes, for the phlegm that congealed in her head and lungs, and as she always did, she began her cookery by imagining what her patient felt and sensed. Mary thought of the cold of the cell, the moisture that clung to every surface, the scratching of rats, the spongy moss growing on the stone walls, and the lurking mold creeping along the wet floor. She imagined the fever that perched on the threshold of health's door. She felt the tickle of a cough starting deep in Agnes's chest, the painful spasm and presence of a foul miasma that signaled the kind of evil sickness in the lungs that could lead to death.

Mary gathered together all these thoughts as she took a small handful each of blue devil's bit and *Carduus benedictus* and tore the leaves into small pieces. She felt the pain in Agnes's nighttime wailing as she boiled it with licorice and anise seeds, felt Agnes's love for Grace as she added the simple syrup and rosewood leaves. And as she prepared the medicine, she hoped and prayed it would be good enough to keep Agnes alive during the hellishness of the coming weeks.

Mary heard rustling in the small room as Tom woke. She fed him a hearty breakfast of pottage and oat cakes and packed her cures in a satchel, and they walked to Verity Martin's house. She hated bringing him there, possibly exposing him to John Martin's sneers and insults, but she had no choice. She had promised Simon, and she would do whatever she could to help Verity.

John Martin was a cabinetmaker, and a skilled one at that, with commissions from Cambridge and even London. Simon, less skilled but more savvy, had helped his business thrive. The house reflected the Martins' prosperity—freshly whitewashed and with glazed windows. Mary noticed, however, that the front had not been swept in some time, and thick cobwebs clung to the gable of the house.

John Martin's success owed much to his skill but even more to his habit of bullying and intimidation. While his strong-arm tactics had won him money and property, they had cost him the good opinion of the people of Bicknacre—and possibly of his own wife. While John insisted she had died of a French pox while visiting her sister, Mary had heard rumors that she had run away with the poor but vastly more affable shopkeeper, Mr. Hodge.

Mary took a deep breath and knocked on the door. Then she waited. And waited.

She heard footsteps in the hall and some rustling.

"Who is it?" a voice barked.

"Mary Fawcett, sir. I'm here to talk to your daughter."

The heavy door swung open to reveal John Martin, his eyes slits of anger and his jaw clenched. His jowls brushed his collar and shook as his head swiveled, scanning the street for onlookers. Simon stood behind him, looking as though he had bitten into an unripe apple.

"What is she doing here?" he asked Simon with a sneer.

Mary pulled Tom more tightly to her side.

"Father, you must welcome her in," Simon coaxed. "She only wants to speak with Verity, to find out how she is, to see if she can help."

"She can talk with me, instead. This . . . woman, I suppose I'll call her that for now . . . keeps company with the beldam who led the devil to my little Verity. Then gave her the poison to rid her of the babe the devil got her with." He raised his voice and looked for an audience in the street to witness his words.

"Father!" Simon protested.

Mary stepped forward, and in her most comforting voice, the one she used on deathbeds and at childbirths, said, "Mr. Martin, I can understand what a shock this is. I imagine I am the last person you want to see standing at your door."

Mr. Martin grunted.

"Nevertheless, sir, I ask your permission to speak with Verity. Agnes did none of the things she stands accused of, and I believe I can help your daughter."

Mr. Martin's face turned an alarming shade of purple, and he'd taken a breath to raise his voice again when his nearest neighbor, William Woods, walked up to the door. Mr. Woods had been a friend of Mary's father and watched over her after her parents' deaths. She had prepared medicine to ease the pain in his mother's belly, the great ache that eventually killed her.

"Mrs. Fawcett, young Tom," he greeted them. "You look well." He gave John Martin a piercing, hostile look. "Is there a problem here?"

"No problem you need concern yourself with, Woods," John replied. "Go home to your shrew of a wife."

Mr. Woods took a step forward. "Now see here," he growled.

"I was hoping to speak to Verity," Mary told Mr. Woods quickly, trying to forestall a fight between the two men. "I've heard she's not well. I would like to help her."

"Surely that poor girl can use all the help she can get?" Mr. Woods said, his jaw clenched, his words directed to Simon and John Martin.

"But she . . ." John Martin garbled his next words in his fury. "It was her crony who caused Verity's condition! She, too, is a witch!"

Again he said this loudly, as though for an audience. Mary saw that many of the neighbors watched, some peeking out of windows, some pretending to be otherwise occupied in the street.

Mr. Woods interrupted him. "If that were true, then the best thing would be for her to face Verity and touch her, wouldn't it? If she's a witch and responsible for cursing your Verity, her touch should cure her. Isn't that what happened with the Pendle witches in Lancashire?"

Mr. Martin pushed past Mary to stand directly in front of Mr. Woods. "I will be damned to hell before I allow that witch near the girl. Do you understand me, Woods?"

Mr. Martin was nearly shouting. Mary saw some of his spittle land on Mr. Woods's face.

Tom whimpered.

Mr. Woods flicked a glance at Tom. "Mary," he said, his voice calm and measured, "do you suppose Tom would like to have some cake with me and my grandchildren? They're visiting Mrs. Woods right now."

Mary sighed with relief. There was no way she would bring Tom into the Martins' house.

"I think Tom would like that very much, and I thank you, Mr. Woods," she said.

"Stay with Simon a moment, young man. A word with you first, Mary," he said, and took Mary's elbow, guiding her out of earshot.

"Simon is a nice young man," he said, his voice low. "And Verity a sweet and kind girl, but you know as well as I that John Martin has always been a mean fellow, and strange. Being his neighbor—well, I will say he has given me just cause to dislike him greatly. And I worry about that poor girl."

Mary nodded, encouraging Mr. Woods to continue despite his obvious reluctance.

"About a week ago, I was working in the garden when Verity ran out as though all the hounds of hell were after her. Her hair was in tangles, and she was yelling up a fright. Her face was covered with scabs. She fell at my knees and begged me to let her into my cottage. I was just about to call out to Mrs. Woods when John Martin came out. He was in a rage. I've seen him angry before, Mary, angry and mean. But I've never seen him like this. He grabbed Verity by the hair and pulled her back inside the house."

Mary caught her breath.

"I'm ashamed to say I did nothing. I didn't know what to do. Finally I got over my shock and went over to the house. John didn't answer at first, but I kept pounding and pounding on the door and he finally opened it. The look he gave me—I thought he would kill me.

"I pushed my way past him before he could object. Verity was lying in her bed, twitching, her eyes rolling around in their sockets. She looked like an animal in a cage. John said Verity was under a spell, that witches had made her insane, made her try to run away. But I saw the way John Martin looked at his daughter. Like he wanted to kill her, like he hated her. And I saw the terror in her eyes. John threw me out. I told the constable, but he said there was nothing he could do."

He looked at Mary, fear and worry and disgust all mixed in his gaze. "Something is amiss in the Martin house, Mary. You need to be careful. That man is a monster."

They walked back to the door. Mr. Woods took Tom's hand and the boy followed him reluctantly, worry for his sister warring with the promise of cake and playmates.

"I'll be just fine, Tom," Mary reassured him. "After all, Simon is here, and you remember how he protected me before."

At the reminder of Simon punching Hopkins, Tom's face split into a wide grin and he went with Mr. Woods.

John Martin snorted derisively and went inside.

Simon opened the door wider, whispering, "I must apologize again for last night."

"This visit has nothing to do with the thatch of my roof," Mary replied. "I'm here to speak with your sister. I want her to admit that Agnes had nothing to do with her misfortunes. You owe me this, Simon."

Simon looked up and down the street, then quickly drew Mary inside. He led her down a dark, dank hallway. The trappings of wealth surrounded them—paintings, rich linens, even a small tapestry on the wall—but it was clear that nobody was cleaning or caring for the home. It had the feeling of a house in crisis, the smell of a sickbed. The gloom and the foul odor and something even darker, something malevolent, shook Mary.

Simon sighed and Mary looked at him more carefully. He looked older and sadder these last few days. He reached out his hand and seemed about to say something when they heard the slam of a door and the echo of stomping boots. Simon looked sick.

"What do you really want, witch?" Mr. Martin shouted.

"As I said, I want only to speak with your daughter, to help her if I can and to hear from her own mouth her accusations against Agnes Shepherd."

"Ha! Then you can leave now," he said. He walked toward Mary and seized her roughly by the elbow.

Mary swallowed a yelp of pain, but suddenly the rough pressure was gone. Simon had grabbed his father's hand and flung it aside. He shoved Mary behind him and loomed over his father. He took hold of Mary's hand, and she could feel his trembling.

"You will never touch Mary Fawcett again, Father," he said in a loud voice.

"Step aside, you sniveling pup," Martin replied. "I will do whatever I want in my own house." He had started to push his son to the side when Simon grabbed his father's forearm and twisted it around his back, turning the older man around. Mr. Martin grunted in pain.

"Listen to me, Father," Simon said slowly in Martin's ear. "You will treat this woman with respect, and you will allow her to speak with Verity, or I will stop paying your bills and every collector in town will come after you."

John wrestled his arm away and turned. Then he spat in his son's face.

Simon calmly wiped the saliva from his cheek and continued staring at his father in open rebellion.

After several tense moments, John yielded and dropped his gaze. "Fine," he growled. "It is no matter to me what this witch does to either of you brats. You and your sister can keep each other company in hell for all I care."

An oppressive silence hung over the three as they walked to Verity's room.

John Martin entered first and sat on the only available chair, arms folded across his chest. Mary couldn't see Verity, but she heard her plaintive cry. "Simon?" she asked, her voice high and shaking. She sounded like a tiny child.

Simon went to the bed and began adjusting the blankets, but Verity pushed him away. When Simon backed up and Mary got her first glimpse of Verity, she gasped.

The poor girl looked close to death. Her arms—thin twigs lying at unnatural angles—lay on top of the blanket. Her face was gaunt, and her skin had a greenish cast. Red veins threaded through her exhausted eyes.

"Mary," she whispered. She tried to lift her arm off the cover, but it took too much effort. Her arm fell back down, defeated.

"Oh, Verity." Mary hurried over to her and put a hand on her forehead. She felt burning hot. Mary sat down next to Verity and bumped into a small bucket. Simon heard the bucket rattle and moved it to the side. "That's for the pins," he said, a scowl on his face.

Verity shuddered.

John Martin barked at Verity, "Good God, child, cover yourself."

Hands trembling violently, Verity rearranged the thin blanket that had slipped off one bare leg, but not before Mary saw that her calf was covered with sores, some of them oozing pus.

Verity turned and looked at the wall.

Mr. Martin snorted with disgust but remained in the room.

Mary began caressing Verity's brow.

"Get your bloody witch hands off my daughter!" Mr. Martin commanded.

Mary ignored him.

"Verity, I've heard that you've been telling tales about Mrs. Shepherd."

Verity turned back to Mary, pain and guilt in her eyes.

"Tell her," Mr. Martin boomed. "Tell the witch what happened, what Agnes Shepherd has done to you."

Verity turned over slowly, clutching handfuls of the blanket under her chin. She looked up at Mary, eyes glistening with unshed tears, and intoned, "I have been through great trials. Agnes Shepherd's curse has made me ill unto death. I have vomited and voided pins and needles, and I dream horrible dreams of the witches' Sabbath in which you and Mrs. Shepherd lay with the devil in turns."

Verity's words shocked Mary, but she was also surprised by how wooden she sounded, as if she were in a kind of trance—or as though the lines were rehearsed.

"Verity," she replied softly, hoping John Martin couldn't hear. "You know that's not true. You know that Mrs. Shepherd is innocent of these accusations."

Verity looked up at Mary and began to reach for Mary's hand when her father stood from his chair. Verity's hand fell.

"What are you saying to her, witch?"

Mary turned to the old man. As a child, she had feared him. Her parents had told her to avoid him—not that she'd needed their warning, as she recoiled from the glint in his eyes when he trained his too-lingering gaze on her. But now she could see that the years had worn him down. He was as sullen as a small child and as weak as an old man. He grabbed Mary's hand to pull her away from Verity, then gasped as Mary gripped back with all her strength. She could feel his anger drain away, replaced by fear. She felt the tremors in his hands and the quickening of his pulse. She simply looked at Mr. Martin, letting him grow more afraid as she held his hand in her strong grasp, and his eyes widened in her gaze. She thought he might hit her, but with a growl he wrenched away and stormed from the room.

Mary had won.

"Simon, may I have some time with Verity alone?"

Simon paused.

With a weak wave of her hand, Verity indicated Simon should go. "Please, brother."

Simon nodded curtly. "I will be right outside the door."

Verity waited until Simon had shut the door tightly before motioning Mary toward her. "Oh, Mary, I am so ashamed."

Mary gently squeezed Verity's hand. It was like holding the bony wing of a bird, as though a single squeeze would leave it crushed. "Why are you telling these stories about me?"

Tears glistened in Verity's eyes. "He made me do it. He's been so brutal, so awful to me. He made me hide the pins in my mouth and in my nightdress. He taught me to make it look like I was vomiting and voiding them." She blushed. "Even in front of Reverend Osborne. Oh, Mary, it was so humiliating!"

"It's your father you're speaking of, isn't it?" Mary asked.

Verity squeezed her eyes shut and nodded.

Mary hesitated to ask the next question. "Not Simon?"

Verity's eyes widened. "Of course not! Mary, how could you think so?"

"I'm sorry, but I had to be sure. And what about the accusations against Mrs. Shepherd?"

Verity hung her head in shame. "She has been nothing but kind to me." Mary took a deep breath and pushed down the anger welling up in her belly.

"But, Verity, why is he doing this to you?"

"He hates me," she said simply. There was no drama in her declaration, just a statement of simple fact that broke Mary's heart. "He has always hated me, ever since my mother left him. He blames me, says I was such a bad child she couldn't bear to be around me anymore. And he blames Mrs. Shepherd. He says she gave my mother a drink meant to lift her spirits, but that it was evil and weakened her will. He thinks that's why she ran away, left him for Mr. Hodge. He never blames himself and his rough ways, of course. Then, when Mr. Hopkins started asking about witches, he forced me to tell these stories. And now I wonder if he himself is starting to believe them."

She paused for a moment, closed her eyes, and gave a small sob. "That's not all."

Mary sat with her patiently until Verity could continue. "Mary, he's done things to me that God intended only to be between a man and his wife."

Mary had suspected as much. She had comforted other women— broken in body and spirit—who'd told her similar tales.

She squeezed Verity's hand gently. "Verity, look at me."

Several moments passed, but Mary waited patiently. Finally Verity looked up, terror and shame in her eyes.

Mary kept her gaze trained on the girl. "You did nothing wrong," she said forcefully. "You have nothing to be ashamed of, and you deserve better. I will do everything in my power to help you."

Verity sagged in relief and Mary gave her a quick hug.

"Did he make you sick to begin with?"

Verity paused, considering. "I don't know. He has the doctor in to see me. And in his only kind act, he helps control my pain. He gave me the cordial you concocted for me."

"The potion I made for your monthly pains? The one you sent Simon to fetch?"

Verity nodded.

"But I made that for you over two weeks ago! And I made only enough for four days."

Verity looked at her with pain and confusion in her eyes. "Are you sure?"

"Where is the cordial he gave you? What does it look like? How does it taste?"

Verity's face screwed up into a mask of disgust. "Oh, it is horrible! It is a wicked green color, and it has great lumps in it and tastes vile."

Mary's stomach twisted with dread. "That's not the cordial I made. Mine was made of clear wine and tasted only slightly of sugar and rosemary."

Verity stopped, rearranged her blanket, and went on in a voice so quiet Mary had to strain to hear her. "So he is poisoning me."

Mary gently lifted Verity's hand and held it in her own. "Verity, you should know that Mrs. Shepherd is in jail and very ill. She's been accused of maleficium based on your testimony, and she may well die in that jail."

Tears filled Verity's eyes. "I did not know what I was doing," she whispered. "He brought the doctor in, and the priest, and that man Hopkins, and he made me vomit those pins, and I thought I would die from the pain. He asked if I had seen her in company with the devil and they would not stop asking. They would not let me sleep. I was so tired, Mary, so tired."

Mary reached out and stroked Verity's hair.

"Shhh," she whispered. "I forgive you. And Agnes will forgive you. You've been tortured, there is no other word for it."

Mary comforted her for several more minutes. When Verity had stopped sobbing—soft little sobs being all she had the energy for—Mary said, "But, you know, you must know, that you have to tell the magistrate you lied about Mrs. Shepherd?"

Verity pulled away and looked at her in fear. "No! No, I cannot, Mary. My father will kill me. Besides," she continued, her voice beginning to rise as she looked wildly around the room and her hands flapped in agitation, "she probably is a witch! Plenty of people have whispered it. I am not the first . . ."

Mary took a breath, ready to argue with her, to plead with her to listen to her better angel, to tell the truth. But just as she opened her mouth, she heard a loud bang in the hallway.

Once again, John Martin burst into the room, Simon following behind. He bellowed, "Why is she still here? Get that damned witch out of my house."

She thought she'd defeated him in their battle of wills, but when she saw the look on his face, a paralyzing fear gripped her. Age may have weakened him, but from the raw fury in his eyes, he looked capable of anything.

She braced for his attack.

But it never came. Instead, he shoved her to the side and grabbed Verity by the shoulders.

Simon leapt to the bed and took hold of his father. Whether from surprise or his own weakness, John Martin took a step back.

"You will not touch her again," Simon bellowed. "You will never lay a finger on her, or so help me God I will make your face even uglier than it is."

Mr. Martin looked alternately shocked and angry, and Mary thought surely father and son would come to blows. Then John Martin took another step back and turned for the door.

He left without saying a word.

Mary sank to the bed. To her surprise, it was Verity who first spoke.

"What am I to do now, Simon?" Her voice shook and she trembled all over. "If I stay, he will surely kill me."

Simon motioned to the bed, and Mary stood to give him her spot. He sat gently on the mattress and took Verity's hand in his.

"We'll ensure your safety," he assured her. "I'll ask Reverend Osborne and his wife if they will take you in. They've always been very fond of you, and they have no children of their own."

Verity started to cry, and Simon took her in his arms, careful to avoid her weeping sores.

Mary left the house. The only words she spoke were silent ones to God, praying for some small measure of good, finally, in the terrible life of Verity Martin.

CHAPTER 9

A broth for those that are grieved with melancholy

*Take the knuckles of mutton and chop them small and
put them into a pipkin with three pints of water and set
them on the fire, and let them boil until such time as the
broth doth smell of the meat . . .*

Simon kept his promise, and Verity moved in that day with Reverend
Osborne and his wife. That was the only good thing to come of Mary's
visit; Agnes was still in peril. Since her imprisonment, Matthew Hopkins
had gathered more testimony from neighbors who'd quarreled with
Agnes—one claimed she'd spoiled twenty brewings of beer, another that
she'd caused his barn to burn down. Several claimed she was the cause of
cream not curdling and crops spoiling too early in the season. Hopkins
had enough evidence to keep Agnes under lock and key until the assizes.

For the next two weeks, Mary visited the jail as often as she could and
desperately attempted to heal the wounds Hopkins inflicted on Agnes
with his tests. One day she'd come to find new bruises on Agnes's wrists
and ankles, the next to find fresh oozing sores the size of peppercorns
scattered all over her torso—Hopkins had used a thick, sharp pin to try to
discover what he called the "witch's third teat," claiming she could use it to

suckle the devil himself. When Mary applied a plaster on the contusions, stopped the blood of the sores, she could feel Agnes's pain and rage—the strength of it rocked her body. But on the outside, Agnes showed only a stoic kind of patience. Sometimes she seemed almost serene.

"Hopkins wants me to be afraid," she explained to Mary. "And I refuse to give that man any joy."

Mary shuddered to think of what else Hopkins would have done had she not been watching over Agnes. And while she desperately wanted to help her mentor, she knew it came at great cost. There had to be a reason Hopkins allowed her access to her friend, and Mary thought she knew what it was: in standing by Agnes, Mary left herself open to accusations that she, too, was a witch. And while that was frightening enough, it terrified her to think her choices could harm Tom. What would Tom do if Hopkins threw Mary in jail? Mr. and Mrs. Woods would care for him, Mary knew, but Tom would be devastated. And worse: What if little Tom, with his wise but strange ways, and the club-foot that had always made the neighbors look at him askance, also stood accused? The thought of Tom in such danger made her stomach roil.

She had no way to gauge how much peril she and Tom were in. She'd avoided town as much as possible since Agnes was put in jail. Simon had tried to see Mary a handful of times, but she let his knock on the door go unanswered, and Sudbury had confined himself to his house. The first few times he refused to answer his door, she was disappointed. He continued to ignore her and her fury grew, and she recalled how they'd talked long into the night about their pasts, their experiments, even their hopes and dreams. What had he meant by confiding in her, advising her, conversing with her in ways that made her heart soar, and then abandoning her? And her other neighbors—well, they avoided her altogether. It seemed that the only people Mary talked to anymore were Tom and Mr. and Mrs. Woods.

Ever since Mary had begun working with Agnes, she had felt a bit of distance, a wariness, in her interactions with the people of Bicknacre. They eagerly came to her with their troubles, and when she helped them—most often with a cordial or poultice, but sometimes just by listening to their woes—they were warm and filled with gratitude. But in public interactions, at the church or market, around other people, she always felt a chill.

But that chill was nothing compared with the hostility she encountered now. Just the past day, a group of some three or four women she had known since childhood passed her on the path through the cemetery without a word, and a little boy screamed in fear when he saw her in the town square. As she walked through the village, she noticed more doors and windows bore marks of protection, conjoined circles with dots in the middle meant to ward off evil spirits—and witches. And just yesterday she'd opened her door to find three old boots cut up and splayed on the step. It was an old trick to protect a family from witches, but usually the boot was hidden in the rafters or in the wattle and daub inside the house. Knowing that a neighbor had trespassed on her property, had come to her very doorstep to leave this talisman, alarmed her more than any of the other offenses.

Her heart ached to know that her neighbors and her friends were so fickle, that they could be so easily manipulated by a charlatan witch-finder. All it had taken was a few well-placed suggestions of bad faith: a word in somebody's ear that the wheat blight had been her fault or that the stillborn son a result of her doing, a raised eyebrow and a nod when her name was mentioned.

People wanted to believe there was a reason for their bad luck and misfortune. Blaming Mary Fawcett was easier than blaming God.

Unwilling to face the betrayal of her neighbors, Mary kept herself mostly at home with her work and her worry until finally the day of the trial arrived, at last marking an end—one way or another—to Agnes's torture.

The assize trial was to be held in Chelmsford at the Market Cross House. The authorities had taken Agnes to the jail in Chelmsford the day before.

The day of the trial, Mary rose early so she could drop Tom off with Mrs. Woods and walk the five miles to Chelmsford. As she gave Tom a peck on the cheek goodbye, she heard a merry noise behind her—a wooden cart carrying some five or six people, drinking ale and laughing.

"That lot's going to the trial in Chelmsford," Mrs. Woods said with a grim look on her face. "They ought to be ashamed, grinning as they are, making bets, acting like they're going to the fair."

Mrs. Woods reached for Mary's shoulder and gave it a quick squeeze.

"Don't worry about the lad," she said. "I'll care for him as long as you need."

Mary thought surely she'd arrive at the courthouse first, but she was wrong. A crowd had already assembled at the Market Cross House. It was an open-sided edifice, tall, with massive oak columns holding up the second story. The accused and the judge—together with all his clerks—sat on the first floor, while assorted benches lined the upper level for the onlookers. The assizes tended to bring a crowd looking for a lively time and a bit of gossip, but the size of this crowd was unusual. Dozens of villagers from Bicknacre had made the trek and were already fighting for seats. Some even straddled the half wall separating the two floors, eager to get a closer look.

Mary was disgusted by the barely disguised glee with which they awaited the spectacle. Most were villagers who'd held grudges against Agnes. Sprinkled among them were a few supporters whom Agnes had helped over the years. Mary spotted one woman whose baby boy Agnes had saved with her quick thinking when she realized the baby was breech in the womb. That lad, a fine, healthy boy of two, sat quietly in his mother's lap, playing with some yarn.

Mary heard a deep voice calling her name and turned to find Robert. She was indignant—was he only willing to talk to her when he couldn't avoid her? She was tempted to ignore him entirely, but then she saw his face. Dark circles rimmed his eyes, and he looked pale and drawn. He, too, had suffered.

She felt some sympathy. "Did you not sleep either?" she asked. She made room for him on the bench.

Robert sat down and sighed. "No, I did not."

Robert buried his head in his hands. "This is just like that terrible day. The day Hopkins had my nurse hanged."

Mary reached out and touched Robert's wrist. He jerked his hand away. He glanced at her from the side but said nothing, and she blushed at his rebuff. Was he not interested in continuing their friendship? Or was he afraid of being held in suspicion by associating with her? If so, why did he seek her out and sit next to her? She was so tired of trying to understand his motives. She pulled up the side of her skirt and scooted farther down the bench, putting some much-needed distance between them.

Finally, a clerk announced the arrival of the judge, a figure cloaked in black. Sudbury sucked in a breath when he saw the man. Mary flashed him a curious glance, but he ignored her. A small host of clerks and a smug-looking Matthew Hopkins accompanied the judge.

Some in the crowd hooted.

"Peace, peace," the judge called. "Quiet, I say! Bring out the accused!"

Tears sprang to Mary's eyes as two strong lads emerged, each holding one of Agnes's thin arms. Mary recognized them as George and Will, footmen at Chamberlen Manor. Mary was grateful to see that they were gentle with her, as they should have been—Agnes had helped them with cures since they were boys. They led Agnes to a seat on a makeshift bench that ran across the length of the room to the side of the judge. The bench was raised well above the other seating, providing for a better view. How odd, Mary mused, that the serious business of determining guilt or innocence should be trotted out for the amusement of the crowd.

Agnes's hair lay lank and greasy, and her dress was torn. Heavy iron manacles encircled her tiny wrists. Mary tried to catch her eye, hoping to convey her love and support, but Agnes's eyes were swollen—from crying or torture, Mary didn't know—and she seemed unable to focus on anything but the floor.

The judge took a seat on a chair slightly elevated from the proceedings and began shuffling papers. Sudbury kept his eyes trained on the judge.

"Who is he?" Mary whispered.

Sudbury leaned close, but he had a faraway look in his eyes. "That's Lord Beatty. He's reputed to be a good man and a fair judge."

Hopkins stood by the judge's side, officiously pointing out salient details of the case. Mary thought she saw the judge sigh and roll his eyes. Finally, Beatty directed Hopkins to take a seat to the side.

The judge looked out over the crowd. "It would appear we have a case of witchcraft to adjudicate. I see in front of me the following charges: 'The record shows that these accusations, collected by Matthew Hopkins of Manningtree, were given in the township of Bicknacre, between the seventeenth day of August in the year 1646 and the twentieth day of September of the same year. In sum, many and sundry gave testimony that Goodwife Shepherd did on occasion give them loathsome and evil potions that did cause them great distress and sickness; that she did some three or four times cause animals, viz., sheep and cows, to give blood in place of milk; that she hath been seen consorting often with a familiar, a black crow by the name of Greedyguts, which creature is directed to perform her will.' What have you to add, Mr. Hopkins?"

"Sir," Hopkins began, an ingratiating smile pasted to his face, "I present the following items of evidence against Mistress Shepherd: First, being directed by the magistrate to keep watch over the forenamed Agnes Shepherd, for the discovery of her wicked practices, I did have conversation with the accused in which she offered to summon her imp, the crow known as Greedyguts, along with other and diverse familiars; myself and Master Stearne, not allowing for this conjuration, did converse with Agnes Shepherd and heard her to say that she had copulation with the devil some six or seven times in the last year. The accused gave witness that the devil came to her in goodly feature but with cloven hooves, and heavy and cold did he lay on her; the exchange for which favors was the promise of revenge on her enemies of the village, in particular of one Verity Martin. Miss Martin's testimony corroborates the accused's own confession, namely in the matter of the devil's intimate relationship with Mrs. Shepherd and her murder of Henry Chamberlen."

A buzzing rose from the crowd. Those who still had pity for Agnes looked about uncertainly.

Hopkins continued. "Further, two women esteemed and trusted in the town, Bridget Jenkins and Catherine Harris, did examine the accused and found her to have two extra paps. The largest, some half the width of a finger, is on her most private area. On questioning, Mistress Shepherd admitted that she gave suck to her familiar from this pap."

Some in the crowd called out, "Witch! She is a witch!" It took the judge several moments—and threats of incarceration for the unruly—to calm them down.

"And finally, myself and Master John Martin did cause to have made a witch cake by mixing young Verity's urine with wheat meal and adding some of her hair and the stumps of a horseshoe, as was seen in the trials held in Pendle. Such a cake will cause the person who bewitched the victim to have a fever and great pain on pissing." Hopkins paused and pointed at Agnes, then thundered, "Judge, you see before you the proof of that trial. Since the cake was made, Goodwife Shepherd has been ill with this very malady. Were her piss to be tested today, it would be found to be dark and sweet, to which I can attest, having been trained by Dr. Coke of London in these very matters."

The judge turned to Agnes. "And what do you have to say for yourself, madam?"

She sat up as straight as she could in her weakened condition, looked out over the crowd, and held her head a little higher.

"I've known the people of Bicknacre for thirty years, and many of you are here today. For thirty years I've heard your problems, cured your ailments, given you medicine, and eased your birthing pains. For thirty years I've held your hands when children and parents and friends have gone to God. And now you turn on me? You've shunned me, and I in turn shun you. I will be declared innocent of these charges in the highest courts, even unto the court of God. My innocence will shine before the Lord Himself, but your lies and petty complaints will condemn you in the eyes of the Almighty. And then shall I have my revenge."

At that moment, rage and fear transformed Agnes into a terrifying, avenging angel, and she seemed capable of any number of supernatural acts.

This, thought Mary, from the woman who'd staunchly defended her friends and neighbors only weeks before. Had she been disingenuous, back when she defended them against Mary's suspicions? Had she come to feel this fierce anger and betrayal since then, or had she always felt this way?

A shiver ran through the room, and Mary felt a sliver of icy fear pierce her heart.

The only person who seemed unaffected by Agnes's speech was Matthew Hopkins. He sat, arms folded across his chest, his face filled with scorn and arrogance. Finally, Hopkins broke the terrible silence that had fallen over the chamber.

"Very affecting, Mrs. Shepherd," he sneered. "Did Satan himself tell you to say that? He does have quite the silver tongue."

The spell was broken. Outraged shouts filled the room, and some of the assembled started stomping their feet.

Hopkins had turned Agnes's righteous indignation against her as damning evidence of the devil's influence.

The judge, however, was unimpressed.

"Quiet!" he shouted. "The assembled will be quiet or be removed." He turned to Hopkins. "I did not give you permission to speak, Mr. Witchfinder General."

Mary could see an unmistakable sneer on the judge's face and she felt a flicker of hope. It certainly seemed as though the judge disliked Hopkins. As an assize judge, Beatty would have already had many encounters with Hopkins and his methods. Perhaps Agnes had a chance after all.

Hopkins turned bright red. He bent his head and looked at the ground.

The judge continued reading. "And further, Goodwife Shepherd did tell Master Hopkins and Master Stearne that she had had relations with the devil in the past, and that some many years ago a daughter was born of their union, one Grace Shepherd, who bore the mark of her diabolical paternity."

A great rage seemed to possess Agnes. She attempted to stand on trembling legs but quickly fell back. She pointed at Hopkins and said, in a great and terrible voice, "You lie. Grace was an angel sent from God. You will pay for your falsehoods."

A spasm seized Agnes. Her body shook violently, and her head flopped to her chest. She shuddered and collapsed onto the rough floorboards. The crowd surged forward to see what would happen, and one little lad almost toppled to his death as his mother leaned over the second-story railing.

Sudbury ran toward Agnes's motionless body, but before he could reach her, Hopkins and Stearne grabbed him by the arms and immobilized him.

"Do not touch her," Hopkins warned. "She's possessed. The devil has her now."

Hopkins fought to keep hold of Sudbury as Mary rushed to Agnes's side. Sudbury, seeing her intent, struggled more furiously, causing Hopkins to curse under his breath.

Mary gently raised Agnes's head off the ground and cradled it on her lap. Agnes's limbs twitched and then stilled.

"Somebody get water!" Mary yelled into the raucous crowd. She knew that Agnes was having a fever-induced fit. She ran a hand over Agnes's flushed brow. To Mary's shock, Agnes's eyes flew open. They looked intent but unfocused, otherworldly.

"Noli me tangere," Agnes said, repeating the words Christ said to Mary Magdalene when he left the tomb. Do not touch me. I am not yet safe. "Avenge me, Mary. Avenge Grace. He can't take her name from me."

As the crowd quieted around her, Mary whispered soothing words and caressed Agnes's brow until her eyelids shut. Soon she sighed and drifted into unconsciousness.

When Mary finally dared to look up, she found Bridget Jenkins staring at her with a fierce hatred.

The judge spoke. "Take this woman back to her cell immediately. You!" He pointed to Mary. "You who are tending her, what's your name?"

Mary tore her gaze from Bridget and looked to the judge. "Mary Fawcett, sir."

"You're to accompany her and ensure that she has good care. And a strong man of the village will go with you."

Matthew Hopkins immediately stepped forward and said in a reedy voice, "Your Honor, I can assure you that Mistress Shepherd is being given every consideration . . ."

The judge threw him a look filled with disdain. "You shall remain quiet. That man over there, the one who tried to help her. You, what's your name?"

"Robert Sudbury," he replied quietly.

The judge looked shocked and stared at Sudbury in disbelief. "Robert? Is it you, really? I wouldn't have recognized you."

Sudbury looked at the ground.

The judge peered at him intently. "Yes, well, go with this woman and see to it that Mrs. Shepherd is well tended. I don't think she's had the best care under Master Hopkins."

Hopkins gaped like a fish and began to object, but the judge had already swept out of the room.

As soon as they reached the street, Mary turned to Sudbury. "We need to stop the trial. She won't survive this."

Agnes had already been taken back to the jail, and Mary and Robert were following behind. A belligerent crowd surrounded them, bellowing insults about "that cursed witch."

Sudbury nodded grimly.

"The assize judges always stay at the Old Bell. The innkeeper, Stephen, was a friend of Jack's, and I'm sure he'll help us," Mary continued. "Lord Beatty seems like a reasonable man, and he clearly dislikes Hopkins. If we speak to him, perhaps we can convince him of Agnes's innocence." Mary paused. "You have some acquaintance with the man?"

Sudbury sighed and looked off into the distance "He was a friend of my father's. He met me when I was a young man at Cambridge. I've changed much since then."

Mary didn't have time to waste on pity. "Yes, yes, you have a scar. Nobody cares about that now. You need to convince him, Robert. He seemed already to be in sympathy with her. You need to work on his sense of justice."

Sudbury stared at Mary for several long moments. Then he nodded, grabbed her arm, and led her to the Old Bell; all the way they endured curious looks from the villagers.

They found Stephen in the yard of the inn, and when he saw Mary, his face lit up. "Mary, it's been ages! I've been so busy at the inn." His face grew serious. "How is Agnes?" he asked.

"Not well. Stephen, we need to speak with Lord Beatty."

He shook his head. "Lord Beatty was very clear that he wanted no visitors."

Mary grabbed his arm. "My friend, there's a good chance Agnes won't last another day of this horrible trial."

Stephen ran a hand through his hair and grimaced. After a tense nod, he led them up the stairs and down the hall to the nicest of his rooms and rapped gently on the wooden door. The knock reverberated and Mary waited, her breath quickening as she heard slow footsteps within.

The judge cracked open the door and peered out. His eyes were sunken, and he gave a deep sigh.

"My good man," he addressed Stephen. "I thought I'd left explicit instructions that I not be interrupted."

"Yes, sir. I am sorry, sir. It's just that, well, I've known this woman since I was a child. She needs to speak with you, and her intentions are good."

Mr. Beatty sighed and opened the door farther, catching sight of Mary and Robert as he did so. His face lightened.

"Ahh, Sudbury. It's been too long."

They embraced.

"How do you fare?" Mr. Beatty asked.

Sudbury waved his hand along the side of his face. "I have my good days and bad, as you see."

Lord Beatty looked a bit sheepish. "Yes, I do. And I'm sorry I didn't recognize you at first. It's not just the scar, Robert—you have grown into a man since I saw you last. And you look much like your father. He was a jolly fellow. And he got me out of more than one spot of trouble. You're the spitting image of him." Beatty grimaced and looked chagrined. "Well, in most ways. Apologies for my lack of tact."

Sudbury shrugged. "Sir, may we come in? We would speak with you."

Stephen took his leave as Sudbury and Mary entered the room.

Beatty motioned for them to take seats, but Mary shook her head. "We won't be long, sir," she said.

"Well, then, you won't mind if I sit? I'm very tired."

"Of course."

Beatty eased himself into one of the chairs by the fire, closing his eyes and wincing a bit as he did so.

"I apologize for my previous rudeness. This tour of the circuits is exhausting. I'm getting too old, and I've seen too much misery and injustice."

Sudbury stepped forward. "That's what we came to speak to you about, sir. We'd like to request that you postpone this trial. Agnes Shepherd is a very sick woman, and we have our doubts that she'll survive the next few days."

Beatty looked serious, and for a moment they thought he might agree.

"I feel great sympathy for Mrs. Shepherd," Beatty said. "I don't doubt that she's innocent and that Matthew Hopkins is a fraud. I've adjudicated some of his cases, read and studied the evidence of others. In only one or two do I believe there was any real witchcraft or maleficium. In most of them, Hopkins simply picked some poor hapless woman, unpopular with her neighbors, and tortured her into giving false confessions. Most judges will be lenient if there has been no real harm, but some of the judges are rigid in their beliefs. And some are susceptible to bribery."

Mary was shocked. "Then why won't you postpone the trial until she's well?"

Mr. Beatty shook his head. "I don't have time to wait. There are other cases to be tried, and then I must visit the rest of the circuit. Mrs. Fawcett, as I said, I've seen many such cases. An accused witch's life is not an easy one. Indeed, right now that cell may well be the safest place for her. If I let her go without a full-throated assertion of her innocence, with even a hint of uncertainty, she'll be hounded for the rest of her days. However, if I judge her to be innocent of all charges, she'll have choices. She can try to reclaim her place in Bicknacre. Or move. If we can finish this trial quickly, I'm sure she'll be a free woman. And now I must excuse myself to prepare. Mrs. Fawcett, it was a pleasure. Sudbury, well met. If only for your father's sake, I will do what I can. I pray to God it will be enough."

Sudbury sat with Agnes overnight while Mary returned to the village to fetch medicine from Agnes's cottage to supplement what she had. She packed everything she might possibly need, her bag groaning under the weight.

As she closed the door behind her, almost as an afterthought, she looked back at the small rug that hid the wooden door in the flooring. Agnes might like to have the comfort of her recipe book. Mary herself liked to read the recipes in bed, to improve her memory of them and to practice the steps in her imagination. She set the bag down on the stone step, lifted the rug, and to her surprise saw that a heavy iron lock guarded the small wooden door.

Agnes must have worried that Hopkins would find and take her recipe book, Mary reasoned, though protecting it with such a massive lock seemed a bit extreme.

Mary shrugged, picked up her bag, and went back to her cottage.

The next morning, Mary returned to Chelmsford to find Sudbury sitting outside the jail, his back to the wall and his head buried in his hands.

Dark fear gripped Mary. "No," she whispered. "Tell me she hasn't died!"

Sudbury raised his exhausted head. "No. As far as I know she's still alive. As soon as you left, Hopkins ordered me from the cell on Beatty's direction. He's ordered somebody else to take care of her, given the suspicions about you."

"What suspicions? Who's made allegations about me?" Mary cried out in indignation.

Sudbury looked askance at her. "You must be aware of the whispers that you and Agnes went into the woods together for the witches' Sabbath. It's nonsense, of course, but Beatty worries that the crowd might become a mob, and he wants to forestall any complaints."

Mary remembered the looks, the sneers, and the sliced boots left on her doorstep.

"Who?" Mary asked with a sense of foreboding. "Who is now caring for Agnes?"

"Bridget Jenkins."

"No!" Mary nearly yelled. "She'll kill her, whether by neglect or malice I don't know, but Agnes will die."

"Mary, why would you say that?" Robert asked.

"I'm surprised you haven't heard the story by now. She seduced my husband, Jack." Mary waited for Robert's gaze to turn sympathetic. It didn't.

"While I was mourning our baby girl." Mary cringed at the defensive note in her voice.

Robert remained silent for a few moments as Mary fumed. Then he asked quietly, "Did you forgive Jack?"

"Well, yes, but . . ."

"It seems to me that Jack's sin was the greater. He was your husband. He was the babe's father."

Mary felt a wave of indignation and anger, but then it struck her that Robert made some sense. She'd forgiven Jack, and he'd meant the world to her. Why had she not forgiven Bridget, who meant nothing? Was she really so petty, her jealousy so potent?

"You may hate Bridget," Robert continued. "But I've seen her with Agnes. She's gentle and respectful to her. I think Agnes will do as well with her as she would with us."

Mary wrestled a growing sense of shame and wondered if she should give Bridget a measure of grace. But then she remembered the look of pure hatred Bridget had shot Mary in the courtroom. "You don't know her as I do! Agnes is in as much danger now as she's ever been."

CHAPTER 10

A medicine or syrup to open the pipes to comfort the heart and to expel melancholy

Take a quart of honey, and put it into a wide-mouthed glass, add thereto so many of the flowers of rosemary as you can moisten therein by stirring them well together, then set it in the sun two or three days, and as the honey waxeth thin with the heat of the sun, so stuff it full with the flowers . . .

That morning the crowd waited restlessly for the trial to start. After almost an hour, they grew vociferous in their complaints. Their questioning whispers turned to loud calls for the judge. The townsfolk did not want to be denied a spectacle.

Finally, Lord Beatty appeared with a bowed head and slumped shoulders. Though he trained his eyes on the ground and looked at no one, an ineffable sadness emanated from him. Mary noticed that he no longer carried the sheaf of papers detailing Agnes's alleged crimes.

Beatty looked out at the crowd. He swiped at his eyes with the back of his hand. "I prayed to God that justice would be served this day, and after a fashion, my prayers have been answered. Agnes Shepherd will not answer for her crimes in man's tribunals. God alone will judge her innocence and His sentence will be everlasting. Agnes Shepherd is dead."

Mary felt the world tilt. She looked at the faces of the villagers—some few seemed grief stricken, but the majority were outraged: they'd been robbed of a hanging.

Mary searched the room for Matthew Hopkins but didn't see him.

Lord Beatty left the room, and the crowd erupted in shouts and jeers. "The devil stole her away," some cried, while others simply chanted, "Witch, witch, witch." The cacophony reached a fevered pitch. Mary wondered if, denied the hanging they craved, the crowd would turn on her. Robert grabbed her hand and pointed to a side door. They ran through it and down several blocks until they found a stone bench.

Mary and Sudbury sat heavily.

"It was Bridget," Mary whispered in fury. "Bridget did this. You let her take over Agnes's care, and now look what's happened."

Sudbury set his hand on Mary's shoulder. She shrugged him off and quickly pulled away. She gave Sudbury a look full of accusation. "Why did you let them give her over to Bridget? Do you suspect me of witchery, too?"

Sudbury sucked in his breath. "No, Mary, no. You have surprising abilities, but I don't think you're a witch, and you'd never purposely do harm."

"Then why have you avoided me?" Mary winced at the plaintive note in her voice.

Robert sighed. "You're only now beginning to experience the ugly suspicion of the people of Bicknacre. I've been their target since I moved here. I didn't want to cause you more troubles because of your association with me."

Mary was taken aback. It made sense, she realized. When had she become so willing to believe the worst? "But why leave her with Bridget? Surely she caused Agnes's death."

"Do not be too quick to make that accusation, Mary," he said. "Agnes already had the look of death about her."

Mary sighed. "Perhaps." She took a deep breath. "I can't help but feel it's better this way than that she be hanged as a witch or a murderer, or that she live to hear Grace maligned again. That would have killed her just as surely as a rope."

Sudbury offered to walk Mary back to Bicknacre, but she rejected his hospitality. She needed solitude and space. Her heart was leaden with grief, the world around her unfamiliar and unwelcoming. She didn't just feel betrayed by the people of Bicknacre—after the events of the last few weeks, she'd come to expect the suspicion and fear she saw in their eyes. She also felt betrayed by the town itself, the buildings and streets and trees—everything she thought she knew so well now seemed to loom over her, threatening, pitiless, strange.

As Mary walked the five miles, her mind buzzed with scenes from the past few days. She thought about Matthew Hopkins, about Simon and Sudbury, but mostly she remembered and mourned Agnes. Her toughness, her wisdom, her gruff, affectionate ways. She pondered how quickly the world could turn itself inside out and destroy every certainty, every security.

Mary arrived at Bicknacre midafternoon, but she continued on. She walked and walked. As the day slid into twilight, she knew she had to go retrieve her brother. The world may have shifted on its axis, but Tom's need for her, and hers for him, would endure.

Tom ran to Mary as soon as she turned onto the Woodses' street and threw himself into her arms. His face was red and swollen with tears. "Mary? Did I hear wrong? It can't be true. I heard that Mrs. Shepherd was . . . was dead!"

Mary put her hands on his dear cheeks.

"No, my child, you did not hear wrong. Mrs. Shepherd was very ill. She is with God now."

"The devil more like." Somebody, a man, stood behind her, and his voice dripped with scorn.

Mary spun around to see Matthew Hopkins with an evil, smirking look on his face.

"Don't worry, young Tom. If I'm successful, she may have your sister for company soon enough."

Hopkins took a step nearer, and they heard an unholy ruckus behind them.

Greedyguts hopped along the path.

Tom clicked his tongue and held out his hand to the bird. "He's looking for Mrs. Shepherd, I think."

Hopkins burst out in a high, cold laugh. "That cursed bird won't find her on this earth. And thanks be to God that the devil has taken back his beldam."

Bridget Jenkins walked up behind them, carrying a basket of herbs and dirtied linens. The sight overwhelmed Mary—were these the herbs and cloths Bridget had used to tend the dying Agnes? The very idea sent her into a rage.

All Mary's grief, all the suspicions she had about Bridget, the pent-up frustration of the last few days exploded inside of her, and she lunged at Bridget.

"What did you do to Agnes?" She pulled Bridget's hair and scratched her cheeks. A primal scream issued from deep within.

Bridget fought back. She bit Mary's hand and tore her dress at her shoulder.

Before she could do more damage, Mary felt a sharp tug on her arm—Sudbury dragged Mary away, her hands pulled behind her back, and whispered calming words. His deep voice brought her back to herself.

As her eyes refocused on her surroundings, she saw that neighbors had pulled Bridget away. Bridget, too, had fury in her eyes.

She spit at Mary, and Mary surged forward, struggling to free her hands, but Sudbury held on tight. As she fought to push her anger back down, she saw Tom walking toward Bridget. His limp seemed more pronounced, but the slow pace lent Tom an uncanny sort of authority. "Tom, no!" she yelled, panic in her voice.

Tom ignored her and stood in front of Bridget. She kicked out at him, but luckily he was just out of reach.

Mary's heart leapt as she heard Tom's small voice pipe up.

"Mistress Jenkins, you've been very naughty. You must not strike my sister again."

The crowd exploded with laughter. The butcher clapped Tom on the back.

When the crowd's laughter died down, Tom continued.

"If you do hit Mary, I'll have to tell Greedyguts, and he will punish you."

The crowd grew very still as Tom pointed to the black crow on the edge of the crowd. Taking Tom's extended hand as an invitation to come get a berry, the crow hopped over to Tom's side. He turned his head to view Tom through his one good eye and gave a raucous caw.

The townspeople murmured as the eerie scene unfolded.

Matthew Hopkins pushed his way to the front of the crowd. "Young man, is that the same crow that I saw by your cottage? The crow known to keep company with Mrs. Shepherd?"

Tom looked at Hopkins and smiled. "Yes, he is my friend, Greedyguts. Mary and I saved him from the bullies."

Mary tried to interject but Hopkins silenced her. Sudbury whispered in her ear, "Don't say a word, Mary."

"Is this crow often at your house?"

Tom was exasperated. "Yes, of course. He's my friend."

Hopkins turned to the crowd. "Good people of Bicknacre, we know this crow, Greedyguts, to have been a familiar of that accursed mistress of the devil, Agnes Shepherd. Moreover, we know that a witch will seat her soul in the body of her familiar, and that when the witch dies, the familiar is left to find another witch as its companion. This crow resembles exactly a creature I read about in Suffolk who visited one Sarah Jones. This crow is a familiar. Mistress Fawcett and her brother must be investigated, and if just cause is found, they must be held over until the next assizes!"

Mary gasped as the crowd turned to her and Tom. Many in the crowd murmured objections, but most of her neighbors looked at her with fear in their eyes—fear of her and worse, much worse, fear of Tom. If the people of Bicknacre could put an innocent pig on trial, could they be capable of trying her poor brother?

A smile lit up Bridget Jenkins's face.

Sudbury let go of Mary's arm and stepped forward. "That's a damned lie!" he shouted at Hopkins. He turned to the crowd. "People of Bicknacre, you must think about this. Has Mary Fawcett ever done anything but help you in your time of need? She's devoted herself to curing you when you're sick, comforting you when you're afflicted!"

A hush fell over the crowd, and then Bridget said in a loud voice, "Mrs. Ridley, didn't you lose that child after Mary Fawcett gave you a tincture for your childbirth pains?"

Mary blanched. Amelia Ridley's baby had gone breech at the last minute, and the midwife couldn't turn it in the womb. Mary had given her a broth made from chicken and some healing herbs to comfort her, but the baby had been born dead. It had been in the hands of God—nothing she'd given the woman could have helped.

Mrs. Ridley nodded, and the crowd murmured.

Bridget continued. "And, Mr. Putnam, wasn't it your sheep that got sick after Tom got into a fight with your son over that same hell-bent crow there?"

Tom had caught Will Putnam throwing rocks at Greedyguts. By the time Tom stopped him, Will had bloodied Greedyguts from beak to claw.

Matthew Hopkins stepped forward. "This woman learned everything she knows from Agnes Shepherd. And let's not forget that she was present at the home of Henry Chamberlen when he was found dead. I think we have enough evidence to investigate both her and young Tom."

Stearne moved forward and grabbed Tom's arm. A fierce rage filled Mary, and she roared, "Don't you dare touch him!" Mary's instincts took hold in a way she had never experienced before. Without knowing how or why, she imagined herself inside Stearne, put herself in the body of the obsequious lickspittle, felt his desire to impress Hopkins, to show the crowd his brute strength.

Somehow, she knew just what to do. She put her hand on her throat and stopped breathing.

Some fifty feet away, Stearne watched her, terror suffusing his face, and after a moment he grabbed his neck, letting go of Tom. He turned red, then a mottled purple, and sank to his knees. Mary lowered her arm but continued holding her breath with all the force inside of her. From a distance, she heard Hopkins shouting, "Do you see, people of Bicknacre? Do you see the power of this witch?"

Mary felt Sudbury touching her arm as he whispered gently in her ear, "Stop, Mary. Stop whatever it is you are doing. Do not put murder on your innocent soul."

Sudbury's voice pierced the fog of Mary's fury, and she took a deep inhale. As she did, Stearne gasped and started panting. He sat up and stared at her in rage.

"You did this to me, witch!" he yelled.

Sudbury answered him. "Nonsense," he said calmly. "How in the world could she affect you without touching you? If she were a witch, she'd have uttered a spell or used a poppet. You simply choked on your own evil intent."

The crowd fell silent, unsure who to believe.

Hopkins stepped forward. "I demand that you, and your brother, accompany me to the jail, Mary Fawcett, before somebody else gets hurt."

Sudbury leaned forward and spoke gently to Mary. "Go with him," he said. "It might be safer for you in jail. Who knows what this crowd will do to you. And I'll get you out, Mary. I don't know how, but I will get you out."

Mary focused on Sudbury's words and then looked at the crowd of her friends and neighbors. The faces of those she'd grown up with. The people she thought she knew. She saw fear and horror and revulsion on every face. She heard children in the crowd crying.

Mary nodded. "I'll go with you, Matthew Hopkins. But I am not a witch, nor is my brother."

⚕

The small jail cell still smelled of the ointments Mary had concocted for Agnes. She held Tom and breathed deep of the valerian and thyme, catching a hint of the wine she'd boiled them in. But the cell also smelled strongly of vomit and piss. And of death.

Mary sat cross-legged on the floor, Tom folded into her lap. He whimpered quietly, the bulk of his tears spent.

Hopkins and Stearne had dragged Mary and Tom to the jail, the crowd parting before them. The men had not been at all gentle, and Mary rubbed the bruises that colored her wrists. They hurt, but it caused her greater pain to see matching bruises on Tom's arms.

"I'm so sorry, Mary!" he wailed when they were all alone. "Is this my fault? You told me not to talk about Greedyguts, but I didn't listen!"

Mary grasped him by the chin and looked into his eyes. "No, child," she said firmly. "This is none of your doing. A madness has gripped this village and it has nothing to do with you."

Tom grew quiet. Mary could hear his breathing slow, and she prayed he might find the sweet oblivion of sleep. She leaned her back against the stone wall, sure she would not be granted the same mercy that night.

A cup of water sat by her side. She took the pewter handle and lifted it to her lips, forcing herself to drink the fetid water. Her lips were dry and cracked from thirst.

She couldn't stop replaying the events of the day—her deep, sharp mourning for Agnes, the uncontrollable rage she'd felt toward Bridget

Jenkins, and the terror and fear on the faces of her neighbors when Hopkins accused her and Tom of witchcraft.

She contemplated what she'd done to Stearne. How had she done it? What strange power had possessed her? And, the most haunting question of all, what would have happened if Sudbury hadn't stopped her?

She closed her eyes and tried to make sense of it all. How could she get Tom to safety? If only she did have some witchcraft at her disposal.

A key turned in the lock. Sure it was the jailer with some loathsome gruel, she kept her eyes closed, feigning sleep.

She heard the door open and soft footsteps approached. She doubted it was the jailer, Geoffrey—when she'd visited Agnes, he'd just thrown open the door and plunked down the bowl and cup, the gruel so thin it splashed on the floor like water. No, these footsteps sounded purposeful. Mary held on to Tom more tightly. Her eyes still closed, she prayed.

She felt a light touch on her shoulder. Her eyes flew open with a surge of terror and fury in her belly.

In the faint light of the candle, she saw the shadowy outline of Simon Martin.

Mary let out her breath and slumped over in relief.

"Mary," he said softly. "How are you? How's Tom?"

Mary was filled with rage. How dare he ask those questions when he himself had welcomed Matthew Hopkins, had fed the man's witch-hunting mania by telling Hopkins incriminating stories about his own longtime friends.

"We're as well as we appear to be," Mary whispered. She kissed the soft brown curls on the top of Tom's head. "Which is to say we have been insulted, beaten, and befouled. Would you like a drink of water?" She offered the cup to Simon, making sure to place the greasy liquid right underneath his nose. Simon gagged. "How did you get in here, Simon? What do you want?"

"I bribed Geoffrey. Mary, I had no idea this would happen. Please believe me, if I had known . . ."

"Simon, I have neither the will nor the desire to hear your excuses. Go to Lord Beatty and tell him what Hopkins has done. He is my only hope for release."

Simon stared at the floor. "Lord Beatty left town in the early afternoon."

Mary couldn't help the whimpering sob that escaped.

"But I want to help you," Simon said. "Please, what can I do, what do you need?"

Mary shrugged. "If you really want to help, you'll find a way to free us."

Simon hesitated. "I'm not sure I can do that. Matthew Hopkins is very powerful, and he's persuasive."

"He's only powerful because the villagers trusted you. This is your doing." Her voice rose, and Tom stirred in her lap.

Trembling, Simon looked at his feet.

"Please, Mary, what can I do for you other than that? I can bring you food, clean water, medicine. Geoffrey will let me smuggle in whatever you need."

"I need my freedom. Until you can grant that, please stay away."

Simon leaned down to touch her shoulder again, but she shook off his hand.

He walked slowly out of the cell. As she heard his footsteps fade down the corridor, Mary regretted her words. How long could she and Tom survive without decent food and water? What did her pride matter anyway?

Finally, the tears she'd held back since before her fight with Bridget spilled out. She tried to hold in her sobs, but she couldn't contain her anger, fear, and frustration. Her convulsions and the hot tears falling on Tom's head woke him. He stared at Mary, confusion in his eyes.

"Is this a bad dream, Mary?"

"Yes, lamb, go back to sleep."

Mary awoke a few hours later with Tom still in her lap. Her neck was stiff from leaning against the stone wall, and she worried her legs would fail should she attempt to stand. She gently moved Tom to the greasy straw. Her joints creaked as she stretched and got to her feet. She limped to the small window and turned her face up to the weak sunshine.

She heard a scrambling overhead, just outside the window, a sort of scratching. Tom murmured in his sleep. As she turned to check on him, a small object pelted her head and bounced to the ground. Then another. She knelt down to investigate.

A bright red sphere glowed in the straw like a ruby, but it was far more valuable than any jewel. It was a wild strawberry.

Another berry rained down, then another. She gathered them and looked up at the window, expecting to see the hand of her benefactor. Instead, she saw a mottled black beak followed by a feathered head and a gimlet eye.

"Greedyguts," she whispered in wonder.

The crow turned his head sideways, and he blinked his one eye at her. He cawed and Mary laughed.

Mary gently shook Tom awake. "Tom, a friend has come to visit. But you must greet him quietly."

She led him over to the window, and a torrent of berries showered them as Greedyguts pushed a pile of strawberries with his beak through the crack in the boards. Mary gathered them up and counted.

"There must be at least twenty here!" she said in amazement. "Greedyguts brought them all."

"Of course he did," Tom said in an assured voice. "He's our friend. He would never abandon us."

They heard another scuffle and the beating of wings as Greedyguts took off into the sky.

Mary moved the berries over to Tom, encouraging him to eat as quickly as possible. Though she was tempted to save some for later,

Mary didn't dare risk hiding them. It wasn't enough to fill their bellies, but the sweetness of the berries cheered them.

They sat alone for the rest of the morning. Just as they were feeling weak from hunger again, Geoffrey brought their gruel.

Unfortunately, he also brought Hopkins and Stearne.

Mary pulled Tom to her and held him tightly. She stood at the ready to muffle him with her hand if need be. She well knew how easily he could say the wrong thing to these two men.

"Mistress Fawcett, I hope you slept well." Hopkins moved a greasy lock of hair that had fallen into his eyes and looked expectantly at Stearne, who laughed at Hopkins's attempt at wit.

"I did not, Master Hopkins," Mary replied, unwilling to play games. "The straw is filthy, the water is not fit for pigs, my brother and I are weak from hunger, and I fear we'll be hanged."

Hopkins gave her a deeply satisfied look. She saw a glint of something in his eyes. Was it excitement? She suspected that her show of spirit—or his learning of her discomfort—gave Hopkins a horrid kind of joy. She refused to give him his sick pleasure, but she could tuck this knowledge away and hope to somehow make it work in her favor in the future.

"Then I expect you're ready to cooperate," Stearne said. "All you need to do is admit to using witchcraft and we'll leave you alone until the trial."

"And it will be a fair trial?" Mary said. "A fair trial in which you've already decided my guilt?"

"As you well know . . ." Hopkins paused. He took a small metal pick out of his pocket and used it to clean his fingernails. After a moment, he held out his hand to admire his efforts. Mary stood tall, her hand weighing heavily on Tom's shoulder. She would not rush Hopkins, must not appear eager to hear his words.

As she remained calm and quiet, he gave her a sour look and continued. "We have many ways to test for witchcraft, all of which have the approval of Parliament. We only seek to punish the wicked and absolve the innocent. If you are pure of heart, you have nothing to fear."

Tom started to speak. Mary immediately put her hand over his mouth and whispered, "Tom, you mustn't utter a word."

Hopkins cocked one eyebrow at Mary. "What's he trying to say that frightens you so?"

"I'm not afraid of what he might say but of the way you might twist his words." She lifted her chin and tried to appear defiant and brave. She had a sinking feeling it wasn't working.

A smug smile spread over Hopkins's face. He turned to Stearne. "Get Geoffrey. Take the boy with you."

Tom protested and kicked out at Stearne, but the boy was tired and hungry, and he could do little. His weaker leg buckled under him. Stearne easily hoisted him over his shoulder and carried him out of the cell. Mary grasped at Tom's jacket, desperately trying to reclaim him. Stearne pushed her away and closed the door. The image of Tom wailing in desperation and reaching out for help was seared in Mary's mind.

She cried out in fear and frustration. She'd always had a solution, a fix, another recipe to try. But now? Now she was trapped and helpless. And she could do nothing to protect Tom. Everything she'd feared, everything she'd tried so hard to prevent, was happening. And it was all due to one man—the man leering at her and licking his lips.

After the door shut, Hopkins strode over to Mary and placed a finger on the wildly beating pulse in her neck. His breath, reeking of onions and ale, fanned her face as he spoke softly in her ear.

"I shall soon delve into your deepest secrets, my dear Mary." He leaned closer, and she could feel his tongue flick the tender flesh of her earlobe.

She reached up to smack him, but he was quicker. He grabbed her hand and twisted it behind her back. He pressed up against her, his cock hard, his pelvis grinding into her belly.

"You are a sweet piece," he murmured. "Do you know how we find the witch's teat, my dear? We strip you naked and shave every bit of you, from your head to your most private parts. Then we take a dressmaker's pin, nice and fat, and find where you suckle the devil, where your skin neither bleeds nor feels pain. Sometimes the mark is here." Hopkins's free hand touched her shoulder. "And sometimes here." The hollow between her breasts. "And sometimes here." He cupped her privates.

Mary stifled a whimper. She would not let him see her fear.

"It's exacting work." He pressed himself against her more firmly, and she tried to wrench away from his foulness. "We will lay you out on the floor, arms and legs spread wide, and we must have witnesses. All of them looking at you, examining your most intimate parts." He rubbed himself against her jutting hip bone. Mary fought the nausea welling deep inside her belly. "But then of course the others will leave, and it will just be you and me, my dear. Just you and me."

Mary heard footsteps outside the cell. Hopkins let go of her and sauntered toward the door. He puffed out his thin chest until it was almost as large as his paunch.

"Yes, I'll enjoy my examination of you," he sneered.

Mary stared at him, defiant. She knew she couldn't show her fear, but she couldn't just stand there. Her pride would not allow it.

Instead, she lifted her arm straight and pointed at Hopkins. He stopped cold and licked his lips nervously.

Mary knew no witch curses. But she took the opportunity to use Matthew Hopkins's fear against him. No longer did she tremble at her own unformed power. No longer did she fear the whispers of others. The worst had already happened—she had been accused of witchcraft, and her brother was paying the price.

"The devil will dance you through hell before you touch me or my brother again," she intoned in a sort of chant.

Mary knew she would pay for this moment, someday, but it was worth it to see the glimmer of fear in Matthew Hopkins's watery eyes as he hurried from her cell.

CHAPTER 11

To make a broth for those that be weak with sickness

Take a good capon of two years old, being well fleshed but not very fat, dress him as you would do to boil, leaving the head and the legs at the body. Then fill the belly full of currants, blend with an ounce of mace, and so sew up the belly . . .

Mary reluctantly opened her eyes. She wanted the oblivion of slumber to last. She had fought hard for the little sleep she'd had, suffering the cold floor, the scurrying of rats, and the fears that crowded her mind.

Tom snuggled against her for warmth and protection. Stearne had brought him back to the cell moments after Hopkins left, looking none the worse for wear, thank God. She had been terrified Stearne would take revenge on her brother after his humiliation in the town square. She'd frantically questioned Stearne about where he'd taken Tom, worried that Tom had been ill used. But Stearne had roughly dumped him in a corner and left, muttering something vile about brats who bite and won't shut up.

Mary gently lifted Tom's arm off her hip to move away from him. She stopped when he stirred. As she waited for him to settle again, she stared at his sweet face, his lips moving as he dreamed, his beautiful brown eyes shut tight against the world.

The quiet lasted only a few moments. Outside in the corridor, Mary heard shouts and sounds of struggle. She remembered Hopkins's whispered threats and grabbed a piece of stone she had chiseled from the wall until her fingernails were bloody and raw. She felt the shard's sharp edge and muttered a prayer.

The door burst open and a man was thrown to the floor of the cell, yelling incoherently, trying to work free of the ropes that bound his hands. He was a furious bundle of fear and rage. And blood, lots of blood.

The man looked up at her.

It was Sudbury.

Mary moved to help him but Stearne jerked her back, leering at her. "Get back in yer corner, slattern," he sneered.

Sudbury lunged at Stearne but tripped on the cords binding him. Stearne laughed and pulled an iron bar from the waistband of his pants. He held it across Sudbury's chest and pushed down until Sudbury grunted in pain.

"Mind your manners," Stearne growled.

Tom whimpered behind Mary.

"Aww, what have we got here?" Stearne asked. "Oh, look at that poor, sweet child. Is he bothering you again, mistress? You know what they say, 'Spare the rod, spoil the child . . .'"

Stearne raised the iron bar and started moving toward Tom, who cowered silently in fear. A panic came over Mary unlike any she'd ever known. She let out a fierce roar from deep inside and lunged at Stearne, gripping his neck in her hands, biting his cheek, thrashing and kicking.

It took Stearne a moment to recover from his shock, but when he did, he acted quickly. He kicked Mary's feet out from under her and threw her into a pile of hay in the corner. Sudbury had managed to stand. He looked murderous, but with his hands tied behind his back, there was little he could do. He rushed at Stearne, head lowered, but Stearne blocked him.

"You little bitch!" Stearne screeched at Mary. "First you choke me with your damned witch curse . . ."

A quiet voice—low, threatening—muttered, "Such violence! I believe we all need to take a moment to compose ourselves."

Mary turned to see Hopkins holding a knife to Sudbury's throat.

"Jonathan, thank you for your service this morning. You have delivered the gentleman to the cell as I asked. You have now completed your duties and may leave."

Stearne grunted and spat at Sudbury's feet. He collected a small leather purse from Hopkins and exited the cell.

"I'm sure we're all relieved that ruffian is gone," Hopkins said. He sounded conspiratorial, as though he expected Mary and Sudbury to chuckle and agree.

Mary and Sudbury said nothing. Tom remained utterly silent, still terrified.

Hopkins put his knife away and took a sheaf of papers from a bag at his side.

"Why am I here, Hopkins?" Sudbury asked with a note of menace in his voice.

"Because you, sir, are being charged with the murder of Henry Chamberlen. According to this testimony—"

"Mary, you will be free!" Simon Martin burst into the cell. He stopped short when he saw Hopkins and Sudbury.

"You do act fast, don't you, Hopkins?" Simon shook his head.

"What are you doing here, you interfering old woman?" Sudbury shouted at Simon.

"Mr. Sudbury, I must ask that you quiet down!" Hopkins said in mock dismay. "We are all civilized here. As I was saying before I was interrupted, you have been charged with the murder of Mr. Chamberlen."

"And you'll be released, Mary!" interrupted Simon. "Verity has testified that it was Agnes Shepherd who directed Greedyguts to visit her, and that all those other misfortunes had been Agnes's doing alone, that you had nothing to do with Henry Chamberlen's murder!"

"Young Mr. Martin is correct, Mrs. Fawcett," Hopkins said. "Miss Martin has thus testified." He stared at Simon, but Simon didn't seem able to meet his gaze.

"No!" Mary shouted. "Agnes Shepherd would never have done such things!"

"Well, according to Verity Martin, she certainly did," Hopkins replied. "Miss Martin gave testimony in front of witnesses that Agnes Shepherd sent her familiar Greedyguts to torment her, that the witch made a poppet of poor Verity and used it to cause her great bodily harm." He pulled out his sheets of paper and began reading. "Furthermore, Verity Martin testifies that Mrs. Agnes Shepherd and Mr. Robert Sudbury sent Greedyguts to her room to convince her to attend a witches' Sabbath. The crow jabbered in the tongues of men. When she refused to go, the befouled bird said Mrs. Shepherd and Sudbury would repeat on her the unspeakable horrors they'd visited together on Mr. Chamberlen."

Mary couldn't believe what she was hearing. "This is absurd."

"Mary, hush." Simon moved to Mary's side and whispered in her ear, "I've taken great pains and paid much money to have you released."

Mary started to protest, but a pained cry from Sudbury silenced her. They all turned to look at him. Sudbury's eyes were squeezed shut, and he struggled to remain standing. He bent his head toward the corner where Tom huddled, hugging his legs and shaking.

"Mary, go," he said in a strangled voice. "Think of Tom."

She froze. Of course she had no choice. She would do anything to keep her brother safe. But that didn't mean others should suffer. She would right this wrong. But first she needed to get Tom to safety.

Hopkins was busy scribbling on a piece of paper. Mary walked over to Tom and picked him up from the floor. She caressed his head and made soothing noises. Simon took her hand to guide them out of the cell.

When they reached the door, she stopped and pointed her finger at Hopkins in accusation just as she had the day before. "Remember what I said yesterday. This is not ended, Witchfinder." She was gratified to see the same flicker of fear in his eyes.

She had found Hopkins's weakness—the man might cynically manipulate others by accusing them of maleficium, but deep down he really did fear the power of witchcraft.

As soon as they exited the jail, Simon began, "Mary, I . . ."

"No!" Mary tried to temper her anger. She nodded toward Tom, who clutched her neck tightly. "We'll discuss this when we get to my cottage."

Mary ignored Simon as he walked them home. She focused on appearing calm and serene under the curious and hostile glares of the villagers. When they finally arrived at the cottage, Simon waited patiently until Tom was washed, fed, and settled on his pallet asleep.

Mary sat Simon down at the table. "Now explain. How did you get me out of that place?"

Simon sighed and buried his face in his hands. "Verity lied about you and Agnes. She told me as soon as she heard you'd been thrown in jail. She took the blame, but my father is the evil behind the original lie." His eyes took on a haunted look. "The things she told me, Mary, about what my father did to her, what he made her do . . ."

Simon shook his head. "This was all my fault, just like you said. I told Hopkins about Verity, believed him when he said she was a victim of witchcraft. I'm responsible. I had to get you out of there."

"How is she, Simon? How is Verity?"

Simon gave a gentle, relieved smile. "She's doing better since she moved in with Reverend Osborne and stopped drinking that vile cordial. She's been eating more, and she's even helping Reverend Osborne's housekeeper. She seemed to be returning to her old self until she heard that you were in jail. She begged me to get you out, to do whatever it took to get Hopkins to release you."

"And how did you?"

Simon sneered. "For all his talk of justice and godliness, Hopkins is very responsive to money. I bribed him to change his mind, Mary. Do you really not know why?"

Simon put his hand over Mary's and looked deep into her eyes. He leaned in.

Mary knew he was about to kiss her, and she allowed him to continue, curious. She had only ever been kissed by Jack, and she had quite liked it. This kiss of Simon's was spontaneous, and Mary thought perhaps he expected her to reject him. But Mary was scared, tired, and lonely. She craved warmth and connection. She missed the oblivion of passion.

When Mary didn't pull away, Simon seemed to freeze, as though he didn't know what to do next. He left his lips on hers, unmoving, unbending, cold. She tentatively licked his lower lip.

Simon jumped, shock in his eyes.

Mary's face burned red with shame. But wasn't that how people kissed? Jack had done that and more, even before they'd married.

Mary bent her head and studied her hands, waiting for Simon to say something. When he did not, she looked up to see a trace of disgust on his face. By some unspoken agreement, they ignored the moment that had just passed.

"But this isn't right, Simon. I can't pay for my release with the wrongful imprisonment of Robert Sudbury."

Simon bristled. "Hopkins was going to throw him in jail anyway. He hates the man. And I don't trust him either. He has too many secrets, and he asks questions to which only God should know the answer. He's capable of great harm, I'm sure of it. Why do you care about the fate of that horrible man, anyway?"

Mary bristled. "Because it's wrong. You know it's wrong."

Simon looked belligerent for a moment and then sighed. He seemed to collapse upon himself.

"You're right, of course you are. I tried to get Hopkins to blame Mrs. Shepherd and leave Sudbury out of it. I felt terrible blaming Mrs. Shepherd and Sudbury, but I couldn't reveal Verity's lies to the world, and Mrs. Shepherd is no longer around to hurt. But Hopkins would only agree to my plan if I promised to implicate Sudbury as well."

"But why should he care so much about punishing Sudbury?"

Simon shrugged.

"I think it's time for you to leave, Simon. I thank you for all your efforts on our behalf." She looked at Tom, curled under a soft blanket on his pallet. "Truly I do."

Mary walked him to the door. The air between them was charged. Simon kissed her hand without looking at her, spun on his heel, and left.

The smell of the jail was becoming distressingly familiar—the mixture of piss, sweat, and blood assaulted Mary's nostrils the minute she set foot inside. And though she wasn't a prisoner, fear weakened her knees and panic set her heart racing. For a moment she thought about turning around and leaving. But using all the will she could muster, she squared her shoulders and followed Geoffrey to Sudbury's cell.

She had forgotten how dark the cell was. As Geoffrey opened the heavy oak door, Sudbury shielded his eyes from the weak light that skittered across the floor. He put his hand over his face, trying to hide the blood and bruises on his cheeks, the swelling lip. She gasped, and Sudbury turned away.

Mary slipped Geoffrey some coins and he left them alone.

Sudbury refused to look up. She walked over to him, slowly, and sat down on the floor.

"Robert," she whispered.

"I was already hideous. I suppose I'm now a veritable monster."

She reached out and gently turned his chin toward her. His eyes, filled with pain, locked on hers. She leaned forward and lightly kissed the spot on his cheek where the bruises bloomed most gruesomely. Sudbury swallowed.

They sat quietly for a minute.

Sudbury cleared his throat. "How's Tom?"

"Still scared, but doing better with Mrs. Woods spoiling him this morning."

He nodded. "How are you?"

She looked down at her hands.

"What is it, Mary?" Sudbury asked, his voice gentle.

She took a deep breath before asking the questions that crowded her mind. She wasn't sure she wanted to hear the answers.

"Why does Hopkins hate you so much? Why does he want to see you hang for Chamberlen's death?"

The response came not from Robert but from the doorway, in a voice that sent chills down her spine. "Because Robert Sudbury did, in fact, commit murder. Just not the one he's in this jail for. God's mighty justice triumphs eventually, doesn't it, Sudbury?"

Hopkins stood at the door, arms folded across his chest, a smirk spread across his face, the same greasy lock of hair tickling his eyebrow.

"Oh, poor Mrs. Fawcett! Did you not know? Did your swain not tell you the tragic story of his lost love?" Hopkins gave a high-pitched giggle that caused him to contort his body with a sickening exuberance.

Sudbury looked at Hopkins. Hatred clouded his eyes. Hatred and shame.

Hopkins entered the cell. "You see, dear Robert hasn't always been the reclusive scholar he is now, disfigured and stoop shouldered from study. Oh no! In his youth, he was quite the dashing young man, a rake-hell, even. Handsome and rich. All the girls in Chichester wanted him. And he wanted all the girls in Chichester, too, didn't you, Robert? But he suffered the ultimate revenge. He fell in love! The hunter was caught in his own trap. She was a beauty, wasn't she, Robert? With that golden hair and those melting brown eyes? And those tits?" Hopkins's voice grew louder and frenzied, ringing throughout the cell. "You wanted my Meg, eh, Robert? You wanted her, and you had her."

"No!" Sudbury yelled. "She was never yours. Nor was she mine."

Hopkins spit at Sudbury's feet. A smug, ugly smile crossed his face. "Oh, I hardly think you're in a position to correct me," he said in a silken voice. Then he turned toward Mary. "And sweet Margery would have gone with him, too—to the altar or to his bed—if not for Henry Chamberlen."

Mary turned to Sudbury. He would not look at her.

"You have not told her, Robert?" Hopkins mocked. "You didn't tell her, my friend, how it was Chamberlen who gave you that scar?"

Mary gasped. "Why would you hide that from me?"

Hopkins turned to Mary. "Oh yes. You see, Chamberlen admired Robert, invited him to work on an experiment together. But then he met Margery, and in his wild lust for her, Chamberlen grew dangerous. When Margery died, Chamberlen threw heated lead in Sudbury's face and claimed it was an accident."

Mary looked at Sudbury, hoping he'd renounce Hopkins's explanation, but Sudbury kept his eyes trained on the ground.

Hopkins's cruel smile disappeared. He turned again to Sudbury. "That's why you came here, isn't it, Robert? That's why you settled in Bicknacre. You wanted to kill Henry Chamberlen, to make him pay for what he'd done to you, for leaving Margery to die giving birth to his bastard."

"No!" Sudbury yelled. His eyes burned, bright and intense. "I wanted to torture his mind, that's all. I wanted to haunt him, to terrify him, to be a constant reminder of his cruelty. But I would never kill the man." He turned to her, his eyes pleading. "Mary, please, you have to believe that."

She blinked. Sudbury seemed to be telling the truth, but how could she know? Why would he keep these secrets from her, secrets that endangered her and her brother? Would she have acted differently if she'd known the depth of Hopkins's crazed hatred of Sudbury and Sudbury's connection to Hopkins and Chamberlen?

She'd trusted her husband, had known him all her life, and he'd played her for a fool. Why should she believe a man she'd known only for a short time? How could he have kept so much of his past a secret when she had come to trust him so completely? She had shared her fears about Mrs. Chamberlen being poisoned, and he'd said nothing of the connection. What cruel game was he playing? She backed away from him, needing space, needing time.

"Come, Mrs. Fawcett—you'll be so much safer with me," Hopkins said, speaking to her in a babyish voice, reaching his hand down to help her stand.

"*Noli me tangere,*" she ordered—the same phrase Agnes had uttered when she'd collapsed at the trial. Something about the memory of Agnes reciting the words, she hoped, would make Hopkins think it was a witch's curse.

Hopkins's eyes narrowed and he let out a low growl.

"Do not touch me," she warned.

Hopkins nodded coldly. "As you wish. Nevertheless, I recommend that you remove yourself from this man's cell. He is not to be trusted."

Mary looked at Sudbury, crumpled in the hay on the floor. He would not meet her eyes.

"Yes, I'm sorry I ever trusted this man," she said. Sudbury flinched.

Mary stepped in front of Hopkins. She let herself out of the cell and hurriedly left the jail. As soon as she was out of sight, she ducked behind some trees and vomited. Then she stood tall, set her shoulders squarely, and set out for Chamberlen Manor to talk to the only person who could possibly give her the answers she sought.

CHAPTER 12

A medicine to preserve a breast that is sore from breaking
and to assuage any swelling or anguish, whether it come
of bruise or otherwise, if it be taken in time

> *Take the ointment called papillon and anoint the place
> therewith: take of rosin wax and deer's suet of each of
> these a like quantity, and one spoonful of the oil of lin-
> seed . . .*

Mr. Chamberlen's death had done wonders for his wife's health. Gone
were the pallor and dark circles under Anne Chamberlen's eyes. And
she'd put on some weight, enough to fill out the lines around her mouth.
She looked like she was flourishing, especially as she sat in her light-
filled parlor, decorated in soft yellows and blues—a striking contrast to
the heavy opulence of the rest of the house.

Yes, Mary thought, her husband's death had given Mrs.
Chamberlen life.

Mary hadn't visited Chamberlen Manor since that terrible day. She
shuddered at the memory of the man's corpse, his glassy eyes and waxy
skin, the green, gelatinous poison covering his fingers.

But Mrs. Chamberlen was gracious and soon put her at ease. She seemed honestly happy to see Mary, and Mary was grateful for a friendly face. They chatted for a bit. Mary asked about Mrs. Chamberlen's health, and Mrs. Chamberlen asked about Tom. When they'd run out of fodder for conversation, Mrs. Chamberlen sat forward in her chair.

After a moment, Mary looked down nervously at her entwined fingers. "Mrs. Chamberlen, I have been told that your husband was well acquainted with Robert Sudbury. Were you aware of that?"

Mrs. Chamberlen nodded. A faint blush stained her cheeks.

"I need to know the story of how they met. And how they fell out."

Mrs. Chamberlen looked out the window, her eyes narrowing as though trying to see far away. "My husband and I lived for a time in Cambridge. Henry was very interested in some of the work done by alchemists there. I told him he was wasting his time and our money, but he didn't care. He swore we would have more money than we could imagine, that he knew people who would soon be able to turn base metals into gold. Mary, have you heard of the philosopher's stone?"

Mary nodded slightly. "I've heard stories and rumors of its power."

Mrs. Chamberlen sighed. "I understand it only imperfectly. According to my husband, it's a stone that alchemists can create, or discover, or some such, through cookery and distillation. It's a divine substance that can change one thing into another and give life. I will admit that I never quite understood his ramblings on the matter. He met Robert Sudbury through these people, these alchemists, but Sudbury didn't seem interested in money." Her mouth twisted. "He was a flirt and a libertine, but he was a far nobler man than my husband. Sudbury imagined the philosopher's stone to be the ultimate source of knowledge and health, not just the means to riches. He soon recognized my husband's greed and they parted ways. Sudbury went home to Chichester and my husband and I went to London. But, Mrs. Fawcett, if you want to learn more about the philosopher's stone, you really should ask Robert Sudbury."

So far, everything Mrs. Chamberlen said matched what Hopkins had told her. Mary's heart constricted.

"Some months later," Mrs. Chamberlen continued, "my husband heard a rumor that Sudbury found a special kind of distillation, a way of cooking away the grosser materials of an element using a new kind of vessel. The method had yielded impressive results. He insisted we go to Chichester so he could confer with Sudbury."

Mrs. Chamberlen sighed and stood up. She walked to the window, clearly struggling with her memories. Mary waited.

"My husband liked other women, Mrs. Fawcett. Many other women. This was something I learned on my wedding night, when he went from my bed to my cousin's. We loved each other, once, my husband and I, but I was never enough. And then, after years of trying to give him a child with no success, he simply ignored me. It was better than his rage, I suppose, better than screaming at me or berating or beating me. But not much better. I wanted a child so badly, Mary, so very badly. And I was so lonely . . ."

Mrs. Chamberlen stopped speaking for a moment, a profound sadness suffusing her face, before she shook herself and took a deep breath.

"There was a young woman in Chichester. Her name was Margery, and she was the town beauty. It was rumored that she was Sudbury's most recent conquest. My husband noticed her. I think he fell in love with her. He was very accomplished at falling in love. Henry insisted we stay in Chichester.

"I don't know what happened," she continued. "I never really knew for sure. One day, my husband left for Sudbury's house in the morning, and in the afternoon he burst into my room and demanded I pack my bags, said we were leaving within the hour. Later I heard there had been an accident, that Sudbury had suffered greatly."

"What happened to the girl?" Mary held her breath.

Mrs. Chamberlen bent her head and studied her hands. "After we left Chichester, Henry left me at our house in London and was absent for many months. When he returned, he was distant—even more so than usual. He had lost his charm, his liveliness. I made discreet inquiries and discovered the girl had died during childbirth. I don't know if the child was my husband's or Sudbury's."

"Did you know Sudbury had come to live in Bicknacre?" Mary asked.

Mrs. Chamberlen nodded. "I did. The servants told me. But I don't go out much, and I still haven't seen him myself." Mrs. Chamberlen paused. "And I don't doubt for a moment that my husband caused those scars on poor Sudbury's face." She looked at Mary. "You don't seem surprised."

"Matthew Hopkins took great delight in sharing some of the story with me," Mary said with a grimace.

Mary and Mrs. Chamberlen were quiet for a moment. Mary remembered the humiliation in Sudbury's eyes as she took in the additional bruises and scars the jailer had left on his face.

"But, Mary," Mrs. Chamberlen asked, "why are you asking about all this? It happened so long ago."

Mary watched the other woman carefully for any signs of duplicity and could find none. "You haven't heard that Robert Sudbury has been arrested for the murder of your husband? He sits in jail even now."

Mrs. Chamberlen gasped. "It was that miserable man Hopkins who put him there, wasn't it? He was there, too, in Chichester. He was obsessed with that girl, told everyone she would marry him. In a rage of vicious jealousy, he attacked Sudbury."

Mary felt a strange pang of jealousy for this long-dead woman capable of igniting such passion. But that sort of indulgence was useless, she told herself. After all, she was alive, and the beautiful Margery was dead.

Mrs. Chamberlen paced the floor, agitated, then sat down next to Mary and took her hand.

"Mrs. Fawcett. Mary. It is clear you have a special interest in Robert Sudbury. You need to know this: I do not believe Sudbury had anything to do with my husband's murder."

Mary watched her closely. "Why not?"

Mrs. Chamberlen stood and resumed her pacing. "The day they discovered my husband's body, after Betsy fetched you, I rose from my bed to see what was happening. I saw movement on the lawn. I saw someone running away . . . and it was very clearly a woman."

Mary gasped. "Why didn't you say anything?"

"I don't know." Mrs. Chamberlen bit her lip. "At the time, I assumed it was one of his lovers. I should have said something when I found out what happened to him, but . . ." She paused. "Well, I suppose I was just too happy he was dead," she said in a rush. "May God forgive me, but I was happy, and frankly I was eager to start living my life."

Mrs. Chamberlen hung her head. Mary reached to pat her hand and found it ice cold.

Mrs. Chamberlen hesitated. "Somebody else killed my husband. And it was not Robert Sudbury."

Mary's head ached from all the revelations. "But you don't know who the woman was?" she asked.

She shook her head. "I could see her skirts, but a cloak covered the rest of her. Mary . . . I believe it was Bridget Jenkins. They were lovers, not very long ago. I don't know how long it lasted—probably a year or more. He finally spurned her around midsummer. We saw her around Bicknacre sometimes. Mostly my husband ignored her. But a few months ago, I came across them together in the woods of Chamberlen Manor."

Mary gave her a look of sympathy, but Mrs. Chamberlen shrugged as she stood once more at the window. "I was used to my husband's philandering. I suppose in a way I was glad because it meant we would stay here at Chamberlen Manor for a while longer." She looked around the parlor. "I love my home. But Henry had been making plans to go to Cambridge again. I believe he and Bridget fought over it—he often came home with scratches on his face."

Mary hesitated to ask her next question, reluctant to cause Mrs. Chamberlen further distress. "Mrs. Chamberlen, you know that I was asked to examine your husband's body?"

Mary watched Mrs. Chamberlen carefully for any signs of distress but saw none.

"Yes, of course."

"Then you may know that I saw him naked." Mary tried to suppress her blush.

Mrs. Chamberlen nodded.

"And that I saw the scars on his stomach."

Mrs. Chamberlen's mouth dropped. "Scars?"

Mary didn't think Mrs. Chamberlen was playacting. She seemed truly taken aback.

"Yes, his abdomen was deeply scarred with various patterns. Mostly shapes—circles, triangles, some that I think I've seen in astrological charts."

Mrs. Chamberlen shook her head. "I haven't seen my husband naked in almost ten years." She nervously twisted the tassels holding back the curtain. "My husband was a beast, but at least he never forced himself on me. When I made it clear that I no longer wanted . . . to be together in that way . . . he left me alone, for the most part. Even when he did ask for those intimacies, he left his nightshirt on and left my bed immediately. He was even rather kind to me until I discovered him and Bridget in the woods. After that day, he grew cold, distant, and he started bringing me that vile poison."

"What did he say was in it?" Mary asked.

Mrs. Chamberlen had worked the tassels into a knot. "When I told him I was too old to bear a child, that my courses were too irregular, he insisted the cordial would overcome those obstacles. At first I believed him. He had become obsessed with his legacy, with begetting an heir.

He wanted me to drink it for three months and then for us to try again."
She blushed. "But as I grew sicker, well . . . we never did. But I trusted it
at first because he told me it was a cordial you yourself had concocted."

Mary grew indignant. "I never made such a thing!"

Mrs. Chamberlen nodded. "Yes, I know. That's why I brought you
to Chamberlen Manor, to see if you would recognize the cordial and
see that note."

"You know I saw it?"

"Of course. I left it there for you. It is, I believe, Bridget's handwriting. It said I should be given the cordial daily, that it would 'do
the job.'"

It fit, Mary realized. Mrs. Chamberlen's suspicions matched what
Mary already knew of Bridget's character. That must have been why she
was spending so much more time with Agnes—so she could steal the
hellebore and learn how to use it. She could have her revenge on Mary
and on Mrs. Chamberlen at the same time. She'd been spurned by Jack
Fawcett and Henry Chamberlen, and with this one act she could be
avenged on their women.

"But why did you tell me you'd keep taking it when you knew it
was poison?"

Mrs. Chamberlen gave a little shrug. "I'd only just figured it out,
and I was planning to dump the cordial once I had confirmation from
you. But I was afraid you might say something to Henry. I know
better now."

"There is more," Mary continued. "When I examined your husband's body, I found, clutched in his hand, a token. I gave it to Agnes
for safekeeping. As far as I know, it's still in her cottage."

Mrs. Chamberlen's brow wrinkled in confusion. "A token? How
strange."

Mary nodded. "Yes, and it had some symbols on it. On one side
was a pelican with her breast pierced, feeding her own children with
her blood."

"The pelican in her piety," Mrs. Chamberlen murmured.

"Yes, that's what Agnes called it when I showed it to her."

"Henry was obsessed with it. It's a symbol for Christ's sacrifice, but it also plays a role in alchemy. It is a kind of joke, I suppose. There's a vessel called a pelican flask that, as I understand it, allows the alchemist to distill a substance without exposing himself to the elements. Henry used to draw it over and over in his diary—I know because I read it when he wasn't looking."

Mrs. Chamberlen thought for a long moment and came to stand before Mary with a worried grimace. "You need to get Robert Sudbury out of that jail before Matthew Hopkins kills him. He hates Sudbury with a white-hot passion and will cause him more pain than any man should bear."

Mary knew Sudbury was in danger, but hearing Mrs. Chamberlen put it so bluntly caused her stomach to clench in fear.

Mrs. Chamberlen wrung her hands and then moved to a little desk in the corner of the room. She took out a piece of paper and began writing, then looked up.

"I've made a decision. Mary, my husband is, was, to blame for the position you and Sudbury are in. I feel responsible. If you can break Sudbury out of that jail cell, I will get you to London. I will send word that you are to stay at our house there. You can remain there until Hopkins leaves Bicknacre and forgets about you both."

Mary's face froze in surprise. "Mrs. Chamberlen, that is too generous."

"Nonsense," she replied. "It is the least I can do." She paused a moment. "Besides, there is something in London you may wish to see."

"What is it?" she asked warily.

"That diary of Mr. Chamberlen's. There are secrets in it, I'm sure. I didn't have many chances to read it, but what I saw was so strange, so fantastical—ciphers that might explain the scars you saw on his stomach and on that token. A key of sorts. I could send for it, but I worry that the servants might read it. And if you bring it back yourself, I can burn it." She paused. "It might be embarrassing if it were found by another."

"But I cannot leave Bicknacre," Mary said.

Mrs. Chamberlen glanced up from the letter she was writing, a look of surprise on her face. "Whyever not? The only way to keep Sudbury safe is to get him away from Hopkins. Mary, this is not a game."

"I cannot bring my brother on such a dangerous trip," Mary replied, her shoulders squared. Most of the skirmishes between the king's men and the New Model Army took place farther west, but she was nevertheless worried about endangering Tom while on the road—not to mention what could happen in London. "And I can't leave him here while Matthew Hopkins remains in town. He's already thrown Tom in prison once—what might he do if I'm not around?"

"He did *what*?" Mrs. Chamberlen almost shouted.

"Yes, but Simon Martin bribed him to release us."

Mrs. Chamberlen's face contorted with rage. "He's done horrible things before, but to throw a poor innocent child in jail? To expose him to all manner of danger and disease? It is unforgivable." Her face took on a fierceness. "Mary, I pledge to you, I swear to our Father in heaven, that I will keep Tom from that monster. You will go to London with Robert, where you'll be safe . . ."

Mary began to protest, but Mrs. Chamberlen gave her a quelling look.

". . . and Tom will stay here with me. I have ample resources to ensure his safety. Besides," she said, an ineffably sad look crossing her face, "I love children."

Mary knew this to be true from what she'd heard in the village over the years. Mrs. Chamberlen had given a substantial amount of money to build a small school in town, and she always had a smile for the children in the village. Indeed, Mary had never heard a bad word said about her.

Mary considered the options. If she refused, Robert Sudbury would surely die, and she and Tom would be even more vulnerable.

If she followed Mrs. Chamberlen's plan, she and Sudbury might put themselves in danger, but at least Tom would be safe. From the fervor and fury she'd witnessed in Mrs. Chamberlen, she believed the woman would do just about anything to protect Tom. And if she could find that diary, they might be able to prove Robert's innocence and put an end to the accusation of her own involvement.

"What does it look like?" she asked. "The diary?"

"It is a vainglorious abomination, to be honest with you. It's small and gilt, and it has the letter *C* embossed in gold on the front. It will be easy to find. As I could barely coax him out of his library, I imagine you'll find it there."

Mary breathed deep and nodded her agreement to the plan.

Mrs. Chamberlen sighed and her voice grew quieter. "Mary, I have another favor to ask of you. It's deeply personal, but I know you to be discreet."

Mary knew well the look of fear in Mrs. Chamberlen's eyes.

"For many months, my breast has pained me, and in the last few weeks it has changed color and shape."

Mary and Mrs. Chamberlen stared at each other. They both knew it was likely cancer of the breast, and they both knew too many women who had died of it.

"Will you take a look and give me something for healing?" she asked.

Mary nodded. "Of course. Go to your chamber and free your breast for me to examine. Cover up as much of yourself as you'd like and ask the maid to send for me."

Mary waited for the maid to send for her and then knocked on her door. Mrs. Chamberlen turned her head to the side when Mary entered the bedchamber. She lay quietly crying.

She was bare to the waist. She did not suffer from false modesty, which in cases like this made Mary's job easier.

"Mrs. Chamberlen, are you ready for me to examine your breast?"

It may have seemed an odd request given that Mrs. Chamberlen had asked for the examination and lay half-naked in front of her, but Mary always liked to give her patients control over when and how she examined them.

"Yes," Mrs. Chamberlen replied shakily. "It is on the left side of my right breast."

Mary rubbed her hands together vigorously to warm them and stepped closer to view the ulcerous wound. The disfiguration was about the length of her thumbnail and varied in color from a dark red to an ominous-looking deep brown. She palpated the area around the swelling. It felt hot and Mary could feel other hard places underneath the skin.

As she prodded the tender skin around the sore, she closed her eyes and imagined Mrs. Chamberlen's life over the last year. Mary felt her joy in the changing seasons: childhood delight in the snow of winter and deep contentment in the drowsy days of summer. She felt pain and loneliness. An image of the bottle of hellebore intruded, and nausea rocked her body.

In her mind's eye, Mary saw the tissue in Mrs. Chamberlen's breast move, jostle, and reorganize. She felt the cancer at its moment of conception, though she didn't know where it came from or what it was. She felt the heat from the skin, the confusion of the body, the eruption of the cancer as it outgrew its confinement and tried to break through the skin.

She knew what she could, and sadly could not, do for Mrs. Chamberlen.

"The sore has not broken yet. That is a good sign. How long has it felt like this?"

Mrs. Chamberlen's face was ashen. "I first noticed it felt strange the Michaelmas of last year, but the swelling has been there for about two months."

"It's not growing as fast as it might," Mary mused. "I have some salves we can use to try and slow the growth, and I can give you something to help with the itching and ease your discomfort by drawing out the hot, dry humors. But I must be honest with you, Mrs. Chamberlen, I have never seen a cancer this advanced be completely treated."

Mrs. Chamberlen nodded. "I knew it was that bad, I suppose, even as I drank the poison my husband gave me. I am dying anyway, after all."

She grabbed Mary's hand. "But you must call me Anne," she said with a sad smile. "You now know all my secrets. Whether you want to be or not, you are now my closest friend."

Mary squeezed back. "It's an honor," she replied.

When Mary got home, she immediately started work on the salves for her new friend. The women who had come before her, her mother and grandmothers and their friends and kin, had shared their knowledge of this disease for decades, centuries probably. She knew of at least five recipes for different stages of growth of the sore, and she and Agnes had made some improvements to the recipes handed down to her.

Mary took her book down from the shelf and flipped to the page with the recipe she knew would best help Mrs. Chamberlen. It was a long recipe, and a bit fussy, but it would work to bring relief. She measured out enough mallow leaves to cover her lap and put them in a large kettle over the fire. She boiled the leaves until they were very soft—"slippery like soap"—and drained them, pressing out the slimy, mucus-like water. She mixed the leaves with some hog's grease, then boiled a pint of cream with three egg yolks and some manchet bread. She roasted some lily roots and crushed them into a fine powder. She stirred everything together and put the mixture into a clay pot.

Mary then went to the garden and spent a great deal of time searching for a dead snail so she could harvest its shell. Some healers, she knew, would not take the trouble and would merely find a live snail and smash it to bits. She didn't blame them entirely. Healing sometimes required death, as when she had to kill pigeons to attain their blood for her eye salve. But when she could avoid death, she did.

Mary eventually found a dead snail and brought it inside. She pulled the desiccated body from the shell—a strange, rubbery thing—and saved it for her other cures. While she worked—stirring, boiling, mixing, stamping, gleaning—she took time to remember what she'd intuited when she'd examined Mrs. Chamberlen. She remembered the sense of betrayal at her husband's deceit, the fury and shame. And she felt a trace of the gaping loneliness at the core of Mrs. Chamberlen's heart.

When she saw Mrs. Chamberlen next, she would instruct her to spread the poultice on a cloth and place it on the sore until it turned red and soft, for at least a day, and then apply the ground snail shell in a thick paste. That would draw out the extra heat and rebalance the humors in her breast.

For a while at least. She hesitated to think what she could do to help once the cure stopped working.

CHAPTER 13

The way how to make rosa solis [for courage and cheer]

Take half a peck of the herb called rosa solis being gath-
ered before the sun do arise, in the latter end of June, or
the beginning of July. Pick them and lay them upon a
board to dry all a day . . .

The next day, Mary conferred with Mrs. Woods for several hours before
doing the impossible: leaving her brother, and the only home she'd ever
known, behind. For how long, she did not know.

She'd gathered Tom's things the night before—packed his small bag
with extra clothes and toys. He'd asked her time and again where he
was going, but she'd just put him off with a mysterious smile and the
promise of a treat. That night, she let him crawl in next to her on her
small bed, and she held him close until her tears subsided.

As she lay there, body still but mind racing, she wondered what
it would be like in London, seeing new faces and hearing new voices.
She'd heard so much about the city. She longed to view the Thames,
to spy the ominous Tower, to visit the booksellers' stalls in St. Paul's
Churchyard. Would she meet new people through Sudbury? Would
he introduce her to his Cambridge friends? If so, would they discuss

the experiments they were working on, the ideas that sparked their curiosity?

Would they want to hear her ideas?

The possibilities sent a frisson of excitement through her. That her mind would once again spark and bubble with new ideas and concepts like it did when she and Sudbury stayed up all night talking. That her ideas would be treated with respect, even questioned with vigor . . . She knew she'd never experience this sort of engagement again if she stayed in Bicknacre for the rest of her life. As much as she feared leaving Tom—and despite the guilt she felt, regardless of Mrs. Chamberlen's reassurances—she couldn't deny she felt exhilarated at the thought of new experiences.

In the morning, Mary told Tom he would stay with Mrs. Chamberlen and that Mrs. Woods would check on him. When she told him that she would be gone for days, maybe even weeks or months, she braced herself for wailing and pleas for her to stay, but Tom was oddly compliant.

"Is Mrs. Chamberlen nice?" he asked.

"Yes. And she will be good to you."

"Why do you have to leave?" he asked.

"I have to go to London to do some business for Mrs. Chamberlen. It's nothing to worry about. I will return as soon as I can."

Tom nodded.

"Are you feeling well?" she asked, surprised at how calm he was. Mary marveled at this precocious boy, this little man-child.

"No," he replied. "I'm very sad and I want to cry. I know you wouldn't leave me unless you had to. But, Mary, I don't want to go back to that jail."

Mary hugged her brother tight. "Mrs. Chamberlen won't let that happen," she promised.

"I'll have Greedyguts with me, right?" Even now, the faithful crow hopped down the path behind him.

"Of course. But remember," Mary said, "I need to borrow Greedyguts overnight. Mrs. Woods will return him to you as soon as she can."

When they arrived at Chamberlen Manor, Mary took the little cage she had carried in her bag and shooed Greedyguts into it. He cawed furiously, but she mollified him by nudging walnuts in through the door.

They left the cage by a tree and went around to the servants' entrance. The cook gave Tom some iced cakes while she fetched a footman to take them to the parlor. Mrs. Chamberlen came to them immediately. Her eyes shone, and she almost looked like a child herself in her excitement.

"Oh, Tom, we will have such fun!" she said, putting her arm around his shoulder. "Do you like fishing? There's a little pond where you can catch the cleverest little fish. And I've brought out all of Mr. Chamberlen's old toys for you to play with!"

Mary cleared her throat. She knew that Mrs. Chamberlen could provide Tom with more fun, more toys, more leisure than she could, but she didn't appreciate the reminder as she stood ready to say goodbye to her brother. Mrs. Chamberlen looked sheepish.

"I'm sorry, Mary," she said. "It has just been so long since I've had a child in the house."

Mary saw the excitement in Tom's eyes and she couldn't bring herself to show her own sadness and worry. Instead, she gave him a quick hug and a kiss on the cheek.

"Be good," she whispered to him. "Listen to Mrs. Chamberlen and Mrs. Woods and do as you are told. Say your prayers, and don't forget to ask for blessings for your sister. Remember to pray for Mama and Papa every night."

She smiled and gave him a squeeze.

"I will, Mary. I will do all those things." His eyes glistened with unshed tears. Despite all the excitement Mrs. Chamberlen promised, Tom would miss his sister. "And you will pray for me?"

Mary nodded.

"And wherever you are going, do not die like Mrs. Shepherd did." Mary bit her lip to keep from crying. "No. I promise."

She took Mrs. Chamberlen aside. "Anne, apply this poultice and let it sit for at least a day, then apply this snail-shell paste daily."

She kissed Tom's head, smiled at Mrs. Chamberlen, and walked out of the room without looking back.

After retrieving Greedyguts, Mary headed immediately to Agnes's small, cozy cottage. She wished she could sit outside in the garden for a bit, breathing in the lavender and mint and thyme, remembering the wisdom and care Agnes had given her over the years.

She had to find some way to get the token Agnes had hidden in her recipe book—if they could find Chamberlen's diary, that token might mean something. But the lock she'd seen on the hidden door the last time she'd been in the room looked formidable.

She found the front door of the cottage unlocked and pushed her way in. The familiar scents of potions and poultices, oils and unguents—and another fragrance that was uniquely Agnes's—nearly overcame her. She lay down on the straw mattress, burrowing in and pulling a blanket over herself as she looked around the small room. Thin light from the one window illuminated the rows of herbs and ointments, the cheese press and churn sitting to the side of a listing cupboard. She took in the ladles and buckets Agnes had hung and left to dry next to the strings of onions and garlic. Mary tried not to think about Agnes getting ready to leave the cottage for the last time, tidying up in the hope she would return to put away the dishes and sweep the hearth. She lay still and let the tears come. But after a few minutes, she took a deep breath and pushed herself up off the mattress.

"Right," she said to herself. "That's enough of that." She smiled at how much she had absorbed Agnes's matter-of-factness.

She moved the carpet away from the little door and sized up the heavy iron lock. Agnes must have known Hopkins would search her cottage, and of course she would want to protect her recipes from his grubby, evil hands.

There had to be a key somewhere. Agnes had barely left her cottage in the weeks before she'd been dragged to the jail, so surely it would still be somewhere in the small house.

At first Mary searched cautiously, with almost delicate care, the sense that she was disrespecting the dead hanging over her. But as the minutes dragged on with no sign of the key, Mary's frustration grew and she became more thorough, emptying all the cupboards and wooden chests, digging through the dried herbs and empty bottles. Nothing.

She sat down, closed her eyes, and tried to imagine herself into Agnes's mind like she did with those she healed. Mary had no idea, really, how her gift worked. Maybe it worked with just the memory of a person. Or with their spirit. Or maybe it was all in Mary's imagination—but she had to try.

She conjured up one of her favorite memories of Agnes. Shortly after Jack died, she found her sitting in a field, spring wildflowers blooming all around her. Even in her plain brown dress, she glowed with the promise of spring. She was playing with Tom, just a toddler then, bouncing him on her knees and singing a lively rhyme:

Mary, Mary, quite contrary
How does your garden grow?
With silver bells and cockle shells
And pretty maids all in a row!

At that last line, Agnes tossed a giggling Tom up in the air, caught him safely in her arms, and gave him a tender hug.

It was the first time she'd seen Agnes look playful. And indeed, from then on, Tom brought out a softer, more tender side of her old friend.

She sat with that memory for a few moments before imagining Agnes in the cottage, puttering over the stove, chopping herbs, and stretching her shoulders. She envisioned Agnes wandering over to the little carpet covering the door in the floor and pulling it to the side. In her mind, she followed Agnes out the front door and to the side of the cottage, watched as she bent down and removed a loose shingle to reveal a small key sitting on the supporting brick.

Suddenly, Mary felt a sharp pain in her head and heard a shriek. She felt dizzy, as though somebody were pushing her away, as though she were falling. She had never felt this before. Holding her head in her hands, she shot out of the chair and looked around the cottage for the source but saw nothing.

She was alone. Had the shriek come from her?

She slowly walked outside. There, just as she'd seen it in her mind's eye, was the loose shingle. She wiggled the small board from side to side until it came clear and revealed a small key.

Marveling at the accuracy of her vision, and still terrified by the strange uproar she'd felt in her head, Mary went into the house and, with trembling hands, fit the key into the lock and opened it with ease.

Inside the carved-out space sat Agnes's recipe book, just as she'd left it. She caressed the soft, worn cover and opened it to the loose index that prefaced the recipes—a folded paper Agnes had inserted into the front. She pulled it away and felt inside the little pocket where Agnes had tucked the token.

It was empty.

Mary's mind buzzed in confusion. Had Agnes moved the token before she was taken to the jail? If so, why?

She decided to save these questions for later—she needed to get Robert out of that jail. She replaced the recipe book in its hiding place and returned the key to its perch behind the shingle. She would have to wait to solve this mystery another day.

That night, Mary and Mrs. Woods crouched on the corner of the side street by the jail, a pile of bright red berries sitting in front of them. They had a view of Geoffrey through the upper window, and they had waited almost an hour for him to finally extinguish the lamp. Greedyguts hopped in circles around them, cawing occasionally.

"I will sit here with Greedyguts," Mrs. Woods repeated the plan for the third time to make sure she had it right, "while you go over to the window and throw a rock into it. Oh, I do hope Robert hears."

"And that he's still capable of standing," Mary added grimly.

Mary took the rock Mrs. Woods handed her and crept close to the window, a narrow slit covered with iron bars. Mary was careful to stay in the shadows. Greedyguts watched her carefully, but luckily he made no sound.

Mary took a shaky breath and threw the rock at the window.

Nothing.

She took another and threw it. Then another. Finally, she saw something move in the dark rectangle of shadows, a flash of pale skin. She hoped to God it was Sudbury and not Geoffrey.

Mary ran back to Mrs. Woods and Greedyguts. She called the crow over to her and gave it a berry. Greedyguts bent his head and looked at her.

"Yes, that one is for you." Greedyguts ate the berry. Mary gave him another, and again the crow cocked his head. Mary pointed to the window, and Greedyguts took off.

Mary could see the pale oval of Sudbury's face in the window. Greedyguts left the berry on the sill and returned.

Mrs. Woods pulled a darning pin from the pocket of her apron and handed it to Mary.

Mary gave Greedyguts another berry and granted him permission to eat it, then gave him another and pointed at the window, directing the bird to take it to Sudbury. They repeated this exercise at least five times, making sure that Greedyguts knew his job. Then she put the pin in the crow's beak and pointed at the window.

Hopefully Sudbury was alone and would know it was Mary sending the pin and know what to do with it. And hopefully he was still strong enough to pick the lock.

Greedyguts returned and let Mary pet his shining black feathers. She fed him more berries as they waited, terrified.

Finally, after Greedyguts had eaten his tenth berry, Mary saw movement in the shadows of the building. It was Sudbury, slowly moving down the alley. Even at a distance, she could see that there was something wrong with his leg—it was bent at an unnatural angle. She hurried over to help him, but before she could get there, Sudbury stumbled and let out a muffled cry.

Sudbury's face was a grim mask of pain as he writhed on the ground, clutching at his ankle, but still he managed to whisper a heartfelt thanks. Mrs. Woods took a handkerchief and wrapped his ankle tightly.

Mary took another handkerchief and gently placed it in his mouth. Sudbury clenched down on it, and each woman took an arm. The cloth effectively muffled his cries, but he could bear only a painfully slow pace.

Mrs. Woods stopped them. "This will take all night. Let's go to my house for a cart."

They slowly walked to the Woods house and bundled Robert into a small manure cart. The sight of the prideful Robert Sudbury bundled into a malodorous cart, a woman pushing on each side, gave Mary a brief sense of satisfaction. Her feelings for him changed by the minute—from sympathy to anger to attraction to frustration. Yes, he'd warned her about Hopkins, tried to protect her from the witchfinder's machinations, ignited her mind, and touched her heart. But he'd also lied to her. She didn't hate him, but she couldn't yet trust him.

As swiftly as they could they carted Sudbury out of town and to an abandoned woodsman's cabin about half a mile away. Greedyguts perched in his cage, quietly munching on dried pumpkin seeds. Sudbury tried to stay upright, but with each furrow in the road and bump of the cart, he slumped farther down. He cycled in and out of awareness—whether he had fainted or slept, Mary did not know—and would occasionally cry out in pain. With each cry, Mary softened.

The cabin had sat empty for several years, but it still had a straw pallet for a bed, and earlier in the day Mr. Woods had brought in kindling for the fireplace and buckets of water for Sudbury to wash in.

Mrs. Woods and Mary waited outside while Sudbury completed his makeshift bath, then they wrapped his ankle again. Understanding that Mary and Sudbury needed to talk privately, Mrs. Woods took Greedyguts's cage and headed for home, promising to return in the morning.

The dark night provided a welcome cover for Mary. She could barely look at Sudbury, could hardly sort out the questions crowding her mind. Mary sensed Sudbury's remorse, knew that he longed to say something, to redeem himself after keeping so many secrets from her. She sat in a chair by the door and waited.

Finally Sudbury spoke. "Mary?" Her name a question—would she hear him? Would she answer? Would she care?

Mary sat, unmoving, for several moments.

Then she wasted no words.

"Did you kill Henry Chamberlen?"

"No," he said without hesitation.

They sat quietly, waiting for the other to speak.

"I'm not the same man I was in Chichester," Sudbury said.

"You are that man," Mary replied, "only then you had a prettier face. Besides, I'm more worried about your lies now than your actions in the past. How could you not tell me all of this? You've put Tom and me in grave danger!"

Sudbury sucked in his breath, then shifted on the straw pallet and turned toward her.

"It's true," he began. "I've enjoyed the company of women. Too many women. My studies were such as could drive a man to the edge of sanity. During the bleakest times, the nights when the dark waters of the River Cam called to me, or the days I could almost watch my hand bring poison to my lips, I found succor in the arms of women. Only in flesh could I seem to find my humanity."

Mary stared at Sudbury across the darkened room, trying to make out his bruised and swollen face. Mary didn't particularly care about his licentious past. He was a man, after all, with human desires and needs. And it would be hypocritical to judge him—since Jack had died, she, too, had missed the warmth of human touch, the fire of passion.

"The day Margery died, the day of the accident—that day scarred me on the inside, too. And while my face eventually scabbed over, my soul remains an open wound. I cannot forgive myself. I couldn't save Margery from Chamberlen, couldn't convince her that his pretty promises were lies. I was responsible for the death of a good, kind woman, a woman who loved me tenderly. She left me because she knew the truth: I could not love her in return. I felt great affection for her, enjoyed her company, appreciated her lightness and laughter, but I did not love her."

Mary thought about Jack, his betrayal, the almost feverish ambition that drove him to work himself to exhaustion, just to earn her forgiveness. She thought of Agnes and her nearly obsessive love for Grace, a love that almost drove her to take her own life. People had their passions, their strange drives, their deep need to love and be loved in return. And Robert wasn't the only man who'd searched for oblivion in the arms of a woman. No, she didn't care about the tomcat ways of his youth. What made her mistrust him was that he had lied to her about knowing Chamberlen and Matthew Hopkins in what seemed like another life. She still had questions, doubts. She didn't know if she could, or should, trust him. But for now, they could make an uneasy truce.

Mary walked over to him. In the dim light of the candle she could see the worry in his eyes, the pleading. She pulled a blanket over his shoulders and then made up her own bed in the opposite corner.

Mary awoke to Mrs. Woods knocking at the door, her arms laden with supplies. Mary was shocked at how high the sun had risen—it must have been midmorning at least. Sudbury was still lying on the pallet on the opposite side of the room.

Mrs. Woods pulled two chairs over to the pallet where Sudbury rested.

"Come. Sit," Mrs. Woods commanded Mary. She then addressed Sudbury. "I heard a commotion at the jail this morning, and as I made my way out of town, two people stopped to gossip with me about your escape."

"We cannot stay in Bicknacre," Sudbury said to Mary. "You may have been acquitted, but people still suspect you. And Hopkins will surely suspect you helped me escape. He won't rest until you're in jail again. He has hated me for years, and now he despises you, too."

"You both must leave as quickly as you can," Mrs. Woods said.

Mary nodded and hurried her friend to the door. Then she turned to Sudbury.

"I have a plan for us to leave Bicknacre. Mrs. Chamberlen has arranged for us to stay at her house in London until Hopkins leaves Bicknacre and the whispers die down, and she has given me a small purse."

Sudbury looked amazed and a little suspicious. "Why would she do so much?"

Mary was reluctant to spill Mrs. Chamberlen's secrets, her hatred of her husband, the burgeoning friendship between them, the cancer eating away at her breast. Her trust in Sudbury was still brittle. "We have a history together," she said, enjoying the look of frustration on Sudbury's face. It felt good to have secrets of her own.

Sudbury nodded, seeming to accept Mary at her word.

"What about Tom?"

"Mrs. Chamberlen will keep him at Chamberlen Manor. She has the resources to protect him."

"And you trust her?" he asked.

"I do," she replied.

Sudbury dropped his head in his hands. "It appears you've thought of everything. When do we leave?"

"Today. Now."

Mary tried to look resolute, tried to hide her shaking hands. Once they left, there was no turning back.

Sudbury looked up. "If that's what you think is best," he said quietly.

"You have no thoughts on the matter?" she asked, surprised at his obedience.

Sudbury sighed. "I've learned not to trust my own judgment, Mary." His head sank again. "I've made so many mistakes."

Mary reached her hand out and rested it on his shoulder.

They had reached a détente of sorts. Whether their uneasy peace could survive the trip to London, she did not know.

CHAPTER 14

To make a seed cake

Take the whites of 8 eggs, beat them very well, then put
the yolks to them and beat them very well together, then
put to it a pound of sugar, beat and sifted very fine, and
beat it for half an hour, then make it a little warm over
the fire, and after that put in 3 quarters of a pound of
flour, very well dried, a quarter of an ounce of caraway
seeds, stir it well together and put it into the pan, it will
take 3 quarters of an hour to bake it.

Mary had never imagined that any part of the world could be so different from Bicknacre. As they approached the outskirts of London in the Chamberlens' luxurious carriage, she was struck by the cacophony, overwhelmed by the shouts of fishmongers showing off their eels and oysters, fruit sellers their cherries and oranges, prostitutes their charms. She saw vegetable stands filled with herbs and garlic, lettuces and long strings of onions. They passed by a large pipe, a conduit that brought water from a nearby stream, where urchins collected water in earthenware jugs while women washed dishes and clothing right there in the street. Men with long rakes cleared the streets of shit and old straw.

The din grew even greater the farther into the city they traveled. Small children, dressed in rags, their feet bare, dodged between the carts and horses, mere inches from being trampled to death. Even the smells were strange and new—one minute she gagged at the sickly sweet scent of rotting fish or piss or decaying vegetables, and the next she was comforted by scents of baking bread and fresh straw sprinkled in the streets.

Sudbury clearly did not feel the same thrill: he peered out of the carriage window with a strange look on his face. She thought she saw interest, perhaps a little nostalgia, in the way his eyes darted this way and that, taking it all in. But she also saw a great deal of sorrow. Mary reached out and touched his arm. He flinched, then gave her a weak smile. It had been a long day of travel, she thought. Perhaps he was tired. Or simply in pain from his injury. Or consumed with memories of his former life.

Mary noticed that the environs became more genteel, the smells less objectionable, as they approached Chamberlen House. The carriage stopped in front of a tidy row of brick buildings, three stories tall—vastly different from the unsteady-looking timber houses they'd passed on the outskirts of town, each floor jutting out a foot or more over the one below.

A large, smiling woman opened the door. She looked around fifty years old, dressed neatly and well. There was a sweetness to her face, though she eyed them with some suspicion. She could not take her eyes off Sudbury's scar.

"Are you here to collect payment?"

Mary shook her head. Where to begin?

Sudbury replied for her. "Mrs. Chamberlen has granted us permission to stay here while we're in London."

The woman stood straighter and smiled a little wider. "Oh, you must be Mr. Sudbury and Mrs. Fawcett. Welcome. Please come in and rest. May I get you some refreshment? My name is Mrs. Stanton, and I'm the housekeeper."

She was friendly but formal as she waved them into the house and led them to the kitchen.

"I thank you for your kindness," Mary said. "We have a letter from Mrs. Chamberlen."

As soon as Mrs. Stanton heard the broadness of Mary's country accent and heard the friendliness in her voice, she relaxed her formality.

Mrs. Stanton pulled two wooden chairs over to a large table worn smooth from years of kitchen work. Mary breathed in the smells of yeast and cooking meat, the hint of cinnamon and ginger, the lingering scent of burnt wood. She smiled—how she loved kitchen smells. She felt at ease for the first time in weeks.

Mrs. Stanton started fussing. "Would you like some ale? I just made a seed cake, and you're welcome to a slice . . ."

Robert shook his head. "No thank you. I was wondering—"

Mary interrupted him. "We would love some cake, Mrs. Stanton," she said. The best way to get on her good side, she knew, was to eat the fruits of the housekeeper's labors.

When Mrs. Stanton set the cake down on the table, warm, sugared on top, and with a robust scent of caraway, Robert wolfed it down. Mrs. Stanton looked on with pride and pleasure.

"Now you may ask your question, Mr. Sudbury," Mrs. Stanton said with an indulgent expression.

Sudbury seemed self-conscious. "Is there still a man named John Weaver working here?"

Mary glanced up. What was this now?

Mary marveled at how quickly Mrs. Stanton's expression turned stony.

"Perhaps," she replied. "May I ask what your business is with Mr. Weaver?"

"He's an old friend," Sudbury replied, a faraway look in his eyes.

The suspicion had not quite left Mrs. Stanton's eyes. "Very well. I'll fetch him. Except for the day laborers, he and I are the only two here when the Chamberlens—well, just Mrs. Chamberlen now, I suppose—are away from London. And I suppose he'll want to read that letter from the mistress." She bustled out of the room.

Mary reached into her leather satchel and brought out the elegant letter. Mrs. Chamberlen's red seal glimmered in the late-afternoon sun.

"What do you suppose it says?" Robert asked.

Mary shook her head. "It didn't take her long to write it. I believe it's a simple letter of introduction, to prove we are who we say we are."

Mary began to feel the effects of the warm fire and delicious cake, reveling in the stability of a solid floor after the rocking of the carriage. Her eyes were starting to close and a warm drowsiness was suffusing her body when she heard loud footsteps in the hallway outside the kitchen. The door opened and Mary almost gasped.

The most remarkable man Mary had ever seen walked into the room. His skin was a deep black—darker by far than the tanned skin of the farmers in Bicknacre in the height of summer. He towered over everybody in the room, as tall as the door frame and almost as broad. He was completely bald, but a lush beard hung almost to his chest.

The man took note of her reaction and grinned.

Mrs. Stanton motioned to them. "Mr. Weaver, this is Mary Fawcett and Robert—"

She was cut off by Sudbury's chuckle, surprised when he reached out to grab Weaver's hand and give him a hearty pat on the back.

Mr. Weaver roared with laughter. "Sudbury! This man's name is Sudbury! It has been a long time, my friend." His voice had the faintest lilt of foreign lands.

"John!" Sudbury grinned openly, and Mary realized she hadn't seen that kind of joy on his face until now. He was usually so wary, so reserved.

Mr. Weaver enveloped him in a massive hug. Sudbury stumbled backward a few steps and laughed.

It was the first time Mary had heard him laugh. It came out as a deep rumble, warm and carefree.

Mary liked it very much.

Weaver pulled away from Sudbury and examined his face.

"But what has happened to you, my friend? Where's that handsome face that used to charm the ladies so well?"

Mrs. Stanton swatted at Mr. Weaver's arm. "John!"

Weaver was unbothered. "Oh, this one was a winner with the ladies," he said. Sudbury looked quickly at Mary, who had already fixed her eyes on the floor. "And he is handsome still in a way. But where did you get that nasty scar?"

"From your late master," Sudbury said.

Weaver froze.

"Chamberlen?"

Sudbury nodded.

"That bastard." Weaver looked thoughtful. "Then again, he left his mark on me, too, I suppose." He pointed to a design on his arm, an inked pattern not unlike those Mary had seen on Chamberlen's corpse, only this one contained a crude *HC*.

"He tried to brand me as his property. What a whoreson he was."

Mrs. Stanton looked at Mary nervously. "John, watch your words," she warned.

"Don't concern yourself," Mary replied. "I bore no love for the man."

Mrs. Stanton nodded. "No, nor did I."

Weaver continued holding Sudbury by the shoulders. "But what happened? The last time I saw you, you and Chamberlen were cooking up those strange brews."

Sudbury extracted himself from Weaver's grip and sat down at the table. "Do you remember Margery?"

"How could I forget her? You stole her away from that pompous ass—Hopkins, was it?" Weaver replied. "A sweet piece—" He cut off whatever he was about to say and looked nervously at Mrs. Stanton.

"But a silly little thing, if I remember," he finished weakly. "Common sense of a bird."

Mrs. Stanton rolled her eyes. "Oh, hush, John," she said. "I don't expect you never to have looked at other women."

Ah, Mary thought. So that was how things were.

Everybody looked to Sudbury to continue the story. He sighed, rubbed his face, and got on with it. "I was wooing Margery. I thought it was time to get married, and she was a good, kind girl. I fancied myself in love. And my only competition was Matthew Hopkins. God, I was so arrogant. And young and foolish, too. Margery was a good girl, but what I needed was a woman who was as wise as she was beautiful."

He glanced briefly at Mary.

"Margery came to visit me one afternoon as Chamberlen and I worked on our alchemical experiments. We were distilling metals, trying to get philosophical mercury. Chamberlen was a womanizer, a cad, as you well know. I should've known to keep her away. He was struck by her beauty. He searched her out, I heard later, bought her jewelry and told her pretty things about setting her up in her own home as his mistress. I didn't learn of her betrayal until some months later when she told me she was with child."

Sudbury looked down at his hands. "I had been careful with her. I only ever kissed her. The child was Chamberlen's. I confronted him. I told him I would never work with him again. He was furious, told me to pack up my things. I was in the middle of gathering the bottles I had brought when I turned and he threw molten lead in my face."

Sudbury's voice remained calm throughout the retelling of his tale, but Weaver had grown increasingly restless. At this last bit, Weaver brought his fists down on the table.

"The bastard!" he shouted.

This time Mrs. Stanton didn't bother to shush him.

Sudbury continued. "Since then, I've made my way in the world with the inheritance from my parents. I continue my experiments on my own. About a year ago, I moved to Bicknacre to be closer to Cambridge." He mentioned nothing of his intent to torture Chamberlen with his very presence, but Mr. Weaver and Mrs. Stanton exchanged looks that showed they suspected as much. "It's only a few hours away. It's there I met Mrs. Fawcett."

Sudbury nodded in Mary's direction, and the other two turned to look at her. She felt an unaccustomed nervousness at the sudden attention.

Mrs. Stanton asked in a gentle voice, "And who are you, miss?"

"Mrs.—I am a widow," Mary replied, steadying her voice. "My husband died five years ago."

Mrs. Stanton gave her a look of sympathy. She patted her shoulder. "Have you any children to lessen the pain?"

Tears sprang to Mary's eyes and she shook her head. "Our child didn't survive her infancy. But I do have a young brother, Tom. Our parents are dead. He's just eight years old and he's staying with Mrs. Chamberlen while we're here."

"Ah." Mrs. Stanton put her arm around Mary's shoulders and squeezed. "She can be a kind woman, especially with children," she reassured Mary. "Your brother will be well cared for."

Weaver hesitated a moment and then asked, "Why are you in London, Robert?"

Sudbury looked at Mary for permission to share their story, and she nodded. She felt instinctively that she could trust these people.

While the others waited patiently, Sudbury stood, as if to pace the floor, then winced and sank back into his seat.

"I've escaped from jail," he finally said, his voice plain and even. "I am suspected of the murder of Henry Chamberlen."

Mrs. Stanton gasped.

"I am innocent of the charge, of course," he reassured her. "And your mistress knows it."

"Well, of course you are," Weaver said. He waved away Sudbury's assertion of innocence as though it were a bothersome gnat.

"What do you know about Chamberlen's death?" Sudbury asked.

"Mrs. Chamberlen told us he died of self-slaughter," Mrs. Stanton answered. "But of course we've heard other rumors."

"He was poisoned," Mary said. "I saw the body, saw the signs. It was hellebore. I don't think one could ingest that much poison willingly."

"May God have mercy on his soul," Mr. Weaver murmured.

"I doubt very much that God wants anything to do with Mr. Chamberlen," Sudbury said, his mouth twisted in disgust. "I hated the man. You know that. But I didn't kill him. It was Matthew Hopkins who had me arrested."

"The man from Chichester that was in love with the girl?" Mrs. Stanton asked.

This part of the story, at least, she knew, so Mary responded. "He's become a witchfinder, Mrs. Stanton. He came to my village in search of evil, and he's stirred up every kind of trouble he can find."

Weaver gave a low whistle. "He's wanted to hurt you for a very long time, Robert. But what was he doing in your town?"

"Chamberlen brought him there to torture me, I think," Sudbury replied, a grim set to his mouth. "And Mrs. Chamberlen knows it. I believe she still feels some guilt for what her husband did." Sudbury waved his hand to indicate the scars on his face.

"And what about you?" Mrs. Stanton asked, turning to Mary. "Why do you leave your brother and your life to come to London?"

"I'm under suspicion of another kind, though once again by Hopkins's hand." Mary paused. A sudden rush of emotion overcame her, and she choked down a sob. She coughed and said, slowly, "I have done some healing, and I learned my trade from a local cunning woman who was arrested for witchcraft. She died before her innocence could be proven. I, too, come under suspicion of murder and maleficium."

Mrs. Stanton laid a plump hand on Mary's forearm. The scrape of the woman's calluses across Mary's wrist brought her out of her reverie. Mrs. Stanton held her hand tightly.

Tears spilled down Mary's face. "Hopkins needed another victim to torment, so he turned the village against me and my brother." Mary angrily brushed the tears from her eyes. "I apologize. I'm not usually so weepy. It has been a sad few weeks."

Mrs. Stanton sprang into action. "Of course, dear, of course! You need some time to rest." She gently pushed Mr. Weaver out of the way and refilled Mary's cup with wine. She brought more cakes for them both before shooing Mr. Weaver from the room and following him out.

"We'll leave you in peace to fill your bellies, and then I'll come back to show you your rooms," she said over her shoulder as she left.

Some of the tension left Mary as the door closed. Sudbury had slumped over, his head once again buried in his hands.

She wondered why Sudbury had failed to mention his acquaintance with Mr. Weaver.

Secrets and more secrets, she thought. Always there were secrets.

Mary was tempted to relax and let the warm fire and wine do their work, but her curiosity compelled her to ask, "How do you know Mr. Weaver? Did you know he would be here?"

Sudbury's voice was low and soft. "I practically lived with the Chamberlens for a month or so when the experiments were at their most precarious. Weaver was a part of Chamberlen's household. He did some jobs around the house, helped the gardener, that sort of thing. Chamberlen would parade him in front of his visitors, to let them gawk at his black skin. We ignored each other for the better part of a week, but then one day when I was walking in the garden, he approached me and started asking questions about the experiments. I learned that he could read and write. He had been taught in fits and starts by the whims of Henry Chamberlen, but it was enough for him to start teaching himself. And he told me he had been following our progress by bits, finding ways to sneak into the room where we did our experimenting.

"He asked me not to tell Chamberlen. He didn't trust him. He hated the way the figures in Chamberlen's alchemy book had dark skin like his. He feared Chamberlen might make use of him in strange ways. Experiment on him. He may have been correct in that. Had Weaver been smaller, weaker, he may well have done. Chamberlen had odd ideas.

"We became friends. We'd meet out in a copse of trees behind the house and talk about alchemy and . . . well, all manner of things. I was very sad to leave him. Because he is foreign, many would look askance at our friendship, but I am glad he's here. He is a good man."

Mary nodded and Sudbury sighed. "What's next?" he said.

"What do you mean? We discussed this. We stay here until Mrs. Chamberlen sends word that Hopkins has left Bicknacre."

Sudbury nodded. "Yes, but I've been thinking. Will Hopkins ever really leave us alone? He's not a man to let slights go. He will hound us. A man capable of putting a boy like Tom in jail is capable of anything."

Mary sat up. "What do you mean? Why are we here, then? Should we return?"

Sudbury sighed. "Tom is safer with Mrs. Chamberlen and her many servants than he ever could be with you. No, Mrs. Chamberlen was right. We needed to get out of Bicknacre. Hopkins wants you. He wants you in jail, at his mercy, available to satisfy his most craven desires."

Mary then remembered Chamberlen's diary. "I wonder . . . ," she said. "Perhaps there is a way around Hopkins."

Sudbury started in again. "I don't see how, Mary. He is—"

Mary interrupted him. "As we were making plans, while you were still in the jail cell, Mrs. Chamberlen told me that Mr. Chamberlen kept a diary, that she expects it's here in this house. Do you remember the ciphers on Chamberlen's corpse that I told you about?"

Sudbury nodded, his eyes wide.

"Mrs. Chamberlen said she saw ciphers like that in his diary. Robert, if we find that book, we might discover who killed him and clear our names. Hopkins will have no more power over either of us."

Sudbury thought for a long moment and then reached over and covered Mary's hand with his. "Hopkins will likely leave Tom alone unless he can use him to get to you. Or to me. Mrs. Chamberlen can protect him, for now at least. You're right, Mary—we need to find that diary."

CHAPTER 15

To make an ointment of swallows good for the shrinking
of sinews or for a strain

*Take of lavender cotton, of hyssop, and of the runnings
out of strawberries, of each of these a great handful, chop
them small, and stamp them with a pound of fresh butter, that hath neither been washed nor salted, and stamp
therewith eight young swallows out of the nest, putting
them in by one and one, feathers, guts, and all . . .*

Mary had been so tired when Mrs. Stanton showed her upstairs, she'd
barely had enough energy to take in the room's luxuriousness. On the
walls hung intricate tapestries saturated in rich maroons and golds with
green vines snaking around the edges. Fine linens covered the tables and
lavender soap and beeswax candles sat next to the porcelain basin and
pitcher. All Mary really cared about, though, was the vast, deep bed
that stood in the center of the room. She'd fallen into it gratefully and
slept for several hours.

When she woke, it was dark, the almost-full moon the only light
in the room.

Mary put on her shoes. She wanted to waste no time trying to find Mr. Chamberlen's diary. She crept down the hall and down the stairs, looking for the library, and noticed a weak, watery light coming from a gap beneath a door. She knew at once it would be Sudbury. He, too, would waste no time looking for the book. They were neither of them good at waiting.

She opened the door softly, not wanting to startle Sudbury. She needn't have worried—he was utterly engrossed in whatever he was reading, his face just inches from the page. He had lit several thick candles, which, between their light and the light of the moon, allowed him to read from the massive book set in front of him.

Mary cleared her throat. Sudbury kept reading. She coughed again, louder this time. Sudbury jumped up, startled, and toppled the candle sitting closest to him. She watched in horror as acrid smoke rose from the paper.

"Robert!" she warned.

Sudbury relaxed when he saw her at the door. "What brings you down here?"

"Robert, the book! The candle!"

Sudbury looked down in time to see the page catch fire. With an alacrity that surprised her, he grabbed a thick woolen blanket lying on the chair next to him and smothered the still-small flame.

"Thank God," she breathed.

Sudbury looked a bit sheepish. "It's not the first time I've caught a book on fire. With my experiments, it's a constant worry. I've learned to always keep a heavy cloth near me."

Mary shook her head. She was always careful to keep her recipe book away from flame. But then, she was poor, and her book was hand-written and thus irreplaceable.

"You couldn't sleep either?" she asked.

Sudbury shook his head. "Did you come here to look for the diary as well?" he asked.

She nodded. "Any luck?"

"No."

She looked at the book buried beneath the cloth.

"What are you reading?"

Sudbury lifted the cloth. "*The Mirror of Alchemy*. I found it here in the library. I should have known Chamberlen would possess it. I hoped I might find some of his notes on the text, perhaps some marginalia. But it's clean."

Sudbury rubbed his eyes.

"Are you well?" she asked.

Sudbury nodded. "Yes, it's just a headache. Reading by candlelight is hard on my eyes."

Mary hesitated. "Jack used to get headaches. It gave him some relief when I rubbed his temples. Would you like me to do the same for you?"

Sudbury's head was still buried in his hands. She couldn't see the expression on his face, but he murmured, "That sounds nice."

She quietly moved behind his chair and laid her hands in the soft brown hair by his temples. With the slightest of pressure, she made small circles with her fingers while her palms rested on the sides of Sudbury's head. Her hands trembled ever so slightly.

Sudbury moaned softly and his head fell back, resting on Mary's belly. He relaxed into her ministrations. She continued rubbing his temples for several long minutes, the only sound in the room Sudbury's occasional sighs.

Then something in the atmosphere changed, an awareness, a tension. Mary's fingers slowed as Sudbury shifted in his chair.

"Thank you," he whispered in a gravelly voice. "Enough."

She removed her hands and placed them on his shoulders. Her fingers still tingled. Sudbury sat up straight and then, after several excruciating seconds, laid his hands over hers.

She bent and kissed the top of his head. She did it again. And then again. Sudbury's hands tightened and he whispered her name.

She surprised herself by sliding her hands down his chest and kissing the tip of his ear. Sudbury's breath quickened, and his response emboldened her. She kissed the pulse at his neck.

At the touch of her lips Sudbury grabbed her hands and threw them off. He stood and walked to the fireplace.

"I cannot." He ran a trembling hand over his face. "I cannot," he repeated. "I need to keep my mind focused if I'm to protect you from Hopkins."

"But who will protect me from you?" she asked softly. His face crumpled and she knew instantly that he had misconstrued her words. She had hurt him, however unintentionally.

"Robert," she said, walking to the fireplace and lifting her hand to his cheek. "Robert, I didn't mean . . ." The words died on her tongue as she saw the pain in his eyes.

He stepped away, leaving her hand hanging in the distance between them.

"Please don't worry, Mary. I understand you. Who could trust such a monster?" But his voice was sad, not bitter, and his eyes remained downcast as he left the room.

Mary came down the next morning to a table laden with a hearty breakfast—eggs and ale and oat cakes—and a look of concern on Mrs. Stanton's face.

"He left this morning without you," she told Mary without preamble. She had been grinding oats in a massive mortar, but she stopped and gave Mary a pointed look. "He said he had to meet somebody and that I wasn't to let you try to follow him."

Mary was thoroughly exasperated. When would Sudbury learn to trust her? When would he quit keeping secrets?

Mrs. Stanton continued. "And so I definitely shouldn't tell you he went to meet somebody at St. Paul's Cathedral." She pulled a lump of dough over to the table and began kneading in the oats. "No, I shouldn't be telling you that at all. And I probably shouldn't have wrapped up your breakfast so you could leave right away. And Mr. Weaver shouldn't have written out directions to St. Paul's."

Mary rushed over to Mrs. Stanton and gave her a tight hug, then grabbed the small cloth that wrapped up her breakfast.

Mrs. Stanton stopped her just before she left. "You be careful. Mr. Weaver would trust Robert Sudbury with his life, he says, but he also says the man keeps strange company."

Mary nodded, patted Mrs. Stanton's plump hand, and walked out.

A wild sort of curiosity washed over Mary when she headed out into the streets of London. It had been taking root in her for some time now, a feeling she hadn't had since before she'd married Jack. She was tired of being cautious and afraid of what others thought of her. She wanted to see marvels and behold wonders: Cathedrals and crowds and paintings. Books and gardens and sculptures. More than anything, she wanted to be surprised by what the world held in store.

Mary had never experienced anything like London. She'd visited some of the smaller villages around Bicknacre with her father, meeting with wool merchants and buying some small luxuries. And once, shortly before her wedding, her father had taken her with him to Colchester to trade some of his more valuable possessions for furniture for Mary and Jack as a wedding gift. They had visited the castle and heard the old stories of Boudica's battles with the Romans and then gawked at what they could see of the old St. John's Abbey. But she had certainly never experienced the chaos and life of a large city.

Mary stopped for a moment to take it all in. The narrow side streets with broken cobblestones and buildings covered in soot. Wooden signs advertising everything from cobblers to pubs to apothecaries hung on every street, creaking in the slightest breeze. And the noise—the people and horses and vendors and, ringing out above everything, church bells.

After a few moments of drinking in all the sights, Mary pulled out the paper on which Mr. Weaver had drawn a rough map. She walked to St. John Street and stopped to wonder at the sight of a large building. It stood tall and sturdy and square, the only two passages to the inside boarded up. It seemed like a building that had once served a proud purpose before it fell into disrepair.

"Do you need help?" an older man stopped and asked. His eyes were kind.

"I was just wondering why this building looks so derelict."

The man gazed up at the building and shook his head. "Ah, I had some good times there, I can tell you. It is, was, the Red Bull Theatre. When I was a lad, they had grand plays there from the Queen Anne's Men, though by my time it was mostly a place for raucousness and tomfoolery. It's been boarded up for a few years now, courtesy of Parliament."

Mary nodded. "I thank you for your help." The man smiled sadly and walked away.

Mary continued walking, past Smithfield and toward the Thames, thinking of the changes Parliament might bring about. There were rumors that they might even abolish the celebration of Christmastide, proclaiming it a Romish holiday and an excuse for drunkenness and debauchery. It was as though joy itself were suspect.

In Bicknacre and throughout Essex, support for Parliament was strong—most people celebrated the victories of Parliament and the New Model Army over the king's men at Marston Moor and Naseby. What would change if Parliament succeeded? Would it usher in a new age, and if so, what would happen to the old ways, the traditions and rituals and ceremonies? She'd been taught that the king had been ordained by God. Would God be so angry with the people of England, with their ambition and pride, that He would strike down every last man and woman?

Or was God working through Cromwell to curb the excesses of the king and his court? Would the king and Parliament find a happy medium? For the sake of everyone, Mary hoped the negotiations worked.

Lost deep in thought, Mary barely noticed when she crested a small hill. She looked up and gasped when she saw the glory of St. Paul's Cathedral spread out in front of her. It was by far the largest and most glorious building she'd ever seen, far eclipsing Colchester Castle. She'd heard that before it was struck by lightning, the massive spire of the cathedral had loomed large, as though its pointed top would pierce the heavens themselves.

As she neared the cathedral, however, she began to notice signs of decay and defacement. Rather than awe, Mary felt only melancholy at the cathedral's mistreatment. Groups of people came and went, chattering and laughing and gossiping; some spoke in languages she had never heard before. Workers dangled from scaffolds, hammering and yelling to one another.

The place seemed less a holy ground than a bustling marketplace.

Mary followed one particularly large group into the cathedral yard, hoping nobody would notice her. She tried to stay inconspicuous even as she gawped at the shops and book stalls set up around the perimeter. As the crowd entered the building, her eyes immediately flew to the arched ceiling and the intricate patterns sketched out in their construction and to the immense stained-glass window on the east side of the cathedral. It cast a goldish-red light with little sparkles of green and blue winking around the periphery.

The place buzzed with conversation and laughter, none of it subdued by the holiness of the surroundings.

What other wonders had she missed all these years? What must it be like to live in a place with marvels around every corner?

Mary dragged her eyes away from the spectacle of the cathedral and realized that the group she'd attached herself to had moved on without her, leaving her alone and exposed. She dashed behind a column and leaned on the cool stone. So much beauty and inspiration, virtually ignored by the commerce and politicking of the world.

She gathered herself together and peered around the column, looking for Sudbury. She slowly slipped from behind the marble column and sidled to the north end of the nave. Just as she resumed her search at the entrance, she saw two men bent forward in whispered conversation. One of the men was quite tall and had flame-bright red hair. The other man was Sudbury.

Mary quickly ducked into a small, musty alcove dominated by a marble statue of John the Baptist. She watched the two men talking with animated gestures. She couldn't hear what they said, but she could make out the occasional curse.

After a minute or two, Sudbury and his companion walked toward the massive oak doors at the entrance. She had just dared to take a deep breath when Sudbury turned back and scanned the shadows, suspicion and confusion in his eyes. After a moment he returned his attention to his companion, who handed him a small cloth. Sudbury checked its contents, nodded brusquely, and walked away without looking behind him. The other man stared after Sudbury for a long time, shook his head, and walked in the opposite direction.

Mary pressed herself against the cold stone and leaned her head on a splintered shelf, absently stroking John the Baptist's marble toe with shaking hands. What had Sudbury been doing? Why hadn't he told her where he was going? And most importantly, what was hidden in that piece of cloth?

With a sigh, Mary left the safety of the alcove and began to make her way back to Chamberlen House. She was tempted to explore the streets of London a little more before returning—she longed for time to walk and think. Whenever she faced a problem with her recipes or whenever she was sad or lonely, she took Tom and roamed the countryside around Bicknacre. She always felt better after her rambles.

As she turned the corner onto Ludgate Street, Mary came upon a charming scene of a group of boys playing Frog in the Middle. She watched for a few moments as the boy in the circle sat with his eyes closed, trying to snatch at the boys poking him—whoever was unlucky enough to get touched was the next frog. She reminisced about all the times she'd played the game as a girl, but her fond memories faded when she witnessed a young boy, with sandy-brown hair and a pronounced limp, approaching the group. Her heart squeezed: except for the rags he was dressed in and his painfully thin frame, she could have easily mistaken him for Tom.

The boys stopped their game and waited for his approach, sneers on their faces. He asked them a question, perhaps whether he could join their game or if they had some scraps of food to share. The biggest of the boys, a stout lad dressed in simple but clean clothing, pushed his way to the front of the group and yelled something unintelligible. Then, to Mary's dismay, he pushed the frail boy to the ground.

"Stop!" Mary yelled. "Stop right now or I will call a constable!"

The group of boys fled, and Mary approached the poor lad still lying in the street. She had every intention of helping him up, giving him some money for food, perhaps even escorting him to wherever he called home. But as she approached, the boy looked at her in abject fear and rallied just enough energy to scramble to his feet and run away.

Mary watched him flee with tears clouding her vision, thinking of Tom and the perilous position he was in. If anything happened to Mary, if she were no longer able to care for him, she knew Mrs. Woods or even Mrs. Chamberlen would take him in. But the Woodses already had five children of their own. What if something happened to Mr. or Mrs. Woods? And Mrs. Chamberlen, bless her, would become weaker by the day from her cancer. Would Tom end up like this young boy, hungry and lonely and afraid?

She must stay safe. She would do whatever it took to return to him.

❦

As Mary struggled with the heavy door to the kitchen of Chamberlen House, she felt something soft brush against her leg. She almost shrieked before she realized it was just the kitchen cat, meowing insistently. She pushed the door open and the yowling cat dashed madly through the crack.

The kitchen was empty, but she heard a soft groaning. She peered around the massive block table to see Mrs. Stanton's still body lying on the ground, eyes shut. Mary panicked. She could only stare at her, watching as she moaned in pain. She'd have to do something, but what? Mary shook herself out of her paralysis and rushed to Mrs. Stanton's side, terrified that she had fallen . . . or been attacked. As Mary bent over her, Mrs. Stanton opened her twinkling eyes.

"Oh, my dear, have I frightened you, or was it that blasted cat?" Mrs. Stanton said, struggling to rise. Relief flooded Mary and she fell to her knees. Mrs. Stanton patted her hand. "I'm sorry, truly. My back, it hurts ever so much. Has since last winter, when I took a tumble on the ice on London Bridge. Sometimes it helps for me to lie on the floor for a bit."

Mary sighed with relief and wondered when she had learned to assume the worst. Probably since seeing Mr. Chamberlen's corpse, purpled and stiff, or Agnes in jail, her body pocked with evidence of Hopkins's cruelty.

"Where does it hurt?" Mary asked. "Is it a sharp pain or dull? Does it spread out after a while or stay in one place?" The healer in Mary took over as she helped Mrs. Stanton stand and led her to a chair warmed by the fire. She began probing Mrs. Stanton's back.

"If you'd like, I can make a warm poultice for you to use at night," she offered. "It has been very welcome to my neighbors in Bicknacre."

Mrs. Stanton sighed with contentment as Mary rubbed her tense and pulled muscle. "That would be lovely, dear."

She helped Mrs. Stanton up to her room and into bed, laying her on her stomach so she could rest a warm cloth on her lower back. Mrs. Stanton complained at first, fretting about how much work she had to do in the kitchen, but Mary tut-tutted her and she finally eased into the straw of the mattress ticking.

Before she left, Mary made sure to lay hands on Mrs. Stanton's back one more time. She closed her eyes and imagined how Mrs. Stanton must have felt before she fell on the ice, the fear as her feet slipped uncontrollably, the way her entire body tensed in order to prepare for the impact, how time slowed and the world spun in the split second before her legs flew out from beneath her.

Mary opened her eyes to find Mrs. Stanton looking at her with curiosity. She'd forgotten that what she did could appear odd. Even magical.

She blushed a bit. "I find this helps me make my cures. I have to ask your body what it's feeling, imagine what your fall was like."

When she explained her process to strangers, to outsiders, she felt keenly how fantastical it sounded. And yet she had no other way to describe it.

"As long as it works, my dear," Mrs. Stanton said matter-of-factly, relaxing into the mattress and sighing deeply as the warmth from the cloth seeped into her aching back.

Mary settled Mrs. Stanton in and went back downstairs. She felt a sort of homecoming as she entered the massive kitchen. She hadn't worked on her cookery since Agnes died, and Chamberlen House held so many resources. She stared in wonder at all the pots and pans and ladles and whisks, at the plentiful wood stored up to feed the fire. Oh, the things she could do in this kitchen!

She pushed away her dreams. She had no way of knowing how long they would stay in London, and all her recipes needed time. Nevertheless, the prospect of making the poultice—a relatively quick and easy recipe—soothed her. She'd longed for the rhythms of her cookery.

Mary pulled down a large pot hanging from a hook on the wall as she considered which of the soothing medicines she would use for Mrs. Stanton's poultice. She usually preferred a cure she had inherited from her grandmother that called for placing twenty or so earthworms on a platter of fennel, letting them consume the leaves for at least a day. In her experience, though, that recipe was best made in midsummer, and besides, where would she find that many earthworms here in London?

Instead, Mary chose a recipe that Agnes had developed. It was not as efficacious as her own, but it required simple ingredients easily found in a well-stocked kitchen. She didn't even need her recipe book for this simple recipe. So many of the villagers had back pain from lifting, from working in the fields or sleeping on rough straw beds, really from any of the myriad rhythms of daily life, that she had made this remedy countless times. She took one of the eggs sitting on the table and pared away the top of the shell and then drained the white, leaving only the yolk. Using a small spoon, she carefully poured in some rose water. She went to the bag of herbs she'd brought with her from Bicknacre and rummaged through until she found the powder of mastic. With a pair of tongs, she carefully placed two small embers from the kitchen fire into the eggshell and stirred to heat the concoction.

A spasm of sorrow hit Mary in the stomach as the familiar smell of the poultice wafted through the room, and she had to sit as memories of Agnes flowed through her. What would Mary do without her? How could she continue on without her guidance and help?

Mary said a prayer and whispered, "Agnes, please help me. I need you now more than ever." She took a deep breath as a wave of peace washed over her. Surely something of Agnes was present now, guarding her. She gently stirred the poultice in its fragile shell, closed her eyes, and recalled the fear and pain she'd felt when touching Mrs. Stanton's back. She allowed her own body to react as if she shared that very moment with Mrs. Stanton. She walked with Mrs. Stanton, slipped with Mrs. Stanton, fell with Mrs. Stanton. Though she sat by the roaring fire in Mrs. Chamberlen's elegant townhome, her mind was on the crowded, ice-covered London Bridge.

She was concentrating so hard she failed to notice the kitchen door open and Sudbury step inside. He stopped to watch her for several long minutes, the admiration in his eyes tempered with anxiety.

When the medicine reached the right heat and consistency, she broke herself out of her trance and opened her eyes. By then Sudbury had left the kitchen and was making his way to his rooms, a small cloth bundle in his hands and a thoughtful look on his face.

CHAPTER 16

A medicine for the stone

*Take the blood of a goat dried and made into fine pow-
der, put a good quantity thereof into a draft of ale and
drink of it.*

Dinner that night was a happy affair. Mary and Sudbury had spent the
afternoon looking for the diary, and they were eager for a break. Mrs.
Stanton felt much better with the help of the poultice, and after the
day servants had left and she'd rested a few hours, she roasted three fat
chickens and brought out all manner of foodstuffs from the pantry.

Sudbury, too, was in a good mood, laughing and far more relaxed
than Mary had ever seen him in Bicknacre. He was witty and amiable, and
Mary wondered if this was what Sudbury had been like before he had been
scarred so badly. Whatever the nature of his transaction in St. Paul's, it
had not dampened his spirits. But the mystery roiled Mary's imagination.

Breads and cakes, tart jellies and sweet jams . . . the four ate until they
could do nothing more but sit by the fire, appreciating their full bellies. And
even then the wine continued to flow and stories poured out of them all.

Mrs. Stanton told of her younger days in London when she worked
as a maid in a great estate. She described the grand lords and ladies

who came to visit, the food, the roasted ducks dressed in the skins of peacocks, the sumptuous clothing and furniture.

Mr. Weaver told of his childhood working in the house of a Captain Melton, who had stolen him away from a faraway land when he was a tiny boy and taken him to England. He didn't know where he hailed from. His only memories of his home were of hot sun and happy songs at bedtime. Captain Melton sent him away from Melton House when he grew tired of him. Mr. Weaver found work with a boatman on the Thames and spent many years rowing all manner of people across the treacherous river, learning its rhythms and tides. He'd liked his job. His gregariousness won him return customers, and eventually attracted the eye of Mr. Chamberlen, who offered him work as his assistant.

After that point, Mr. Weaver looked to Sudbury and, wordlessly, ended his story.

Even Sudbury shared stories, though of the four of them, he spoke least of his past. As a child, he'd delighted in causing mischief of the milder sort—putting salt in the sugar jar, hiding the curry combs from the head groomsmen, stealing the butler's shoes. At first Mary found it surprising that he would play such tricks on the servants, but after a few more such stories, she realized that the servants had been Sudbury's only playmates—not once did he mention his parents or cousins or friends.

She ached for the lonely little boy that Sudbury's stories revealed.

Eventually the fire died down and the stories and laughter slowed. Weaver excused himself from their company and extended a hand to a blushing Mrs. Stanton.

After they left, a pleasant kind of sleepiness fell over Mary and Sudbury, and they chatted lazily, watching the flames before making their way upstairs.

The late hour, the conversation, even the flame of the fire reminded Mary of the moment she and Robert had shared the night before in the library. How soft his hair had been when she'd kissed the top of his head, his quick intake of breath when she'd touched his shoulder.

But she also remembered his pain, his insistence on misunderstanding her.

Sudbury walked Mary to her room. As she began opening the door, he put his hand over hers on the knob.

"Mary," he whispered. "It has been a long time since I enjoyed an evening such as this. Thank you."

His face glowed from the candle in his hand. The warm light softened the harsh lines and canals of his scars. She'd always thought him handsome, but never before had he seemed tender.

Slowly, tentatively, Sudbury bent his head toward her. He cupped her cheek with his palm, and she felt the gentle scrape of calluses. She had expected the soft hands of a scholar. Her eyes closed as she anticipated his kiss, but instead she felt the light brush of his lips on her forehead. Then her cheek. And then her other cheek. She held her breath waiting for him to kiss her lips, but instead she heard him whisper, "Sleep well, Mary."

"Would you like to come in?" she asked, voice shaking.

Sudbury gulped and nodded wordlessly, following Mary as she stepped backward into the room.

He stopped abruptly, grabbed Mary by the shoulders, and moved behind her.

"Mary, go back into the hallway," he commanded.

Mary bristled at his tone. "I will not," she said. Sudbury attempted to block her view with his body, but Mary managed to peek around him. She gasped, pushed him aside, grabbed the candle out of his hand, and approached the bed.

There on her mattress lay a pinkish monstrosity, all pale flesh and hair like wires. Mary stifled a scream.

Sudbury moved toward the bed and prodded the fleshy lump.

"What is it?" Mary asked.

"I think . . . I think it's a pig."

Mary shook uncontrollably and held back the urge to vomit. She took a deep breath and moved closer. With one trembling hand, she reached out and poked the pink flesh. It was cold. The pig was dead and had been for a while.

Someone had arranged the animal's corpse to make it look like a slumbering figure, on its back with its eyes closed. How she would look, had she gone to bed earlier.

Sudbury laid a hand on Mary's shoulder and she flinched. "Look," Sudbury said, pointing at a square of white glowing on the bedsheets. It was a note. Sudbury picked it up and handed it to Mary.

"Remember Grandley's pig," she read out. The handwriting was heavily slanted, and the hand that produced it must have been shaking. There was something familiar about it, but Mary couldn't put her finger on what it might be.

Mary turned to Sudbury and saw the horror in his eyes.

After several moments examining the bloated corpse, Sudbury wrinkled his nose in disgust. "It stinks. It's been dead a few days already. Look there—its throat and abdomen are slit, but the blood at the neck is clotted. And its stomach has been opened."

"What does that matter?" she said, her voice rising in panic.

Sudbury looked away. "It means the pig wasn't killed today, nor was it killed and placed here on a whim. Somebody planned this."

Mary took a deep breath. "Someone who knows how to get into the house. Someone who was watching us and knew when we were gone."

Sudbury nodded.

"Not Mrs. Stanton or Mr. Weaver," Mary said adamantly. She could not think people of such great kindness could be capable of such an evil trick.

"No," Sudbury agreed.

Mary couldn't stop staring at the fleshy corpse.

"We should get it out of here," she said.

Sudbury nodded. "I'll need help. I'll get John."

Mary instinctively wanted to keep this thing hidden from Mr. Weaver. For some inexplicable reason, she felt guilty, complicit in some sort of horrific secret. But she knew they couldn't get rid of the bloated corpse splayed out on her bed without his help. Mary nodded.

As they approached Mr. Weaver's room, Mary blushed at the gasps and guttural moans of pleasure coming from inside.

Sudbury looked at Mary with a mixture of embarrassment and amusement.

"Perhaps we should give them a few moments," Sudbury whispered.

They retreated to the kitchen to wait. The energy between them before was nothing compared with the tension in the kitchen.

"Mary . . . ," Sudbury had begun to say when Mr. Weaver clomped into the kitchen, whistling a jaunty tune. He caught up short when he saw Sudbury and Mary. He took in Mary's pallor and Sudbury's furrowed brow.

"What's wrong?" He noticed Sudbury's hand on Mary's arm. "Am I interrupting anything?"

Sudbury snatched his hand back. "John," he said, "I'm glad to see you. We need your help."

Sudbury immediately walked out of the kitchen, and Weaver followed him without saying a word. Mary trailed behind.

"What is it, man?" Weaver demanded, puffing slightly as they walked quickly to Mary's room.

"It would be better to show you," Sudbury replied.

They stopped outside Mary's room, and Sudbury turned to Weaver. "Brace yourself, John," he warned.

Sudbury opened the door. Weaver stepped inside and let out a shout and a string of curses.

"What is that thing? And what's it doing in here?"

"It's a pig. Or it was a pig. As to what it is doing here, we don't know," Mary said quietly. "But we found a note." She reached into the pocket of her skirts, retrieved the wrinkled paper, and handed it to Mr. Weaver.

When he finished reading, he looked more perplexed than before.

"Who is this Mr. Grandley, and why is his pig in your bed?"

Mary explained the reference to the pig that had been tried for witchcraft in Bicknacre.

Weaver gave a low whistle.

"So whoever did this has known you for some time."

Sudbury nodded, a grim look on his face.

"I'll go tell Mrs. Stanton what happened. She's tough as nails, but she'll need some warning before she sees"—he pointed to the bed—"that."

They returned to the kitchen. Mary sat at the table, her head propped in her hands.

"Who can have done this, Robert?" Mary asked, her voice muffled.

"It must have been somebody from Bicknacre," Sudbury said thoughtfully. "Just as John said."

"Or they knew somebody from Bicknacre."

"And they knew you had been accused of witchcraft."

"And whoever it is, they hate me."

"Or me," Sudbury replied gently.

Mary looked up in surprise. "If they're trying to scare you, why leave the pig in my bed?"

"I can think of no other way to terrify me than to threaten you."

Sudbury refused to meet her eyes.

"What do we do now?" Mary asked, trying to keep her voice from shaking.

"You cannot go back to that room," Sudbury said, his voice firm. "You'll have to sleep with me tonight."

Mary stared at Sudbury, and he blushed a little.

"You can sleep in the bed and I'll sleep on the floor. I can't let you be alone."

Mary agreed. As they waited for the other couple to come to the kitchen, Sudbury reached out and held Mary's hand.

When she arrived, Mrs. Stanton immediately went to Mary and embraced her in a tight hug. Tears sprang to her eyes.

Mr. Weaver whispered something in Sudbury's ear, and they left the room. Mrs. Stanton settled herself next to Mary at the kitchen table.

"John told me what you found in your bed—about the pig." She shuddered. "My dear, how horrible."

Mary took a deep breath and looked into Mrs. Stanton's concerned face. "Yes, it was. I must ask, do you know of anyone who might do such a thing? Perhaps as a prank?"

Mrs. Stanton thought and then shook her head slowly. "We have very few staff here when the Chamberlens are in Bicknacre. Those who come through work only during the day. Most I've known for years, but they often bring in extra help for big projects. I'll ask."

They heard a clatter in the doorway as Sudbury and John, bearing the pig between them, heaved the corpse into an alcove in the kitchen and covered it with a tattered old blanket. Mary could see one little hoof sticking through a rip in the cloth—bent at an unnatural angle, clods of dirt still clinging to its ghastly pale skin.

As the men stepped away, Robert stumbled and cursed. "This blasted ankle still hurts, and that pig is heavy. Who could have been strong enough to put it in Mary's bed?"

"We'll talk about that tomorrow," Mrs. Stanton said. "But now we all need to get some rest."

"Mary's staying with me tonight," Sudbury informed the pair, his voice brooking no dissent.

Sudbury took Mary's hand and led her upstairs to his room. It was far smaller and simpler than hers. Sudbury gathered one of the many blankets and a pillow and lay down in front of the fire.

"Go to sleep," he said to Mary in a gruff voice.

Mary burrowed under the covers. A wave of exhaustion came over her and she almost immediately fell asleep, but not before she noticed that the bedclothes smelled of Sudbury. She burrowed deeper.

The next morning, Mary awoke confused, worry gnawing at her stomach. At first she couldn't figure out why—she only knew that she felt a great reluctance to leave the comfort and warmth of her bed. She pulled a blanket over her head and tried to drift back to sleep, but something was wrong—the smell and the feel of the sheets were strange to her. She sat up with a gasp when she remembered she wasn't in her own bed but in Sudbury's. She recalled the eerie glow of the pig's pink corpse in the moonlight, the pervasive smell of rotting flesh, the crinkled note with its tidy and precise writing promising death.

Mary looked around the room for Sudbury, but he had already left. She dressed quickly and walked down to the warm kitchen, the smell of yeast and woodsmoke calling to her. Mrs. Stanton had been awake for some time, it would seem. Immediately Mary looked to the corner where the pig corpse had lain. It was nowhere in sight.

Mrs. Stanton easily guessed Mary's thoughts. "Robert and John moved it early this morning. They're taking it to the butchers in Smithfield and paying them to toss it with the offal." She hesitated and looked down at the dough she was kneading. "Robert was very insistent that you not see it again this morning. He was worried about you."

Mary blushed and set to work wiping down the table. She and Mrs. Stanton worked together silently for a half hour more before the men came back. They came in quietly, but their presence felt like a rough invasion of the women's comfortable sanctuary.

Mary had been thinking about the pig corpse all morning. Now as Sudbury's presence filled the kitchen, other memories from the night before surfaced, memories of soft lips and calloused hands.

Sudbury's eyes bored into hers with an intensity that made her shiver. "Mary?" His voice was quiet, a whispered question. "Will you come with me?"

Mary nodded and wiped her hands on a cloth.

Sudbury took Mary's hand. He led her up to his room and settled her in the hard wooden chair. He began pacing by the bed.

"Mary, I've been up all night. Thinking. I've been less than honest with you."

Mary snorted. "Indeed."

Sudbury ignored her sarcasm. "What happened last night"—at first, she didn't know whether he meant their tender moments or their ghastly discovery—"has convinced me that keeping you in the dark does you no favors. You're in too much danger for me to leave you ignorant."

He paused and took a deep breath. "The symbol you saw etched on Chamberlen's body, after his murder . . . I told you I knew little about it. That's not true. In fact, that symbol has haunted me for the last five years."

Mary sat still in her chair, afraid that any small move would interrupt his disclosure.

Sudbury reached into his pocket and pulled out a small cloth bundle—she recognized it as the package the man had given him in St. Paul's. He removed the cloth, unwrapped a book, and opened it for her to see. Mary stifled a gasp at the intricate pictures and colors within. Sudbury waited while she skimmed the pages, taking in strange images of malformed and magnificent creatures.

"This is called the *Atalanta Fugiens*. It is an emblem book by a German physician, Michael Maier. Brilliant man. He was fascinated with the figures and geometry of alchemy. Let me read to you: 'Make of a man and woman a circle; then a quadrangle; out of this a triangle; make again a circle, and you will have the Stone of the Wise. Thus is made the stone, which thou canst not discover, unless you, through diligence, learn to understand this geometrical teaching.'"

Sudbury pointed to a symbol. It was the same strange glyph that looked like a small one-eyed man that she'd seen on the medallion and etched in horrible mimicry on Henry Chamberlen's corpse.

"It's called the *monas hieroglyphica*," Robert explained. "It comes from the work of John Dee, Queen Elizabeth's physician and a great scholar of alchemy. He used it to guide him in his work, said it was the key to conversing with the angels."

"You knew about that symbol?" she said. "You knew then and said nothing?"

Sudbury had the grace to look ashamed. "I was afraid," he said simply. "I was afraid to put you in danger, and I didn't know how it was connected to me. You know that Chamberlen and I worked together when we were in Cambridge and Chichester. He sought me out. He had heard rumors about my work." Sudbury took a deep breath. "Mary, in your medicines, you have used the bezoar stone before, yes?"

"I've made tinctures with it, yes." The bezoar was a small stone sometimes found in the bellies of animals—cattle and goats and such. It was an ugly little thing, a little smaller than her thumb. It looked for all the world like a regular rock, but it was known to save a person who'd ingested something foul or poisonous. She'd last used it when a young boy had eaten the flowers of a monkshood plant. Sadly, the remedy hadn't worked, and the boy had died.

Sudbury gave a great sigh and flexed his hands as though trying to expel the memories through his fingertips. "I was working with the bezoar, trying to purify it and determine its properties. Chamberlen convinced me to let him help, promised me money and connections. At first I thought he and I were after the same thing, that we both valued the bezoar for its curative properties. After some time, I realized that he had other ideas."

He paused.

"Chamberlen thought that the bezoar was the key to making the philosopher's stone. You have heard of the Great Work?"

Mary nodded. "Mrs. Chamberlen told me something of it. She said Mr. Chamberlen sought the philosopher's stone for riches and wealth, to use it to turn base metals into gold."

"At the beginning, yes. But he grew more ambitious." Sudbury's eyes clouded. "At first, Chamberlen was interested only in amassing gold. But as he read more, as he delved deeper into the secrets of nature, he became curious about the stone's other properties, how it can connect a magus to the angels. He became obsessed with knowing the divine. With that knowledge, a man could control kings, could make the world move at his bidding. He could even learn how to live forever."

Mary shook her head. "And Chamberlen thought the bezoar could give him that power?" she asked, a note of disbelief in her voice. She couldn't imagine such an ugly, insignificant object having such powers.

"Not on its own, no," Sudbury said. "I'm doing a poor job of explaining. This is difficult. You know that there's a vast body of work on how to make the philosopher's stone, stories of its creation, books written about its coction and rarification. But nobody has ever succeeded. The process involves locating exactly the right ingredients, purifying and distilling them, in precisely the right order."

"Like the recipes in my book?"

Sudbury nodded. "Yes, exactly. I told you when we first met—do you remember?—that we do similar work with our fires and our coction. And, like your recipes, the process involves cooking certain ingredients over heat. Chamberlen's ideas were strange but brilliant. He thought that the magical properties of the bezoar proved that it was key to the philosopher's stone but that the vehicle we philosophers use was too base for such a divine object."

Sudbury paused and closed his eyes for a moment. When he opened them, Mary almost gasped at the pain she could see in their depths. "He thought that rather than cooking the stone over fire, he'd cook it in a vehicle of flesh and blood created in God's image. Just as the bezoar is formed in the belly of beasts, he would cook it in the flesh of man himself . . . in the stomach, to correspond to God's work in a woman's womb. He experimented time and again with different animals: dogs, cats, mice." He hesitated. "And pigs. Then he decided he was ready to try with a human vessel. He thought that if he could get the right ingredients into the body, the stomach would provide the coction needed to transform it into the philosopher's stone."

Mary thought she might vomit. "And how would he get those ingredients into the body? How would he retrieve the stone?" she asked, afraid she already knew the answer.

Sudbury looked up at the ceiling while he spoke. "He would poison someone and then cut open their body after death. I didn't believe he would actually go through with such madness. And I certainly had no idea that was what he planned to do with Margery. He gave her hellebore. She and her child died of the poisoning."

"That dog we saw in the forest, the one Tom found. It had its belly cut open and those symbols carved on its skin."

Robert nodded. "Yes, and the scarring was not fresh. Clearly Chamberlen was still experimenting before his death." He continued pacing, agitated. "Chamberlen tried to get me to agree with his heretical ideas; I told him he was mad. I thought that would stop him. I was a fool.

"Chamberlen went wild with joy when Margery told him she was with child. He'd been giving her a cordial that had bezoar in it. He was convinced that it was the philosopher's stone, not a child, growing in her womb. Or perhaps he thought it was both—his ideas were beyond reason. I found Chamberlen with Margery's body. I'd gone to her home and found her lying on her bed, naked. She was unconscious, poisoned, already near death." Sudbury turned pale at the memory. "Chamberlen stood over her, a knife in his hands. He had carved that symbol into her belly in the belief it would transform the poisons into the angel stone. I tried to stop him. I rushed over and grabbed the knife. I could see the wildness in his eyes. And the terror. He told me to think about this, about how Margery would be transformed by the angelic matter into an eternal being, and that if it were not so, that her sacrifice would be worth it. With just this one small death, he thought, he could banish death forever."

"What did you do?"

"I hit him. Again and again until I knocked him unconscious. I nearly killed him. To this day I don't know what stopped me. Then I picked Margery up, dressed her, and carried her to the midwife. The ordeal killed the child, a boy. Margery's body expelled it, and she followed soon after in death."

Mary put her hand on Sudbury's arm. He was trembling.

"I went to Chamberlen's house and confronted him. That's when he threw the lead in my face."

Sudbury's hand went up to his scar, an unthinking attempt to hide his disfigurement. Mary reached out to his hand and gently lowered it.

"Since then I've tried to watch Chamberlen, to see if he had another victim in mind. I confronted him in Bicknacre, told him I would watch him until his last days. Little did I know that would be so soon."

They sat for a few moments, Mary trying to make sense of this new revelation, Sudbury wrestling with the ghosts of his past.

"The tattoos on his belly," Mary whispered. "Was he trying to concoct the stone in his own body? Mrs. Chamberlen thinks Bridget Jenkins murdered him because their affair had ended, but what if he killed himself trying to make the philosopher's stone?"

Sudbury nodded. "Possibly. But how would he do it? He would need a catalyst of some sort for the next stage of the process. A metal, perhaps."

Her belly churned with the realization that she had, unwittingly, kept vital information from him.

"Robert, I never told you . . . I found something when I examined Chamberlen's body. A token with strange markings. I showed it to Agnes, and she said one of the symbols was a pelican in her piety. Chamberlen had been clutching it in his hand. Do you suppose that was the catalyst?"

His eyes were filled with surprise—and some frustration.

"Where is that token now?"

She shook her head. "I don't know. I hid it in Agnes's recipe book, in her cottage, but when I went to retrieve it, the token wasn't there. I thought perhaps Agnes had taken it out to look at it before her arrest."

Robert closed his eyes, deep in thought. "That symbol on it, the pelican in her piety—I think that's the key. Perhaps he meant to pierce his own chest as the pelican did, or slice open his own viscera? Sacrifice himself, as Christ did? I just don't know. We shall always have to guess, I suspect. But I'm trying to piece together his thinking. Mary, if we can prove that he killed himself, we will be freed from suspicion. When you saw me yesterday, with that man in the cathedral, that's what I was trying to determine—what Chamberlen's thoughts and plans were in the last year of his life."

Mary looked at him in shock. "Yesterday? You saw me?"

Sudbury nodded. "Yes, there in St. Paul's Walk. I was surprised you didn't ask me about it. I worry that you've been imagining all sorts of scenarios."

Mary blushed. "I admit I have."

"The man I met with was a tutor of mine who also knew Chamberlen. I wanted to know if he had heard from him—or of him. He had."

"When? What did he find out?"

Sudbury hesitated. "That man, Thomas Bradford, invited me to visit him at his house on Fleet Street. He let Chamberlen stay there a few months ago. Bradford refused to tell me what happened—said he didn't want to talk about it in the middle of St. Paul's—but he said Chamberlen left some books at his house and welcomed me to examine them. We've had no luck locating the diary here, so I thought it best to look there."

"And the bundle he gave you?"

"That was this book, the *Atalanta Fugiens*. As far as Thomas could tell, Chamberlen was obsessed with it."

Sudbury took her hand. "Mary, I want you to come with me. No more secrets."

CHAPTER 17

A broth to keep the back from slimy causes and from the
breeding of the stone

*Take a knuckle of veal and a young cock or pullet, lay
them in water to soak out all the blood an hour or two,
and set them on the fire in a gallon and a half of water,
and so fair skim it, then take two ounces of french barley
and wash it in a little warm water, and seethe it . . .*

Thomas Bradford's dwelling was located on a tidy street of modest but
newish buildings. It didn't stand out in any way but for the knocker
on the door, a disembodied hand, long fingered and elegant, with one
finger pointing to the lintel. It jutted out from the wood and swung up
and forward so that the pointing finger tapped on the door, as though
the house were a person and the visitor tapping its shoulder.

Curious, Mary looked up to see what the finger pointed at when
the knocker was at rest. Carved into the frame of the door, visible only
to the person standing directly underneath it, was a ceramic plaque
aglow in red and orange, with a bird, wings outspread, feeding three
baby birds from drops of blood spurting from its chest. Mary sucked
in her breath. The pelican in her piety.

Bradford opened the door himself. He was a tall man, taller even than Sudbury. He looked to be some twenty years older than Sudbury, and while he had a scholar's pallor, he seemed well fed and healthy. A broad smile spread over his face and he immediately enveloped Sudbury in an embrace.

"My friend," he said, "how glad I was to hear from you again!"

He pulled back and eyed Mary. "And this must be the woman you told me about."

Bradford gave her an assessing look. She felt as though he was taking her measure, waiting to see how she'd react to his bold stare.

Mary gave him a nod. "I am Mary Fawcett," she said, not bothering to wait for Sudbury to introduce her.

Bradford's expression changed from critical to appreciative. He gave a little bow. Mary instantly felt that she would like this man.

"Please, please come in," he said, motioning them inside.

Mary entered the parlor and recognized implements and tools she'd seen in Sudbury's house. Scattered everywhere were glass flasks with narrowed openings, bellows, various small instruments, and books—many, many books.

Bradford cleared glassware and notes from a set of chairs by the window.

"Please, have a seat while I finish this distillation."

"Is there anything I can do to help?" Sudbury asked. Mary heard eagerness in his voice.

"No need," Bradford replied.

Mary sat down and Sudbury reluctantly followed suit. His eyes tracked Bradford's movements as he gently stoked the fire until the flames barely licked the iron sides of the grate, then lifted a large glass flask with a pair of tongs into the center of the flames. When the flask started to teeter, Mary heard Sudbury's breath catch. But Bradford stayed steady and confident in his motions, and the flask righted itself.

Mary could not contain her curiosity. "May I ask what that is, Mr. Bradford? Are you working on some sort of potion? Something to do with the philosopher's stone?"

Bradford blinked a few times and then roared with laughter. "No, no indeed, though I probably should be." He reached over to a shelf and pulled down a jar of golden liquid and showed it to Mary. Was it honey? "No, I'm just preparing my next batch of mead."

Mary wondered if Bradford was laughing at her, but she saw such good humor in his face, heard such warmth in his voice, she, too, had to laugh at her question.

Bradford pulled three wooden cups from a low cupboard, poured a generous measure of mead, and handed a cup to each of them.

"There, now we're nicely settled. Robert, Mrs. Fawcett, what can I do for you?"

Sudbury took a deep breath. "Last time we spoke, you told me Chamberlen had been here to work."

Bradford glanced at Mary.

"She knows who he is, what he was," Sudbury said, answering Bradford's unasked question. "She knows it all."

Bradford nodded. "Well then. Yes, Chamberlen came to me some months ago, asked if he could lodge here. I was about to visit my mother in Essex anyway, so I told him he could use the whole house. I never liked the man, but it gave me comfort to have someone here while I was away."

"What was he working on?" Mary asked.

Bradford rubbed his eyes. "He didn't tell me. But I came home earlier than expected. There was a contagion in the village, and I took my mother to my sister's house in Kent." He paused and shuddered. "That afternoon I returned home to find my laboratory filled with a horrible smell."

He turned to Mary. "That's not unusual in this work, but this smell was not chemical."

"What did it smell like?" Sudbury asked.

Bradford hesitated. "I've been to several anatomies at the Cutlerian Theatre. The smell was similar—rotting corpse, aqua vitae, and vinegar. I couldn't find Chamberlen right away, so I wandered around the house calling his name. Every piece of my equipment was in use, every flask and jar and pot, even those from the kitchen. But he had paid handsomely for the right, so I wasn't too angry. Not until I found him in my basement. And not until I saw what he had done there."

Bradford looked away, his hands tightly gripping the arms of the chair.

Sudbury prodded him. "What had he done, my friend? I don't think we will be surprised."

Bradford looked up and held Sudbury's gaze. "He butchered animals down there, all in the name of alchemy. But no, that is not right. He did not just butcher them. He tortured them. There were all manner of animals, some dead, some alive, some in a horrible place in between. All the dead ones had their guts cut open and all the living, or near-living, ones had been poisoned. The stink was unimaginable."

Sudbury nodded his head sadly. "What did you do?"

"First I vomited. Many times. I could hardly believe what I saw. Then I grabbed him by the collar and demanded to know what he was doing. He told me to calm myself, that he was engaged in a great work that would benefit us both. He said . . . it sounds impossible . . . he said he was cooking the philosopher's stone in the bellies of those poor creatures, transferring it from one to the next."

Sudbury looked surprised. "You mean it was just one stone? I had thought he was trying to create more."

"You knew about this?" Bradford asked, a look of shock and disgust on his face.

"Only afterward, I assure you. I had no part in his heretical experiments. But from things he had said and things I had seen, I pieced it together."

Bradford took a deep breath. "But Chamberlen is dead now. How did it happen?"

Sudbury didn't hesitate to tell Bradford the story. Mary thought it must speak to his deep trust of the man.

After Sudbury had told Bradford about the markings on Chamberlen's abdomen, however, he hesitated. "Mary, too, plays a role in this story. She examined Chamberlen's corpse."

Bradford raised his eyebrows.

"I'm a healer," Mary said. "I have much experience with poisons, and the constable asked me to examine the corpse."

"Did you find anything else?"

Mary hesitated only a moment, mostly out of the habit of keeping her own counsel.

"As Robert said, there were strange markings, tattoos, on his abdomen. And in his fist he clutched a sort of medallion."

Bradford sat forward in his chair. "What kind of medallion?"

"It was about the size of a small egg. And it had markings." As Mary described the series of circles and triangles and the pelican in her piety, Bradford gave a low whistle, then stood and walked to his shelves and pulled down a book.

"That would explain the book I gave to you at St. Paul's, Robert," Bradford said. He turned again to Mary. "I found it in the basement after Chamberlen left. If he had reached the pelican stage of the Great Work—then he was further along than I would have guessed."

"Mrs. Chamberlen mentioned a diary. She said she saw similar ciphers in it."

Bradford looked at Mary and said, hesitating, "And you're sure she is not guilty herself?"

Mary answered, "We can't know that for sure, I suppose, but I trust her. And I'd like to see the diary, as well. What Robert hasn't told you is that he stands accused of Chamberlen's murder. If we can find that diary, explain what Chamberlen was trying to do, we can clear Robert's name."

Bradford snorted. "If Robert were capable of such a thing, he would have done so long before now."

Sudbury gave a twisted little smile. "We've searched Chamberlen's library inside and out with no sign of the diary. Is there any chance he might have left it here?"

Bradford looked around the room. His eyebrows drew together in thought.

"After I threw that madman out of the house, I hired some discreet men to help me clean up. I had to pay them handsomely to stay quiet about what they had seen, but of course some rumors must have gotten around because I'm having the devil of a time hiring a housekeeper. They removed the animal corpses in the basement and did a rough cleaning, but everything is much the same as Chamberlen left it."

Bradford led them down some steep stairs to a surprisingly well-furnished basement. She had expected something like those she'd seen in Bicknacre, used mostly for wintering potatoes and onions. But this basement was spacious, with a fair amount of light coming in from windows at the ground level. Bradford removed a dustcloth that covered a table and an upholstered chair. "This is where he did his writing. Robert, you and Mary look here, and I'll go look on the shelves."

Mary immediately began searching the drawers while Sudbury tapped lightly on the wood of the recessed desk to check for hidden compartments. Bradford, meanwhile, took every book off the shelves and checked them thoroughly.

They searched for over an hour before taking a break. Sudbury gave a frustrated sigh and plopped down in an opulent-looking red velvet chair. After several long moments sitting with his head in his hands, he shifted suddenly and stood up.

"This is a very lumpy chair," he announced.

Bradford kept flipping through the books. "Yes, well, it's just an extra I keep down here for convenience. I do like my small comforts."

Sudbury grinned. "No, I mean that is a *very* lumpy chair."

Understanding dawned on Bradford's face as Sudbury leaned down and began patting the velvet cushion. Bradford opened the top drawer and pulled out a sharp knife. Mary wondered whether it was one of the knives Chamberlen had used in his anatomizing and shuddered.

He offered it to Sudbury. "Here, slice into it!"

Sudbury shook his head. "We don't want to cut the book." He tugged the cushion upward, and after some initial resistance, it popped off. Sudbury turned it over. The fabric was folded like an envelope, and all Sudbury had to do was move the extra material to the side. He reached in and pulled out a small leather book with a brass clasp. A large, elaborate initial C edged in gold shone up at them. Sudbury held it up triumphantly.

Mary's breath caught as she took in the sight and thought about what horrors and secrets might be inside. The room, so recently cozy and comforting, suddenly seemed too dark and noisome.

"We should take it upstairs," she said, trying to keep her voice from shaking. "Somewhere in better light."

Sudbury was studying the cover. "Good idea," he said absently.

Bradford gave her a sympathetic look and led them upstairs, back to the chairs he had set by the window.

With deft fingers, Sudbury worked the small clasp until it popped open. Mary noticed that his hands shook as he opened the cover.

Bradford leaned close to Mary and Sudbury for a better look. On the very first page was a diagram of a human body, astrological and alchemical symbols superimposed over the head, heart, liver, hands, and feet.

Sudbury turned the page.

Mary recognized the form of the text: square blocks in black ink with titles in red. She couldn't read the words, but she knew exactly what she was looking at.

"They look like recipes," she exclaimed.

"Of a sort," Sudbury replied. "They're alchemical experiments. This first one is for the dissolution of gold, and then there are some for the chemical wedding—the process by which the philosopher's stone is made." Mary peered closer as he pointed to a rather elaborate drawing of a man and woman, naked and holding hands. The woman's belly was swollen, as with child, and she stood near a peacock and what looked to be a phoenix rising from the ashes. It reminded her of the tapestry she had seen at Chamberlen Manor with the magnificent phoenix rising in the background.

Sudbury turned several more pages, revealing recipes in Latin and more illustrations, these of cats, dogs, and rabbits. They looked roughly similar to the anatomized man on the first page, but the symbols were in different places.

Though she couldn't make sense of the Latin text, Mary was transfixed by the pictures and diagrams in the book. It felt like a puzzle that, if she were clever enough, she could solve.

As Sudbury flipped the pages, one image kept recurring: that of a little human form in the bell of a flask.

Sudbury stopped on a page with that very image and read slowly, in Latin. As he finished, his voice quavered. Mary looked at him and then at Bradford.

"He wasn't trying to make the philosopher's stone," Sudbury whispered. "Or, that wasn't all he was attempting."

Bradford's eyes were wide. "He cannot possibly have been that ambitious, surely?"

Sudbury began turning the pages again. "I knew he was troubled, but I had no idea the extent of his plans."

"What is it?" Mary demanded, her voice rising.

Sudbury shook his head as if to clear away some mental image.

"Let me see that," Bradford said. With trembling hands, Sudbury passed him the book.

Bradford gave a low whistle.

"What are you looking at?" Mary ground out slowly, her frustration building. Why wouldn't they tell her what they saw?

"This is impossible," Sudbury muttered. "He can't actually have achieved anything like this."

Mary grabbed the wooden cup that had held her mead and banged it on the table. The two men looked up, shocked.

"What. In the world. Are you talking about?" she nearly shouted.

Sudbury blinked several times, coming back to the present, and then took the book from Bradford and held it out to her. "He was playing God, trying to make a homunculus."

Mary had no idea what a homunculus was, but the look of horror on Bradford's face when Sudbury said the word sent a chill down her spine.

"And what is a homunculus?" she asked in her most commanding voice, daring the men to continue ignoring her.

"It's a little man born of alchemy rather than of a woman's womb," Robert explained.

Bradford took over. "Paracelsus says a homunculus may be made from man's seed if it is baked in a horse's womb and fed with human blood. Do you think Chamberlen attempted it here, in my home?"

"I think he may have tried something like it," Sudbury said.

Bradford looked like he might be sick.

Sudbury pulled the book from Mary's hands. "May I take it?" he asked, looking to his friend.

Bradford shrugged. "Please do. I have no use for such a thing, nor do I want it under my roof."

Sudbury put the book down on the small table and reached out to take one of Bradford's hands in both of his. "I thank you, friend," he said.

Bradford frowned. "For what I don't know. I've done nothing but let you look in my basement and deface a very ugly chair."

"You have done much more," Sudbury said. "You've been my friend when others have turned from me in disgust." He pointed vaguely at his face.

Bradford gave an irritated harrumph. "Frankly, I prefer you like this. You are not as arrogant."

After a shocked pause, Sudbury laughed. "Yes, I suppose that's true. I'm glad you said it. Perhaps that will convince Mary here that I am, indeed, a changed man."

Bradford turned to Mary and bowed. "He has always been clever, but now he's also wise. Trust him, Mrs. Fawcett."

Mary gave a little curtsy. "It's been a pleasure meeting you, sir."

Sudbury tucked the little book into his coat pocket, and they took their leave.

Bradford watched them go, a thoughtful look on his face. After a few moments, he sighed and closed the door. If he had watched only a few seconds more, he might have noticed the bent, hooded figure following them down Fleet Street, skirting the horses and the crowds, becoming one with the shadows.

CHAPTER 18

A medicine for such as make water like clear blood

Take a good handful of betony boiled in new milk of a cow that hath not been at bull, and drink it warm every morning and evening.

Mary sat in an oversized chair in the library of Chamberlen House and thought about the strange couple of weeks they'd had. She'd been frightened, overwhelmed, and disgusted in turn, but she had to admit that she'd felt more alive than she ever had. She had seen new sights and gained knowledge that unlocked great and terrible secrets—experiences she would never have in Bicknacre. Her heart and brain thrummed with the energy of the city. If it weren't for how much she missed Tom, she might never want to go home. But even as she admitted that truth to herself, an image of a smiling Tom flashed in her mind. She missed him so very much.

She returned her attention to the diary Sudbury examined. They had searched for clues that would explain Chamberlen's death, but much of the diary was written in Latin and incomprehensible to her. Mary resolved to learn some Latin—she felt so frustrated seeing all this precious knowledge in a code she couldn't break. For now, however, she let Sudbury take the lead: the world of alchemy was Sudbury's, not hers. But, as she was quickly learning, all knowledge was precious. While Sudbury read the stained pages and muttered to himself, sometimes even pantomiming the directions Chamberlen had painstakingly recorded, Mary studied the pictures and marginal notes, trying to decipher some sort of logic.

She could barely believe her eyes when she studied the pictures Chamberlen had drawn. The looping tails of dragons swept across the pages, while figures of men and women stood posed in circles, triangles, and squares—sometimes copulating. Fires burned. Strange birds pranced. Animals preyed. Suns and moons dotted the pages with strange glyphs that Robert explained represented different minerals or celestial bodies, and some stood for different stages of the alchemical process.

She doubted she would ever be comfortable in this bizarre world, but she was starting to recognize the symbols and, in some cases, could even "read" the symbols in the entry to know what it represented. A circle with an arrow pointing up and to the right, for example, stood for iron, and a circle with a dot in the middle represented gold.

And, most important to their theory of Chamberlen's experiments, a strange little mound—like an upside-down horseshoe with curved ends—stood for the bezoar.

Halfway through the diary, the content changed, and there were fewer diagrams and pictures. The entries, in Latin, were written like recipes, but instead of harmless herbals, as in her book, they contained different kinds of minerals and poisons. The recipes became simpler, too, listing only a few ingredients.

"They're notes on his own experiments," Robert said in disgust. "He was refining the process."

"At Mr. Bradford's house?"

"Likely, yes, but perhaps even before." He pointed to a word in the margin that said, simply, "Bicknacre."

After a few pages, intricate drawings accompanied the recipes, always of an animal splayed on a table, a man above him with a knife. There were drawings of pigs, dogs, and calves.

Mary had just begun taking notes on a new page when she heard a noise coming from the kitchens.

"Did you hear that?" she asked. She had to repeat the question, as Robert was thoroughly immersed in his reading. When he finally looked up, they heard a great ruckus, and a woman's scream echoed through the hallways.

They leapt up, books, papers, and quills falling unheeded to the floor, and rushed to the kitchen. Mrs. Stanton was lying on the floor in much the same position she'd been in that day a few weeks before when her back was hurting. Mary breathed a sigh of relief before noticing that, unlike the last time she had encountered Mrs. Stanton in this position, her eyes didn't open and sparkle up at her, and no tinkling laugh dispelled her fear.

Just then, John Weaver burst in, his eyes frantically surveying the room. "Where is she?"

Sudbury ran to Mrs. Stanton. "She's here, John."

Weaver's eyes widened. He rushed to her side and pushed Sudbury away, then felt for a pulse.

A chill ran down Mary's spine. Mrs. Stanton was bent in an awkward position, her arms akimbo at an unnatural angle. There was an ugly red gash in her forehead made even starker by her distressingly pale hue, and her eyes failed to flutter open at the sound of their voices.

"She lives," Weaver said in a trembling voice. When he ran his hands over Mrs. Stanton's bent arm and tried to straighten it, she let out a low groan, and finally, finally her eyelids fluttered briefly.

Weaver sobbed once, gently, and bent to lift her up to lean against his kneeling body.

Mrs. Stanton groaned again. This time her eyes opened, and she looked around in confusion.

"What happened?" she asked.

"You tell us," John replied, his voice gruff. He smoothed her hair tenderly. "What do you remember?"

Mrs. Stanton closed her eyes and grimaced. "I was in the wine cellar when I heard a crash in here. Just as I opened the door, I was hit on the head. With that, I suppose." She looked to one of the broken jars lying next to her, and then to a corner by the stove. "I think it fell on me from above."

Mary walked over to the corner Mrs. Stanton pointed to. "Look!"

A light coating of ash on the floor next to the oven hearth showed the faintest impression of a shoe.

Sudbury took a deep breath. "It wasn't an accident, then. Somebody did this."

"I'll kill them." Weaver's voice was flat, but his fists were clenched tightly, and a vein throbbed in his temple.

Mrs. Stanton let out a quiet groan.

In one swift motion, Weaver picked her up in his arms and carried her out of the kitchen.

"I'm taking her to her room. She will rest for the remainder of the day."

Sudbury and Mary simply stared at the retreating figures.

"What do we do now?" Mary asked.

"Whatever Weaver tells us to do. He's the best one to know what she needs. And in the meantime, we keep watch and figure out what's in that diary."

As they made their way back to the library, Sudbury grabbed Mary's hand—for comfort or safety, Mary didn't know. But she didn't object.

Sudbury kept hold of her hand until they reached the fireplace in the library, when he abruptly dropped it.

"Mary, did you take the diary with you to the kitchen?"

Mary shook her head and looked at the desk.

It was empty.

In all the chaos and confusion, somebody had taken Chamberlen's diary.

⚶

Mrs. Stanton stayed in bed for several days as they waited for rest and Mary's remedies to take effect. She treated her with her most trusted recipes: yarrow mixed with cream to treat the ghastly cut on her forehead and *Sanguis draconis* crushed with sugar for her eyes. With Mary's ministrations, Mrs. Stanton eventually regained her strength and insisted on returning to her duties.

After a week of paralyzing fear as the mystery of Mrs. Stanton's attack went unsolved, a letter arrived from Mrs. Chamberlen. It was short and to the point.

> *Mary,*
> *I promised I would send word the moment it was safe to return to Bicknacre. I believe that now to be true. Hopkins has left, though not under the best of circumstances—indeed, his absence is a mystery. He had been ill for several days, desperately ill, and then two weeks ago he vanished, only a few of his belongings packed, the rest left undisturbed. I don't know Hopkins's fate, but he seems no longer to be a threat to you. I believe it's safe for you and Sudbury to return, though you must still remain hidden here in my home. The murder charges against Sudbury stand, but I believe without Hopkins's influence, Sudbury won't be actively pursued. I have spoken with the magistrate and seen to it that he will be left alone should the two of you return.*

Mary had been waiting impatiently for Mrs. Chamberlen to send word that it was safe to go back, but the missive left Mary surprisingly melancholy. She wanted to go home, didn't she?

She thought of Bicknacre, of the neighbors who suspected her of terrible acts, of the former friends who looked askance at her. Villagers she had helped for years with her cures and her talent, avoiding her in the street. She remembered the dreariness of her days, the endless gleaning and mixing and cooking, always the same recipes with the same results. Then she remembered the glistening world she had glimpsed that day at St. Paul's: new, enticing, enchanting.

Did she want to return home? Was that really the life she wanted?

But there was a postscript: *Tom requests that I add his entreaties for your return. He says, "Tell Mary I've finally learned to skip rocks."*

Reading this last bit almost made her sob. The longing to see her little brother squeezed her heart and stole her breath. She need not think further—she would do whatever necessary to reunite with Tom.

Sudbury had been waiting patiently while Mary read the letter, but he finally gave a little cough.

Mary turned to him with tear-filled eyes. "Tom is fine."

Sudbury breathed a sigh of relief, and she continued. "Robert, Hopkins is gone. And now that the diary is missing, there's no longer a reason to stay. We can go home."

Sudbury nodded. "I'll arrange our travel."

Not two days later, they were back in the coach on the road to Bicknacre. They'd said their goodbyes to Mrs. Stanton and Mr. Weaver with tears and hugs. As Mary gave Mrs. Stanton further instructions on using the store of poultice for her back and the medicines for her head, Mr. Weaver pulled Sudbury aside and whispered in his ear. A look of fury came over Sudbury's face, and Weaver patted his arm, attempting to calm him.

As they pulled away in the coach, Mary turned to Sudbury. "What did Mr. Weaver say to you? You looked livid."

"He discovered who attacked Mrs. Stanton," he said slowly. "It was the same people who put the pig in your bed." Sudbury's jaw was clenched.

Panic consumed Mary as an image of the gash in Mrs. Stanton's forehead and the ghastly, bloated pig corpse flashed in her mind.

"Weaver has been asking around, letting it be known he would pay good money for information. Finally two boys came to him—Mrs. Stanton hires them occasionally to clean the fireplaces. They thought it was better to confess than for Mr. Weaver to discover their guilt. They say they didn't mean to hurt her. They were told to cause a ruckus, so they were smashing crockery in the kitchen. One of the pitchers hit Mrs. Stanton in the head when she came to investigate."

"Why did they do it?"

"These boys are very poor. For causing this damage, they were paid enough to keep them in food for a month. Which is why after he tweaked their ears, Weaver gave them two loaves of bread. But, Mary, that diary went missing during the fuss. I'm sure they were hired to draw us away from the library, away from that diary."

"But who paid them? Who would do such a thing?"

"All they could tell him was that it was a woman. She was cloaked. She approached them shortly after we arrived from Bicknacre and paid them handsomely to carry that pig to your bed. It was the same woman who paid them to cause a commotion."

"A woman," Mary repeated. "Did they describe her?"

Mary braced herself to hear mention of Bridget's bright golden hair, but Sudbury just shrugged. "Her face was covered by a hood. They said they wouldn't recognize her again but by her voice."

They sat quietly the rest of the journey, contemplating this new information. With Hopkins gone, they thought they might be safer returning to Bicknacre, but were they walking into a trap?

As they turned in to the grounds of Chamberlen Manor, Mary felt inexplicably nervous about seeing Tom again. She had never left him before. He was so young. Would he understand? Would he be angry with her for leaving?

She needn't have worried. As she and Sudbury walked up the path, they saw Tom playing by the old stone well with Mrs. Woods and her children. They were dropping rocks in the well and hopping on one foot until the rock hit water, laughing as they teetered and toppled.

Mary laughed, and Tom's head shot up at the sound. As soon as he spied her, he ran as fast as his limp would allow. He launched himself into his sister's arms, and if Sudbury hadn't been there to catch her, Mary would have fallen backward with the force.

"Mary, Mary, you're back!" he cried out. Mary held on tight.

"Tom, be gentle with your poor sister!" Mrs. Woods called out, laughter in her voice. "Welcome home, you two! Oh, Tom, see, I told you they'd be just fine!"

Tom would not let go of Mary's waist for several minutes, and Mary was perfectly content to let him cling to her. She answered all Mrs. Woods's questions about London. Sudbury, standing some ways back, added a detail or two, but mostly he remained quiet, watching Mary and Tom.

Mary looked down at her brother. "Will you go play with the other children while I speak with Mrs. Woods some more?"

Tom looked mutinous and clung tighter to her waist.

Mary put her hand under Tom's chin and gently lifted it so Tom couldn't look away. "I will stay right here, Tom, right here where you can see me. I promise."

"And when we're done talking, I'll take you back to Chamberlen Manor and Cook can give you a sweet cake," Mrs. Woods promised.

Tom reluctantly pulled away and walked toward the children, looking back every few paces to check that his sister was still there.

Mary was filled with guilt. "My poor boy."

Mrs. Woods laid her hand on Mary's arm and said in a firm voice, "He enjoyed staying here with Mrs. Chamberlen—he missed you, but he made friends with some of the servants' children, and he has been happy. You did what you had to do to keep him safe. You couldn't have stayed in Bicknacre while Hopkins was here."

Mary took a deep breath.

"And how have the people of Bicknacre taken Hopkins's disappearance?" Sudbury asked.

Mrs. Woods sighed. "I thought that with Hopkins gone, the village would go back to the way it was. And things have improved, but everyone is still so suspicious of each other. It's as though we removed the source of a stench, but the stink remains. I fear a drought or some dead cows may bring more accusations of witchcraft and once again turn us against each other."

Mary nodded sadly. "And what of Robert? Is the magistrate still content to leave him be?"

"I think so. Nobody really believed Robert was guilty of Chamberlen's death, I think, but they didn't want to anger a witch-finder. Now everybody is too scared about what happened to Hopkins to worry overly much about Robert. Not that I advise going into the village right now. But, Robert, if you stay at the manor, you should be safe."

"And what do you think happened to Hopkins, Mrs. Woods?" Sudbury asked.

She hesitated. "He was very ill. I would have thought he had caught some deadly contagion, except that he simply disappeared. No corpse, no sign of a struggle. Not even Stearne knew where he'd gone. There are rumors, of course. Stories of witches carrying him off and practicing his own techniques on him, giving him the swim test, pricking him to death."

After a few moments of quiet while Mary and Sudbury absorbed this news, they took the children to the kitchen for the promised cake and went to speak with Mrs. Chamberlen.

Mary couldn't help cringing a bit as they stepped inside the grand entrance of the manor. She was still wearing her travel dress, and she smelled of sweat and horseflesh. Sudbury looked like death, his face pale and drawn from exhaustion and the pain in his leg, exacerbated by the long carriage ride. Mary winced at the thought of her grimy gown touching the delicate silk of the couch.

But when Mrs. Chamberlen entered the room, all such thoughts disappeared as she swept Mary into a hug. She smelled of the expensive perfume she favored and was dressed exquisitely. Despite Mary's dishevelment, Mrs. Chamberlen welcomed her warmly and generously.

She extended a hand to Sudbury and bade them sit. "Welcome home. Tom will be so happy to have you back, Mary." Mrs. Chamberlen looked a bit wistful at that. "As I said in my letter, I think you'll be safe now that Hopkins is gone."

"But what if he comes back?" Mary asked, tears threatening to fall. "I don't think I could leave Tom again."

"We shall figure out a plan," Mrs. Chamberlen reassured her. "Meanwhile, did you find my husband's diary?" She sat forward in the chair, eagerness in her eyes.

"We had it, we think," Mary replied.

Mrs. Chamberlen frowned. "What do you mean?"

"I don't know if it was the same diary you were looking for, but it was definitely his. I know his handwriting when I see it," Robert said.

"Well, what was in it, then?"

"Mostly recipes and drawings," Mary replied. "Mainly in Latin."

"Recipes?" Mrs. Chamberlen asked. "What kind of recipes?"

Mary looked at Sudbury, who nodded.

"Alchemical," Mary answered. "But we didn't get much of a chance to look through it before it was stolen."

Mrs. Chamberlen gasped. "Stolen? By whom?"

"We don't know. There was a commotion; Mrs. Stanton was hurt—"

Mrs. Chamberlen sat forward again. "Why was I not told? Is she well? Has she recovered?"

"She is shaken, but fine," Mary reassured her. "Mr. Weaver found the culprits. Two young lads making mischief."

"As Mary said," Sudbury continued, taking over the story, "the book holds more than just recipes. There are some accounts of experiments Mr. Chamberlen conducted."

Mrs. Chamberlen's eyes widened, but she didn't say a word.

"There are descriptions of feeding a bezoar stone, with several other substances, many of them poisonous, to a variety of animals. Then the outcome of Mr. Chamberlen cutting into their guts, some of them while still alive."

Mrs. Chamberlen flinched but didn't interrupt.

"He experimented on pigs and dogs and cats." Mary hesitated. "The experiments got more complex, more detailed."

A faraway expression settled in Mrs. Chamberlen's eyes, an absence. "Was it just animals?" she asked warily. "Just animals he experimented on?"

Sudbury bit his lip. "In the diary, yes. But he may have worked on people as well. It may have been what he intended for Margery, back in Chichester," Sudbury said.

Mrs. Chamberlen looked up, her eyes infinitely sad. "And for me?" she asked.

"Perhaps," Mary whispered. She took the other woman's hand.

Mrs. Chamberlen nodded. "I see. So I was indeed married to a monster."

Mary and Sudbury said nothing.

After several long minutes, Mrs. Chamberlen said, "And you have no idea who may have stolen the diary?"

Mary responded, slowly, "I have a suspicion. I wonder if it might be Bridget Jenkins."

"Bridget? The woman my husband was bedding?"

Mary's jaw tightened, remembering Bridget and her threats. "The same."

"But how could she be in London? Has she the means to travel there and back?"

Mary paused. She couldn't answer that. But she knew in her gut that Bridget was somehow responsible for the pain caused in the last several months. Years, even.

"Well, whoever it may be, it's clear you're still in harm's way. You must stay here at Chamberlen Manor, with Tom. You cannot return to the village. I have men here who can protect you."

Mrs. Chamberlen called to one of her servants to prepare rooms, then turned to address Robert.

"Now, Mr. Sudbury, I need to speak with Mary and I must ask that you leave."

Sudbury shot a look full of curiosity and concern at Mary, but she ignored him.

"Certainly," he said. "I will join young Tom in the kitchen for sweet cakes."

The moment Sudbury left the room, Mary asked Mrs. Chamberlen, "How are you feeling? Did the salve work?"

"The pain has lessened, and I can move more freely—the salve has helped with that. But I'm not getting better. Will you take a look at it?"

"Of course, Anne. I'll meet you in your room when you've disrobed."

Mary noticed the smell of rotting flesh when she entered the room. It had not yet reached the putrescence of the deathbed, not even yet of the sickroom, but it lay under the surface, a hint, a warning, like a bushel of apples about to go bad.

Mary set her face into a passive mask, trying to hide her concern.

"Are you comfortable with me examining your breast?"

Mrs. Chamberlen nodded.

Mary warmed her hands and placed them on Mrs. Chamberlen, more gently than she had before. By the looks of it, the cancer had progressed.

The sore was bigger, and the skin over the burgeoning lump was taut. It felt hot to the touch, and Mary thought she felt another lump next to it. At the side of the cancerous sore was a small moist area. She squeezed the area lightly and pushed out a small trickle of pus.

"I'm pleased that the salve has given you relief. And the snail shells?"

"At first, but not lately, perhaps not for the last two weeks."

"I have another recipe I can try. It works well when the sore has broken."

Mary prodded the area to determine the extent of the growth. When she'd finished her examination and pulled a linen cloth over Mrs. Chamberlen's chest, she gave a wobbly sigh.

Mrs. Chamberlen turned to her, her eyes glistening. "I will die of this, won't I?"

Mary saw no reason to lie in these situations.

"Yes, eventually."

"How long?"

"There is never a way of knowing. I've been wrong on that question too many times to try and guess again. But it would be wise to get your affairs in order in the next several months, Anne."

Mrs. Chamberlen nodded. "At least there is one bright spot: that bastard of a husband died before me and let me have some of the happiest months of my life."

CHAPTER 19

To make a syrup cordial good for such as have taken thought

Take half a pint of the juice of borage, as much of the juice of bugloss, the like quantity of the juice of balm, put all these juices together, and seethe them in a skillet, and the green will rise up thick, like a posset curdle, then clear it with the whites of two eggs, well beaten, and scum it clean . . .

It was no good. Despite the long day of travel and the deliciously soft bed, Mary simply could not get to sleep with all the thoughts and fears crowding her head. Tom, having refused to sleep in his own room, snored in a little trundle bed next to hers. Rather than tossing and turning, risking awakening Tom, she got up and sat in the chair by the dwindling fire. She pulled out her recipe book and felt a shiver of anticipation. Now that she was back in Bicknacre, she could begin work on her cures once again.

With a pang, she thought of Agnes's recipe book, regretted leaving it behind. She would retrieve it as soon as she could. Though she already had copies of most of Agnes's recipes in her own book, she still wanted to have a reminder of all that Agnes had meant to her, to see her handwriting and touch the pages she had lovingly written over the years.

She was just starting to feel drowsy when she heard a strange noise, a strangled cry. A paroxysm of fear gripped her stomach. She waited, listening, for several more minutes. She heard it again, only now it sounded a little softer. In horror, she realized it came from the room adjoining hers. From Sudbury's room.

Mary fought her fear. She checked to make sure Tom slept soundly and then grabbed the heavy iron candlestick. Once outside her room, she crept down the hallway, testing each floorboard to make sure it didn't squeak before she stepped on it.

She didn't dare knock, so instead she very slowly turned the knob. She raised the candlestick over her head and burst through the door, hoping to use the element of surprise to her advantage.

She didn't know what she expected, but she knew what she feared: the sight of Sudbury's body, bloody and bloated, like a horrible reproduction of the pig corpse in her bed in London, or the pale, ghastly body of Henry Chamberlen splayed out on his bed. Relief washed over her when she saw Sudbury was alive, lying in bed, his body drenched in sweat, moaning in his sleep.

"Not the lead!" he cried out. "Set it down! I burn!" He thrashed wildly, trying to protect his face.

Mary pulled the door closed behind her and sat down by his side. She set the candlestick down by the bed and very gently laid her hand on his brow.

"Be still," she said. "All is well."

He quieted.

She continued rubbing his brow and whispering in soft tones as he calmed. Then, just as he seemed ready to drift into a peaceful sleep, his eyes opened. He took in her presence with shock and fear that quickly transformed into wonderment.

"Mary?"

"Yes," she whispered.

"But I dream of you so much," he said, confused. "Is it really you?"

Mary knew how to reassure him. She leaned down and pressed her lips to his. She kissed him softly, just allowing their lips to touch, no more. Then she kissed each eye, then the deepest whorl in his scar.

"You are safe," she said.

Sudbury shuddered.

"You are safe," she repeated. She kissed him again. This time it was passionate and curious.

"You are safe," she said a third time, and Sudbury put his arms around her waist, drawing her to him.

Sudbury returned her kiss. His hands moved to her hair, smoothing and tangling it by turns as he tried to pull her even closer.

"Mary," he gasped. "Mary, do not leave. Do not ever leave."

"I must. Tom sleeps in my room tonight. I can't leave him to waken alone."

Sudbury gulped several times, pushing down his fear and panic. His face grew calmer, and he nodded.

"Of course," he said, his tone becoming distant and formal. "I shall be fine." He paused. "Thank you for checking on me. It's been a long time since anyone . . . since anyone cared."

Mary took a deep breath. How could she leave him now?

She thought to stay for only a few minutes, to lull him to sleep and return to her room with Tom. But the steady pulse of his breathing and the warmth of his body soon caused her to join in his slumber.

From below came a crash and a scream.

The sun had already risen, and she had left Tom alone all night.

Mary jumped out of bed and ran to her room to check on Tom. He had awoken, but he showed no fear. He rubbed his eyes with one small hand.

"Thank you, God," she said in a whisper.

"What's happening?" he asked in a sleepy voice.

"Nothing for you to worry about, pet," Mary reassured him. "The puppies sleeping in the kitchen got loose, I imagine. Go back to sleep."

She needed to find out what was wrong, but she couldn't take him downstairs. He had already faced so much danger.

"Tom, you must not leave this room unless I say. Do you understand?"

Tom nodded and collapsed back into the little bed, his eyes already closing. "Yes, Mary, but hurry back."

Mary kissed his forehead and rushed downstairs toward a loud buzz of voices.

"We need to see them," a woman's voice pleaded. "Please, lives are at stake!"

Mrs. Chamberlen emerged from her room in her dressing gown and called to the footmen. "What's happening? Who is there?"

A maid turned and bowed. "Please, madam, Reverend Osborne is here to see you, and he's with Verity Martin."

Mrs. Chamberlen frowned. "That is most unusual. But why have you not let them in the house?"

The maid looked frightened. "Miss Martin, she is not . . . she is in a fit of sorts."

"Let them come to us immediately," Mrs. Chamberlen demanded.

When Reverend Osborne and Verity Martin finally entered the room, Mary gasped. The reverend looked frightened and confused. And Verity—Verity was splattered with blood and dirt, and her bodice had been ripped in several places. Her eyes darted around the room in terror.

Verity ran to Mrs. Chamberlen and grabbed her hand.

"Whatever is the matter, child?" Mrs. Chamberlen asked.

"He's dead. Or, I think he's dead. I don't know!" she wailed.

They all looked to Reverend Osborne for answers.

"Mr. Sudbury, Mrs. Fawcett, Mrs. Chamberlen," he addressed them with a little bow. Verity's head shot up as she heard Mary's name. She gasped and ran to Mary, throwing herself into her arms.

"Mary, Mrs. Fawcett, you are home! You'll help us, I know you will!" She motioned to Reverend Osborne. "Tell them what happened! Tell them!" Verity said. "They won't believe me. Nobody believes me anymore."

"It's been a long night, and I don't feel well," the reverend said. "May I sit?"

Mrs. Chamberlen nodded.

He sat and rubbed his tired eyes. "We've been very happy to have Verity with us since the . . . the unpleasantness with her father. She's a good girl and has been helpful to us. We have no children, and my wife has taken to thinking of her as a daughter."

At this, Verity gave a tremulous smile.

"We asked Verity to stay with us indefinitely. We couldn't imagine sending her back to that father of hers."

He looked at Verity. "Sorry, my dear."

"Don't apologize. He's the very devil."

"We were delighted to offer Verity a place in our home. When John Martin found out that Verity had accepted our invitation, he became enraged. He wrote letters to us—horrible letters threatening us with terrible harm."

Verity interrupted and, with a wavering voice, finished the story. "He forced himself into the house this morning and attacked me. He slapped me and ripped my dress. Pulled out chunks of my hair. He called me an ungrateful slut, and worse. He suggested things, horrible things, about the Osbornes and me. I could listen to him no more."

Her voice became softer and her eyes grew unfocused. "There was a pile of logs by the fire. I grabbed the largest one and hit him as hard as I could, right across his temple."

Mary sucked in a gasp. Then the reverend continued the story.

"As soon as John Martin pushed his way into the house, my wife ran to get me. We rushed into the front room to find Verity crying and cradling her father's head in her lap. As soon as Verity saw us, she fainted dead away."

"I was weak," Verity said. "Useless. I'm so sorry."

"Nonsense, child," Mrs. Chamberlen said briskly. "You reacted as any of us would."

Verity reached up a bloody hand to wipe away a tear and then clutched her fists.

"Shhh," Mary comforted her. She rubbed her back while Reverend Osborne continued.

"After we revived Verity, my wife took her to her room to rest while I went to find help. I left Mr. Martin by the fireplace and told the maid to check on him, but I didn't think he would recover. Indeed, I assumed he would soon be dead. I ran to the Martins' house. Simon was home. I told him as quickly as possible what had happened, and we hurried back to my house."

A look of remembered horror crossed Reverend Osborne's face. He clearly struggled with what to say next.

Mrs. Chamberlen gave a frustrated noise. "Go on, man! What happened?"

Reverend Osborne looked up with haunted eyes. "He was gone."

"Who was gone?" Sudbury asked.

"John Martin. He was just . . . missing."

Verity gave a little sob, and Mary stroked her hair and rocked her.

"That is impossible," Mrs. Chamberlen said imperiously. "From the sound of it, the man was either dead or incapacitated by that head wound."

Reverend Osborne nodded. "He was indeed. But he was gone. There was still blood on the floor, and the log lay where it had. But John Martin, or his corpse, was gone. I worried Simon wouldn't believe me, but he did. He stopped only to check on Verity before going into the woods to look for his father. He thought perhaps he might have recovered and, in his confusion, begun to wander." The reverend looked doubtful at this. "Though his wounds were severe indeed."

"And where is Simon now?" Sudbury asked.

Verity looked up. "He's still looking for our father, I think," she replied. "He hasn't returned. What if something terrible happens to him? What if my father is alive and hurts Simon? Oh, this is all my fault."

She buried her face in her hands.

Sudbury looked stern. "Mrs. Chamberlen, I must go help look for Simon and Mr. Martin. May I borrow a few of your strongest footmen?"

"Of course." Mrs. Chamberlen nodded to her butler. "Round up George and Will. They're the youngest and strongest."

Mary stepped forward. "I'll be ready in a few minutes."

While the rest of the room looked at Mary in surprise, Sudbury gave her an appraising look.

Reverend Osborne sputtered, "You shall do no such thing, Mrs. Fawcett," but Sudbury interrupted.

"She's right. She should go. With all her foraging for plants over the years, she knows those woods better than anybody."

Mary turned and hurried out before anybody else could disagree. She ran to her room and changed into her dress and sturdy boots. Tom remained fast asleep. She gently kissed his forehead.

As she approached the front door, a soft, whispered voice stopped her. "Mary?"

Verity had been cleaned up—the blood was wiped away, and she wore a fresh dress. But her face couldn't hide her fear and pain.

"Mary, you must hate me. I don't like myself most of the time. I think about the accusations I made against you and Agnes, about what I said, every day. Every hour. But I want you to know that I've become a better person since those dark days. My father poisoned me in body and mind, but I . . . I think my time with Reverend and Mrs. Osborne is helping me."

Mary opened her arms, and Verity, shaking, embraced her.

"Verity, I saw what your father did to you. And I'm sure what I saw was only a small fraction of what you suffered."

Verity shook with sobs.

"I cannot fathom your pain and confusion. I don't hold you responsible, and I'm sure Agnes also forgave you before her death."

Verity pulled away and looked up at Mary with tear-filled eyes.

"Be careful," she pleaded. "My father is capable of any evil."

Mary gave Verity's hands a squeeze, took a deep breath, and left the room.

They located the footmen and left the house. A fear overcame Mary that she could not name. Something was profoundly wrong, something beyond the disappearance of Matthew Hopkins and John Martin.

Sudbury put his arm around her shoulder and squeezed tight but didn't say a word.

Before leaving, they had conferred with Mrs. Chamberlen, Verity, and Reverend Osborne about where to look for Simon and his father. The Martins' house had already been searched, as had the church and graveyard. Since Mary and Sudbury didn't want their return to Bicknacre known, George and Will went to the village while Mary and Sudbury began searching the woods. Mary had told the footmen to meet them midmorning at the same woodcutter's cottage they'd sheltered in after Sudbury escaped from his cell.

The sun hovered low in the sky, and the trees cast long shadows that provided cover and secrecy. Mary was unsure whether that benefited them or their quarry.

She and Sudbury took a path through a particularly thick copse of oaks that opened up to a sunlit meadow.

Despite the sudden warmth of the sun, Mary felt a chill. Her gut clenched as the tang of blood—and something worse—assaulted her nose.

Sudbury stopped her in her tracks and pointed to a small circle of trampled grass. There lay the corpse of a rabbit, its viscera splayed out around it.

"What do you think happened?" she whispered.

"Probably attacked by a stray dog," Sudbury replied, but he didn't sound sure.

The bright red blood matting the rabbit's fur glistened in the sun, suggesting that it had been freshly killed. Probably that very morning.

Sudbury fetched a long stick. He prodded the lifeless body and flipped it over and back again.

"What are you looking for?" Mary asked.

Sudbury didn't answer.

"You're looking for the mark, aren't you? The mark that was on Chamberlen's corpse and on the poor animals in Mr. Bradford's house? The *monas*."

Sudbury nodded. His mouth was set in a grim line.

"Do you see it?"

Sudbury nodded again, and Mary held back a whimper of fear.

"But Chamberlen is dead, and this rabbit's corpse is fresh."

Sudbury poked at the rabbit again with the stick, then moved some of the offal that had spilled to the blood-soaked ground underneath. Scratched into the black earth, Mary could make out the mark that had haunted her dreams since examining Chamberlen's corpse.

Robert cocked his head. "Mary," he said slowly. "Do you hear something?"

Mary tore her gaze from the eviscerated rabbit and froze. She could hear a barely detectable moan coming from behind a thick oak trunk.

Her chest deflated and her stomach clenched.

Robert hoisted the stick over his head, and Mary took a small knife from her pocket. As quietly as possible, they inched to the other side of the tree. The moans, though getting louder, sounded pitiful and weak.

Wordlessly, Robert pointed to one side of the tree as he went to the other in order to round the trunk at the same time.

But they didn't need that advantage, for Matthew Hopkins lay before them, bloodied and naked, a gash across his tattooed stomach.

Mary turned to the side and vomited. Even in this state, close to death, his eyes nearly swollen shut, Hopkins became alert.

"Who's there?" he whispered. "If it is you, beldam, begone!"

He looked closer. "You!" he spat. "Mary Fawcett, the witch that ran away. Lord, the many ways I've suffered since you left, and you have no idea of it." He tried to laugh, but the pain made him sputter instead. "I still say you would've been a pretty little cunt to add to my collection."

Robert looked at him with cold eyes and turned to walk away. "Come," he said to Mary, "we have more important things to do than comfort the devil's helper."

Mary wanted to. She wanted to walk away from this man who had harmed her and so many she loved. But she could not. Something in her, a voice whispering to her soul, told her she had no right to withhold her gifts from anyone who needed them. She knew, somehow, that only by helping this damned soul could she preserve her own.

She kneeled in the bloodied dirt. She touched Hopkins's feverish temple. With his eyes closed, his face nearly in repose, she could almost see what he had looked like as a boy, small and vulnerable. Who could have done this to him? Then he opened his eyes and sneered at her.

Then, with a cry, he frenetically turned his head from side to side, looking up to the sky with cold terror.

Robert growled and took a step away. "What is he looking at?"

Mary turned to Robert in confusion. "I have no idea."

"No!" Hopkins screamed. "Martha Clarke? How are you still alive? Mrs. West? And Rebecca?" Blood oozed from the wound below his ribs as he writhed on the ground. "You were hanged! I saw you all hanged!"

Robert looked around in confusion. Mary could see nothing either, but she thought she could hear, up high, in the whispering of the trees, the eerie sound of laughter.

"Why do you bind me?" Hopkins squealed. "What will you do with that pin? I am no witch, I have no witch's teat!"

Robert and Mary looked on, unsure what to do, as Hopkins thrashed in misery. Then he began gurgling. Phlegm and blood slid from his lips down his chin.

"I cannot breathe!" he gasped. "There's too much water, and I cannot float."

With a trembling hand, Hopkins reached out to grab Mary—whether to save himself or take her with him to whatever hell he was in, she could not know.

Robert and Mary stood by in a state of shock as they watched him take his last agonized breath.

"We should go," Robert finally muttered.

Mary nodded, and then in an act of kindness he did not deserve, she closed Matthew Hopkins's eyes, which were frozen in terror at whatever penance he had faced.

As they hurried away, Mary heard a sound and turned. Above the trees, turning the sky to black, dozens of crows descended. Mary grabbed Robert's sleeve and they ran, turning in horror to see the crows, jostling and cawing and fighting to land on Matthew Hopkins's flesh.

They ran for several long minutes. Mary's lungs burned with the effort, but she had to put as much distance as possible between them and whoever, or whatever, had tormented Matthew Hopkins.

"Slow down!" Sudbury called. "We should probably look around in this meadow."

Mary took a deep breath and nodded briskly. "Yes. I will start over here and you begin at that berm on the opposite side."

They took sticks and beat the grass from either side until meeting again in the middle.

"Did you see anything?" Mary asked, knowing the answer.

"Nothing. Where should we go next?"

Mary thought for a moment. "The cottage isn't far. We should see if George and Will are there."

They hurried the half mile to the cottage in silence. As they drew near, Sudbury stopped abruptly and put his arm out in front of Mary. She stumbled and let out a startled cry. Sudbury stepped behind her and held her tight to his chest, his hand covering her mouth.

Panic rose in her belly. What was Sudbury doing?

Mary's knees buckled and she struggled to breathe. Sudbury kept one hand wrapped around her mouth, and with his free hand he pulled a knife out of his belt.

Mary stifled a scream and forced herself to breathe through her nose. She wriggled her hands out of Sudbury's grasp and curled them around his forearm. She took a deep breath and pulled, while biting down on the soft flesh of his palm as hard as she could.

"God's teeth!" Sudbury swore as he let go of Mary and pulled his hand away in pain. Mary grabbed the knife out of his hand. "Why did you do that?"

"I might ask the same of you! Why did you attack me?" She poked the knife against his chest.

"Keep your voice down," he whispered. "I was trying to warn you. Look!"

Sudbury pointed to the clearing below, where the cottage stood. Mary saw nothing amiss.

"There's smoke coming from the chimney," Sudbury said. "George and Will wouldn't have started a fire. Somebody is in there." Sudbury looked at the joint between his thumb and forefinger, where a semicircle of tooth-shaped marks had started to redden. "Praise be, another scar," he grumbled, his mouth twisted in a grimace.

"Oh," Mary said. She looked at the knife in her hand and handed it back to him without saying a word.

"You scared me," she said by way of explanation.

"I could say the same," he muttered.

Mary started to reply and he once again shushed her. "Don't apologize. Right now, we need to find out what's happening in that cottage."

Mary studied the thatched house. The early-morning light bathed it in a deceptively innocent glow.

"What do we do?" Mary whispered, her voice barely audible.

Sudbury merely shook his head. "Nothing for now. We wait. We watch. If John Martin was strong enough to build a fire, he's still a danger."

They stood, frozen, watching, for nearly an hour. When they finally saw some movement, it came not from the cottage but from a little shed some distance away.

Mary grabbed Sudbury's hand as the door inched open. He nodded to indicate that he, too, had noticed the movement.

They both gasped when the door opened a little wider and the sun glistened off bright blond hair.

Bridget.

"What's she doing here?" Mary whispered. She moved to rush down the hill and tear the woman to pieces, but Robert stopped her.

"Be patient. We need to know what she's going to do."

They watched as Bridget slowly exited the shed, staying close to the walls and ducking behind an abandoned cart.

As Bridget fumbled with a small bag at her side and withdrew a knife, a scream rent the air.

That scream would haunt Mary to the end of her days.

The scream came from the cottage.

It was the scream of a young boy.

Tom.

Mary's blood thrummed in her head, and a cloud of fear and horror fogged her thinking. She started forward, with no thought besides rushing to the cottage to save her brother.

Sudbury grabbed her arm, and she fought to throw him off.

"Stop now," he hissed. "Stop or you will get him killed."

Fear pulsed through her, but she managed to focus her eyes on Sudbury and listen to him.

"We need to think this through. We have no idea who took him from Chamberlen Manor."

"It's that bitch Bridget! Obviously it's Bridget!" She could hear the panic in her voice. "How did she steal him away?"

Sudbury gave Mary a little shake. "Stop, Mary. Think. Look. Bridget is still by the shed. That scream came from the cottage. Bridget is hiding. What, or who, is she hiding from?"

Mary forced herself to focus. "I don't know, but Bridget, that devil's dam—she can't be trusted. I need to go to him. Now."

Sudbury sighed. "John Martin hates you. If he's in there, you'll die and be of no help to Tom at all."

"We need to do something!" Mary whispered, willing him to understand her desperation.

"We need to be careful," Sudbury replied. His calm voice infuriated her. "Can you honestly tell me that you would be able to see Tom, hear his voice, and not rush to save him no matter who was with him?"

Mary closed her eyes and took a deep breath. "What's your plan?"

"This may be the hardest thing you ever have to do, Mary," he said, looking steadily into her eyes. "But you're going to have to wait here."

Mary shook her head vigorously, but Sudbury continued.

"I'm going to climb that sycamore behind the shed and create a diversion, try to draw out whoever's in there. You wait until the cottage is empty and fetch Tom."

"Then what?"

"We have to be smart," Sudbury continued. "If you can free Tom, do it. Then grab him and run as fast as you can back to the manor. But this is important—if you can't free him quickly, you must leave him there and meet me back at this spot so we can plan. You *must*, Mary."

Mary nodded. She didn't think she could possibly leave Tom in there alone, but if she didn't agree, she would never get inside that cabin.

Sudbury gave her a stern look. "Promise."

"I can't. I won't."

Sudbury sighed. "Then promise me you'll do what you can to stay safe."

Mary nodded. "But what about you?"

"I'll be fine," Sudbury said grimly. "At worst I'll get a few more scars to add to my collection."

Without another word, Sudbury disappeared into the trees.

Mary sat down gingerly in the dew-wet grass. Fear seized her. She tried to control her breathing and keep her hands from shaking. She couldn't help Tom if she couldn't even control herself. He must be frightened and could be in pain. Could even be dead.

For a long time, the only sound was her own short, tense breathing.

Though she knew to expect noise from Sudbury's diversion, she had to stifle a scream when she heard more yelling, followed by great, booming crashes. The noise came from the shed.

It didn't take long for a response from the cottage—grunts, muffled curses, and the sound of a heavy lock. Mary's eyes were fixed on the front door, desperate to rescue Tom and, if she had time, to kill Bridget Jenkins with her own hands. She waited to see if John Martin emerged.

Mary held her breath as the door opened and she saw a slight figure in a brown dress step out. She expected to see Bridget's bright golden curls, sure she had somehow snuck into the cabin from the shed. But instead she saw gray hair piled in a bun. Instead of Bridget's tall, proud step, she saw the bent shuffle of an older, sicker woman. No, it was not Bridget Jenkins leaving the cabin.

Mary covered her mouth to quiet her gasp, for below her, hood down and face turned to the sun, stood Agnes Shepherd.

CHAPTER 20

To make a water good for the passion of the heart and for
those that have taken thought and it is to be made only in
the month of May

> *Take four great handfuls of rosemary flowers, buds and*
> *all, and of sage, of elecampane roots, being scraped and*
> *sliced, and of thyme that is blown, of each of these two*
> *good handfuls, and of primrose flowers, and cowslip flow-*
> *ers a platterful, and of violet flowers, bugloss flowers, and*
> *borage flowers, the like quantity; of dried red rose leaves*
> *two handfuls, and put thereto as much of balm, as there*
> *is of all the rest . . .*

Mary sat, frozen. Agnes was not dead. Agnes was alive and standing in
front of the cottage.

Then the sound Mary feared the most pierced the silence again:
Tom, her own Tom, crying in agony. A great and horrible rage filled
her. Her mind buzzed and her body acted on its own accord, her feet
carrying her toward the cottage. Fortunately she maintained control;
she knew she had to be quiet, quiet as death, or she'd put Tom in even
more danger.

Mary slid down the slippery grass of the swale, behind a large rock, to watch Agnes walking toward the woods near the shed with a large, vicious blade in her hand.

Mary waited a few more minutes after she could no longer see Agnes, then went to the cottage door.

As Mary got closer, she noticed strange smells coming from inside. She detected smoke and the smell of cookery—mallow and holy oak, probably, and burning dung. But she picked up a metallic scent, too, along with the earthy and unpleasant odor of hellebore. She gagged.

She took a step into the cottage, but all she could discern were large, ominous shadows, as though she were seeing underwater. A small fire flickered in the corner, but it seemed to give off more smoke than light, and a cauldron suspended above it blocked what little illumination the flames cast. Mary took another step in. As her eyes adjusted, she took in the horrific scene. The sunshine streaming in from the door fell on an array of knives and scalpels laid out on a black cloth and coated with blood. Next to the cloth were dozens of glass bottles arranged in bunches. Mary guessed at least one of them was a bezoar extract.

In the opposite corner, a board stood upright, as though it were blocking something.

Or hiding it.

The too-familiar metallic tang of blood grew stronger, and Mary caught the stench of rotting flesh. She pulled a handkerchief over her mouth and tried not to gag as she walked over to the board and, trembling, peered behind it. She saw nothing but a bare corner and some stray pieces of crockery.

Then, right next to her ear, she heard a small, high voice groan.

Mary jumped back, heart pounding, arms crossed over her face. She was ready to claw, bite, and kick anything that came near her.

But there was nothing.

She lowered her arms and peered at the backside of the board. She saw a lump in the middle, covered by a thick embroidered cloth.

Hands trembling violently, Mary reached over and, in a swift motion, pulled at one end of the cloth.

Hidden underneath was Tom, unconscious.

Mary bit her fist to keep from crying out. Tom was strapped to the board, his arms pinned on each side, his torso slumped in the middle.

Like Christ on the cross, she thought.

Tom's head lolled to the side with his eyes closed. Mary sobbed and felt for his pulse—it was strong, but Tom was unresponsive.

Expertly knotted cord held Tom to the board. Mary frantically worked at the knots for several long minutes, her tears mixing with the sweat and blinding her. The knots were so tight, she feared using a knife to cut them.

Tom remained eerily silent.

Finally Mary gave up. She needed help. She needed to go get Sudbury.

Mary leaned over and pressed a kiss to Tom's brow. "I will return soon, I promise."

She hurried to the door, gave a quick look around outside, and saw nobody. She took a deep breath and just as Mary stepped into the sun, she felt a sharp stab at the back of her neck, not strong enough to pierce her skin, but painful nonetheless.

"Well, look who I found," a female voice said softly. "If it ain't the Fawcett bitch."

Mary didn't have to look behind her to know it was Bridget Jenkins.

Bridget pushed the knife in a little farther. "We're going to go to the shed now, and you aren't going to make a peep or I'll slit your pretty throat."

Mary swallowed her rage. She had to stay calm to save Tom. She allowed Bridget to guide her to the shed. After they'd walked through the rough door, Bridget closed it softly.

"Sudbury, I know you're in here!" she said in a loud whisper. "I have your lady love with me, and I will happily kill her if you try to hurt me."

Mary tensed up to tackle Bridget, but Sudbury, as if sensing her intent, immediately emerged from the shadows.

Bridget looked at Mary and sneered. "You may not believe this, but I just saved your life."

Mary snorted, then immediately regretted it as the knife grazed the flesh near her pulse.

Bridget laughed. "Yes, I know, Mary, you would like to think that I am the cause of all your woes. You don't like me. Believe me, I feel the same about you. But know this: I would never hurt a child. I can't say the same for your good friend Agnes Shepherd."

Mary bit back the curses she longed to spit in Bridget's face. She needed to get back to Tom.

She steadied her voice. "What do you know?"

"Agnes took Hopkins, or what was left of him, to a copse of trees beyond that field. Those two footmen from Chamberlen Manor? Agnes has been paying them for months. They dragged John Martin here." She gave a short, bitter laugh. "They'll regret that soon enough, if they haven't already paid with their lives.

"Your brother hasn't been here long, but she's already drugged him and plans to 'experiment' on him, as well." Bridget's voice became gruff. "No child should suffer the fate of Matthew Hopkins and John Martin."

She cleared her throat and pointed the knife at Sudbury. "Now that you've made such a fuss out here, she'll carry out her plans even sooner."

Bridget put her knife away.

Mary felt her chin tremble. She mustn't cry, not here, not now.

"Are you going to start bawling like a baby? How useless you are. If not for that poor boy in there, I'd have left you to your fate. It'd be what you deserve."

"And why is that?" Mary said, lifting her chin in the air. "Unlike you, I have committed no sins."

"Hush, both of you!" Sudbury called out. "There will be time for your squabbles later. Right now, Tom needs you."

Bridget nodded reluctantly, and Mary looked at the ground, ashamed.

"How do you know all this?" Mary asked.

Bridget grimaced. "I've been watching Agnes since you two left for London. During her trial, I was sure she would either die in that jail or swing on the end of a rope, so I helped her escape. We disguised her and bribed the jailer to leave the cell door open and tell everybody that the gravediggers had taken the body. That was before she told me everything she's done."

"Why have you turned on her now?"

Bridget spit on the ground. "You're not the only one who's lost a loved one, Mary Fawcett."

Sudbury laid a hand on Bridget's arm. "Henry Chamberlen?" he asked.

Bridget shrugged his hand off and wiped at her eyes. "I seem doomed to love other women's husbands.

"She killed Chamberlen, too, you know," she continued. "It was she who poisoned him. He was a bastard, but he treated me good, the only one who ever did. I couldn't help myself. I loved him. And I may not have your book learning, Mary, but I'm loyal as they come. So I started watching her after you left. I wanted to see what she was up to."

She took a shuddering breath. "Things were different after I helped her escape. She used to teach me about herbs and healing, but she started telling me all manner of strange things, about stones and angels and her dead child, Grace. Then she ignored me altogether."

Mary felt abashed. Had her resentment of Bridget blinded her to Agnes's doings? What else might she have missed?

Mary and Bridget eyed each other warily.

"What do you know about Simon? Do you know where he is?"

"What, did he go looking for his father? Pfft, why bother? John Martin is a bastard, and I would gladly dig his grave for him."

"And I would throw the first handful of dirt," Mary added. She and Bridget briefly shared a look, a reluctant camaraderie.

Bridget broke eye contact first. "Agnes won't be distracted from her plans for long."

"Now or never, then," Sudbury said. He pulled out the knife from his belt. "Bridget, you keep watch. Mary, you stay here and I'll go in and get Tom."

Sudbury turned to go, and Mary grabbed his arm and tugged him backward.

"The devil take me if I stay here safe while my brother is trapped in that house, scared and alone. I'll need your knife. That woman can tie a sturdy knot, and your knife is sharper than mine. You keep watch with Bridget while I go in. If I don't come back shortly, come to the cottage."

Sudbury started to object, but Mary cut him off.

"It has to be me. Tom won't willingly go with anybody else, and we can't risk him balking or crying out."

Sudbury nodded reluctantly. He handed her the knife. "Be safe."

Mary set her shoulders and walked to the house, careful to avoid any sticks or leaves that would snap or crack. Her hope that their plan might work grew with every step toward the cottage.

She entered and walked as softly as she could to the board that bore her brother. Her heart was racing. She expected the worst.

She found him with his head bent at an unnatural angle, staring right at her.

"You're back," Tom said in a singsong voice. "But you're just a ghost like the last one. You're not real. You're not my Mary."

"Oh, Tom," Mary cried as she rushed to his side, sobbing. Tom's eyes widened.

"You didn't talk before. But that doesn't matter. You must still be a ghost."

Mary sobbed as she brushed his hair off his forehead. "My sweet little boy. What has she done to you?"

Mary ran her finger across the dark marks on Tom's shoulders. They were not raised or enflamed, which meant Agnes had only drawn the symbols, not burned them onto his skin. Not yet.

She recognized two of the symbols on his arms and stomach. They were the same alchemical marks she had seen in Chamberlen's diary. Agnes planned to brand them on Tom, she was sure.

"Mary?" Tom buried his head in Mary's shoulder. "Mary, is it really you?"

"Yes, Tom. Yes, it's me, your sister—me, your Mary."

Mary would never, for as long as she lived, forget Tom's sobs of fear and relief.

She held him for a few moments before reluctantly pulling back.

"Tom, we have to get out of here before she returns."

"Mary, was that really Mrs. Shepherd? I thought she died. Is she a ghost? She's a very mean ghost. She says nice things to me, but I think if she were really nice, she wouldn't have brought me here and made me drink that nasty tea."

"I don't know, Tom." Mary didn't think twice about the deception. "Perhaps she is a ghost, or maybe even the devil pretending to be Mrs. Shepherd, in which case you need to be very quiet so we can hide you away safely."

Tom nodded and closed his eyes. He looked to be unconscious again. With trembling fingers, Mary used Sudbury's knife to saw through the cruel cords that held Tom to the board. Sudbury's knife was sharp and thin, making the job easier, but she still had to be careful not to cut into Tom's tiny wrists. Mary resisted the urge to massage the blood back into his hands. There would be time for healing later, when they were out of danger.

She had almost untethered the first strap when a horrible croaking sound issued up from somewhere around her heels. She looked down and saw, to her despair, Greedyguts cawing happily in greeting. He began flapping wildly and hopping about, jerking his head left and right.

Agnes stood in the doorway, staring at her with a mixture of sadness and pity.

"Mary," she said, shaking her head. "How I wish you had not come today."

Agnes held out her arm and gave Greedyguts the signal to come to her. The crow ignored her, gave a shriek, and flew up to the rafters. He turned his head sideways to stare at Mary as Agnes scolded him.

"Ridiculous bird," Agnes muttered. "I don't know what has gotten into him."

"How could you, Agnes?" Mary asked. "How could you do any of it?"

"Oh, Mary," she said softly. "If you knew what I know, had lived the life I've lived, you would understand. So much has been taken from me."

Agnes read the confusion on Mary's face. She went to the fire and stirred the pot set atop it.

"Grace," she said simply. "My Grace was taken away from me, ripped from my bosom."

Mary tried to make her voice gentle. "Agnes, Grace died of small-pox. You did all this because you're angry at God Himself?"

Agnes gave a bitter laugh. "Oh, I am furious with God, as well. But no. Grace was not taken by God but by man. One man, specifically. Henry Chamberlen, he took my girl from me."

Mary shook her head in confusion. "Why would you think that? Why would he do such a thing? Did he even know her?"

"She was his daughter."

Mary froze.

"I know it seems impossible, but I was young once, too. Only ten or so years older than Henry. He took me to his bed, shortly before his marriage and about a year before Mr. Shepherd died. Lord knows I went willingly enough. My husband had been ill for some time. Far too ill to lie with me. Henry was young and hot blooded, and he yearned to learn the secrets of the bedchamber. He got me with child. My husband knew the child was not his—he had not visited my bed in almost a year when Grace came along. When the scrofula carried him off, he took his revenge by giving all his possessions to the church. He left me penniless."

Agnes grew quiet, lost in memories of the past. Mary feared that when she returned to the present, she would continue in her mad experiment. She needed to keep Agnes talking until Sudbury and Bridget arrived.

"That must have been very hard," she said softly, sympathy filling her words.

Agnes looked up. "Grace was less than a year old when my husband died, Mary. We were starving. Grace couldn't stop whimpering from hunger. I went to Henry Chamberlen, begged him to give us some money, anything to help us survive. I thought it was the very least he would do for his own flesh and blood. But I misjudged. When I went to Chamberlen Manor, his new wife answered the door. I was hooded and wore a scarf high on my neck, so she didn't recognize me—but she saw Grace in my arms and suspected something. She called Henry to the door. He was furious with me. He threw us out into the cold. I went to the church, and Reverend Osborne gave us some money and some soup, and in return I gave his wife a salve for a rash. She put the word out that I was a healer, and that saved us."

"But, Agnes, Grace died of smallpox when she was thirteen years old. The child you describe was just a babe. How could Chamberlen have killed her?"

"I swore I would never ask him for a thing again. I swore it, Mary. How could I face that monster after he'd thrown us out into the cold to our death? But when Grace got sick, I swallowed my pride. Once more I made my way to Chamberlen Manor to beg for just a little money to buy the ingredients I needed to make medicine for her. This time I was careful, and I waited until Mrs. Chamberlen was in London. But I had no better luck. Henry beat me. Left me black and blue. Luckily Grace was at home, or he would have beaten her as well."

"But what has that to do with"—Mary gestured to the foul evidence of death all around the cabin—"with all this?" At first, Mary had simply been trying to keep Agnes talking to stall her, but now she wanted answers to the questions swirling in her head.

"It was then I swore I would have my revenge. He was a terrible man, Mary. And he did terrible things. Oh, I watched him carefully, waiting for the right time. I roamed his rooms after I delivered medicine to his wife—I told her to keep my visits a secret, that he'd be furious she wasn't consulting with a London doctor. I read his diary. Not the one you found in London—that just had his recipes. No, I read the diary in which he kept his most brilliant thoughts and ideas. Sudbury has told you of Henry's interest in alchemy. He found out about Sudbury's research, thought it was brilliant. But he didn't think Sudbury had gone far enough. He felt the bezoar needed to be cooked in a more purified vessel than the vulgar air."

Mary knew what was coming next. "A human vessel."

Agnes cocked an eyebrow. "You have been paying attention. Chamberlen was too much of a coward to try a human body, at least at first. He practiced on animals. Initially, I thought he was filled with delusions, but then I realized that God had led me to him to learn his secrets. And then"—she shrugged—"to kill him."

"But I saw the note by Chamberlen's body. He died by self-slaughter."

"I forged it. And every word in it was true. The man led a life full of sin and misdeeds."

"So you did the same? You've tried his experiments yourself!" Mary shook her head. "And that pig corpse—you put that in my bed?"

"Oh, heavens no, that corpse was far too heavy for me to lift! But yes, I did hire some boys to put it there. I wanted to scare you, Mary, to keep you from Bicknacre. I was trying to protect you by keeping you away from Hopkins until I could deal with him."

"This is madness, Agnes," Mary said. She kept her voice neutral. "But you don't have to continue in this. You can stop now, and we can help you."

Agnes chuckled. "Ah, my dear, I believe it's a little too late for that."

She walked over to another angled board, one Mary hadn't noticed earlier in the gloom, and turned it ever so slightly. Mary gasped.

There lay the naked body of John Martin, his arms and legs splayed, stiff and blue.

His was the foul odor in the mix. His corpse the smell that made Mary gag. Mary walked forward, legs shaking so violently she thought she might tumble, and took in the awful details of his condition. His skin had turned waxy, and his head lolled to the side, his engorged tongue sticking out. It made him look like a cheeky youth. How strange that Martin should look so boyish in death.

Then Mary registered the most horrifying details. His belly was blistered and burned, and on his stomach, shining faintly in the light of the fire, she could see alchemical symbols—etched out in what Mary thought might be blood. Across the bottom of his abdomen, at hip level, was a large surgical gash in the form of an X.

A wave of nausea swept over her, and she feared she would vomit. She put her sleeve over her nose again and took several deep breaths.

"He was a terrible man, but I really thought I might not have to use him. I thought my work on Hopkins might do it," she said. "I kept the witchfinder drugged until I was ready to experiment on him—he felt no more pain than he inflicted on me. I fed him the bezoar extract, heated his stomach, did everything right, but nothing happened. I had to keep him alive, of course, or it never would have worked." A note of frustration entered her voice. "I cut in so carefully, searched so thoroughly, but could find no philosopher's stone. It should have gleamed like the sun and shone like the moon. But all I found was this."

Agnes reached over to the makeshift table next to the instruments and picked up a glass flask. Inside was a grayish, round mass. "Kidney stones," she said with disgust.

Mary noticed a flask sitting nearby holding another object. "Agnes, that is the token I left with you, the one I took from Chamberlen's hand."

Agnes tilted her head thoughtfully. "Yes, I've been intrigued by that medallion since you showed it to me. I thought it must be a part of Chamberlen's experiments. I placed it in Hopkins's abdomen, but it didn't work. The stone needs more coction, more time to reach its perfect state." Her voice took on a singsong quality. She was breaking with reality. "It needed a better vessel. Purer. Younger."

"And so you snuck into the house after we had all started looking for John Martin. That's why you took Tom," Mary said. She couldn't believe what she was hearing. "You are willing to kill him for this damned stone?"

Agnes looked at Mary in surprise. "My dear, of course he will be fine! He's like a son to me! That's the entire reason I practiced so thoroughly on Hopkins. You must admit they deserved their deaths. No, I'll give Tom enough medicine so he won't feel a thing, and then I'll use the stone to bring him back to life." She gave Mary an accusatory stare. "After all these years, how can you think I would hurt that boy? What kind of monster do you think I am?"

"I had thought you were a dead monster," Mary replied.

"Ah, yes, I'm sorry about that. I thought you might worry. But that is enough, Mary." Agnes walked with great confidence over to the fireplace. Mary stood, frozen, unsure what to do. Were Sudbury and Bridget nearby? Had they heard all this? When did they plan to make their presence known?

Agnes reached out and grabbed one of the knives arrayed on the black cloth. Mary trembled.

"What are you doing, Agnes?" She started inching toward Tom.

"Stay where you are," Agnes barked out. She sharpened the knife on a nearby whetstone and walked over to the board where Tom hung. "If you come closer, I shall have to kill him, and I really don't want to do that. He will be fine, my dear—better than fine! He will be the first to benefit from the great philosopher's stone! It will heal him of his limp and he will be stronger than any man alive. This is my legacy to him."

Mary froze.

Agnes motioned to her. "Now walk over there very slowly and grab that rope. Bring it to me."

Mary did as she was told, giving the rope to Agnes with hands trembling violently.

"Turn around."

Just as soon as Mary had her back turned, Agnes grabbed her wrists in a viselike grasp. She used her other hand to put the knife in her mouth, and then tied a quick, strong knot. She kicked the backs of Mary's knees, and Mary fell to the straw-covered ground.

Tears sprang to Mary's eyes. They were tears of frustration, not self-pity. How was she to help her brother? Would she be forced to watch him suffer, to die in front of her while she lay, impotent, on the floor?

Agnes walked toward Tom. Mercifully, his eyes remained closed, his body motionless. Mary hoped to God he was unconscious.

She watched in horror as Agnes consulted a book set on a stand nearby. She recognized the cover. It was Agnes's recipe book. This must have been why she'd kept it hidden, under lock and key, in her floorboards.

Agnes lifted the knife, ready to carve into Tom's stomach. Mary whimpered and pleaded, "Agnes, please, have mercy!"

Before the knife could pierce Tom's skin, Mary heard a shriek and saw a swirl of motion and bright hair, and the knife fell to the ground.

Bridget had Agnes in a chokehold, her own knife pressed against Agnes's ear.

Sudbury arrived a moment after, breathless. He took in the scene and breathed a sigh of relief.

"Oh, Bridget, you've always been courageous," Agnes said. She looked unperturbed by the sharp knife pressing into her skin. "You are still, however, as much a fool as ever. When will you learn to control your temper?"

Bridget looked at her with disdain. "I hardly think you're in a position to lecture me now," she said. "I am, after all, the one holding the knife."

"Yes, but not for long." Agnes looked up into the rafters and made a gesture. Immediately, in a blur of feathers and raucous cawing, Greedyguts swooped down and pecked at Bridget's hands until she let go to protect herself. A scrabble ensued, and Agnes emerged, triumphantly holding the knife. She hurried to Tom and lay the knife next to his neck.

Bridget collected herself and frowned. "I hate that godforsaken bird," she muttered.

"Not, I think, as much as he hates you," Agnes replied. "Now, take that rope and tie up Mary's beau over there. And do it nice and tight, or I'll know. And if you fuss, Mr. Sudbury, I shall have to kill my darling Mary. I don't think you'd like to have another young woman's death on your conscience."

After Bridget had finished tying up Sudbury, and Agnes had inspected her work, she ordered Bridget to sit in a chair by the fire. "If you move, I'll direct Greedyguts to peck out your eyes. But if you are a good girl and sit still, you may stay and watch my great work. You and Mary may be my pupils yet."

Agnes adjusted the recipe book. "You should have taken this when you had the chance, Mary."

Agnes turned to a page at the end of the book and began reciting something in a low voice. Sudbury looked up in shock.

"She's still trying to make the stone," Mary explained. "The philosopher's stone. She's reading the instructions for cooking the bezoar."

As they looked on helplessly, Agnes laid the knife down. Mary hoped Bridget would take the opportunity to tackle Agnes, but it seemed Agnes's threat had worked—Bridget was eyeing Greedyguts in fear. Agnes picked up two glass flasks. She poured a gelatinous substance from an earthenware vessel into the flask containing the medallion. "You know," she said as she turned toward them and gave a thoughtful look, "I'm glad of your company. An occasion such as this should be witnessed."

She swirled the mixture in the flask a few times and put it over the fire. As she did so, a reddish smoke began to rise and swirl.

"The Red Dragon!" she said triumphantly. "This is the last step of the Great Work. You see it, don't you, Mr. Sudbury? You see what I have accomplished!"

Mary turned to look at Sudbury and was shocked at the look of interest on his face. Agnes also noticed.

She raised an eyebrow. "You want to know how I did it, don't you, Mr. Sudbury? You want to know how I achieved this stage of the process." She looked thoughtful for a moment. "I'll tell you, but I want something in return."

Sudbury looked at her warily. Panic struck Mary. Surely he wouldn't betray them, she thought. But did she really know how much his life's work meant to him?

Bridget shrieked, "You fool! Do not listen to her lies—she has no special knowledge!"

A look of fury crossed Agnes's face, and she raised her hand as though to slap Bridget, but her fist fell, twitching, to her side. "Be quiet, Bridget. What do you know of these things?"

"I don't believe you. It's a false result," Sudbury said. "I've attained that step myself. Something is missing. All your work has been for nothing."

"You lie," Agnes sneered.

"Prove it. Why test it on this boy when you could test it on me? Let him go, and I will work with you, share my knowledge with you."

Mary felt the tears prick her eyes again. She was wrong. Sudbury wasn't tempted by the wisdom of the alchemists. He was trying to save Tom's life.

Agnes snorted. "I am not such a fool."

"You think I don't know what this stone can do? Why waste that power on a simple boy? You can test it on me, and when I have absorbed the power of the stone, I will do the same for you."

"You lie!" Agnes screamed, and she threw an empty glass bottle at Sudbury's head, missing him by only a few inches.

Mary had never seen Agnes like this. It wasn't the elements in the vessel that had transformed, it was Agnes's soul. "Why are you doing this?" Mary wailed. "Agnes, please, what are you doing? How can this possibly be worth all this pain?"

Mary's voice seemed to soothe Agnes, and she returned to some semblance of sanity. She took a deep breath and moved to the fire. She picked up a long-handled spoon and began stirring the substance propped above the flames. "Chamberlen, the bastard, only wanted gold and power, but I learned more of his secrets. I want the power to converse with the angels. Imagine, Mary, a chance to talk with my sweet Grace, to sing her a lullaby, to tell her I love her."

Mary couldn't contain her sob. Agnes caused all this pain and death just for the chance of talking with her beloved daughter. Mary glanced over at the board to which Tom was still bound. Could she say what she wouldn't do if Tom died? Or if she had a chance to talk with Jack once more? To embrace her father and feel her mother's smooth hand on her cheek? To rock her sweet baby girl just one more time?

Mary looked at Agnes with tears running down her cheeks. "Oh, Agnes."

"I knew you'd understand, my dear."

Mary and Agnes looked at each other for a long moment, once again sharing the bond of friendship forged over the years.

And then Agnes grabbed the knife. "So you understand what I must do. Don't worry, I promise to bring him back." She moved toward Tom.

"No!" Mary cried.

She felt the same surge of energy as she had on the street by the Woodses' house, when she somehow managed to choke Stearne before he could take Tom.

That was it! She had no idea what kind of magic she had used to strangle Stearne. She hadn't wanted to think about how she had done it. She had no desire to repeat it. That kind of power was dangerous. But once again Tom was in danger. She needed to conjure it again. For Tom.

She closed her eyes and imagined what Agnes was feeling. She rocked back and forth as she felt the crushing sadness of Agnes's loneliness and her craving for Grace. Then she reached out to make a connection with Agnes.

"What is she doing?" Bridget asked Sudbury.

"Remember what happened before, with Stearne?" he whispered.

Though Mary's eyes were closed, she knew that Agnes faltered, that she slowed her footsteps and lowered the knife. Mary opened her eyes just long enough to see Agnes reach out a hand and touch Tom's cheek instead.

And then, with a great scream, Agnes severed the bond with Mary.

Mary hadn't experienced this resistance with Stearne. Did Agnes share Mary's strange power?

"It's not working," she said. She felt the sweat on her brow from the force of her concentration.

"You'd better make it work if you want to save your brother," Bridget shouted.

Sudbury reached back with his tied hands to touch Mary's fingertips. "Mary," he said, "have you ever tried to use your gift with animals?"

Of course! Greedyguts was waiting in the rafters just above them. "No. But I'll try now." Mary's voice shook.

Mary conjured a mental picture of the crow, remembering the day she and Tom had found him, bloody and near death, on the road, the small band of bullies standing nearby with rocks in their hands. She heard herself scaring the boys away, yelling at them to go home. She saw Tom's shadow as he bent down and gently petted the crow's back. She felt the fear gripping the crow as Tom stroked his ruffled feathers, then the gentle relief flowing through his body when the boy's touch soothed. As though through a fog, she remembered applying a salve to the bird's wounds, recalling his growing strength as Tom fed him with a small spoon. Then she felt the animal sense of loyalty the crow had for her brother. And she reached out and connected with Greedyguts.

Mary swayed back and forth as she and Greedyguts communed. It was the strangest thing she had ever felt—everything in the room came into the sharpest focus, and time itself seemed to warp and condense. Then she sensed Greedyguts's confusion as he watched Agnes bring the knife up over Tom's chest, felt his driving need to save the young boy on the table. Somehow, she knew that she was simultaneously herself and Greedyguts. She could feel her head whip back and strike at Agnes's eyes with precise force. She flexed her talons and, with a driving need, dragged them across Agnes's face as Tom's small, high voice called out, "Mary? Where are you, Mary?"

Mary collapsed as the connection with Greedyguts disappeared with no warning. She felt Bridget cutting the ropes at her wrists and then freeing Sudbury, who ran to Agnes and held her hands behind her back in a tight grip.

Mary shook her head and took a deep breath, filing away these memories and feelings to study later. She and Bridget rushed to Tom and gently worked to free him of the ropes tying him to the board, soothing him with soft words. When he whimpered in pain, Sudbury bound Agnes's wrists even tighter, ignoring her rage-filled howls. By the time they had freed Tom and he'd stumbled away from the board, Agnes had grown silent.

It took some time for Tom to come fully to his senses, and what he did next Mary would never forget in all her days.

Tom walked over to Greedyguts, who still stood by Agnes. Her eyes were bloodied, and deep scratches from Greedyguts's claws ran crisscross, from ear to ear and forehead to mouth, like the warp and weft of a cloth. Tom whispered something to the bird. As he approached, Agnes turned her head to the side. Tom bent and gently placed a kiss on Agnes's cheek.

Sudbury, nervous to have Tom anywhere near Agnes, squeezed her arms and she whimpered.

"Mr. Sudbury," Tom said softly, "please don't hurt Mrs. Shepherd. Everybody makes mistakes."

A sob—deep, wrenching, filled with the utter horror of a soul that recognizes its own twistedness—escaped from Agnes's belly.

"He is just like my Grace," she whispered.

But for one, they were the last words she would ever say.

With superhuman strength, Agnes twisted out of Sudbury's grasp and took hold of the knife. She ran to the book and threw it to Mary.

Then she grabbed the flask containing the medallion and held it out in one hand while her other held the knife poised over her breast.

"Run," she ordered them. Then she threw the contents of the flask into the fireplace and with both hands plunged the knife into her heart.

Mary rushed toward Agnes, her instinct still to protect her, but Sudbury pulled her back.

"Get the boy," Sudbury yelled to Bridget as he grabbed Mary's hand and began running. "That potion will explode!"

They made it to a small copse of trees before the boom. They all looked behind them to see the cottage engulfed in a ball of flame. Nothing, no one, could survive such a burst of fire. And shooting out of the flames, a comet of black against the deep blue sky, was Greedyguts.

CHAPTER 21

To make a salve called Gratia Dei

Take half a pound of rosin, so much of sheep's tallow, set them upon the fire, with a quart of fayre water, and when it is melted, put into it of barrel soap, half a quarter of a pound, then let it boil well the space of half a quarter of an hour . . .

The group assembled in the graveyard was small, but nobody expected any different, as hated as John Martin was.

Simon and Verity stood on one side of the freshly dug grave, Mary and Sudbury on the other. Verity held her brother's arm for support. Reverend Osborne intoned the funeral mass from a few feet away, and behind him the gravediggers leaned on their shovels, looking bored.

Enough of John Martin's corpse had been found in the ruin of the cottage to warrant a coffin and a burial. The footmen hired by Agnes had fled, sure they would be blamed for his death. From his charred corpse, the constable couldn't determine whether he'd died from a blow to the head or Agnes's knife, and it didn't matter much to anyone in Bicknacre.

They couldn't imagine asking Verity to prepare John Martin's body for burial, so two of the women he had hated most—Mary and Mrs. Woods—were the last to see him, exposed in all his naked humanity.

No bells were rung for John Martin, and no watch was kept.

There were no further questions about the death of Henry Chamberlen—it was clear to everyone that Agnes had killed him and that her horrific secrets had died with her.

As for Matthew Hopkins: nobody searched for him, and when a hunter found a skeleton in the forest some months later, picked clean and surrounded by black feathers, no one asked any questions.

After the burial mass—terse and cold—the gravediggers came forward, and each grabbed a loop of the rope secured around the coffin. But before they could begin lowering John Martin into the cold ground, Verity stepped forward.

"Stop," she cried. "I have not yet shown my father the full extent of my respect."

Verity stepped forward and spit on the pine box and then turned and walked away.

Simon looked up, and Mary could see that his eyes were dry. He had not shed a tear. Simon turned to the gravediggers. "Continue," he said, and he followed his sister home.

❦

Later that night, Sudbury and Mary sat next to the cheerful fireplace at the Woodses' house, set off a bit from the laughter and chatter of the others. They had gathered together—Sudbury, Mary, the Woods family, Mrs. Chamberlen, and even Bridget Jenkins—to share dinner and each other's company. Tom lay asleep in Mrs. Chamberlen's lap. She looked tired, but a deep happiness shone in her eyes when Tom scrambled up into her arms.

The horrible events of the previous day hovered like a dark cloud on the horizon. But for tonight, gathered together, they would ignore it.

"It's a pity Simon and Verity didn't wish to come," Mary said. She sorted a tub of elderberries for drying, grateful she had the work to concentrate on.

Sudbury nodded. "I can't blame them, though I wish they didn't feel such shame about their father. They cannot be held responsible for his actions."

"Reverend Osborne has told them as much," Mary replied. "And he and his wife have again offered Verity a home. She doesn't know whether to accept it or to live with Simon, but it gives her a great deal of comfort to know she still has friends in the village."

Sudbury turned to her and said softly, "About that . . ."

Mary slanted a curious look at him.

Sudbury coughed into his hand. "Do you? Do you feel you still have friends in Bicknacre?"

"Well, of course!" Mary replied. "Look around. The most precious people in my life are in this room." She chuckled and looked at Bridget. "Some perhaps less precious than others, but I'm working on that."

Sudbury laughed. "I admire your generous spirit. She's had a hard life, but her heart is good, I think."

"Why do you ask if I still have friends here?"

Sudbury looked into the fire. "Mary, I'm leaving Bicknacre. Bradford has invited me to live at his home. You know I only came here to keep an eye on Henry Chamberlen, and now that he's dead . . ."

Mary's heart fell. She focused on sorting the berries. "Now that he's dead, you have no reason to stay."

"No," Sudbury replied. "That's not true. I have one reason." He looked at her meaningfully. "Mary, if you were to leave with me, you and Tom, we could . . . well, we could be happy, I think. I am eager to return to my studies, and Bradford said he's looking for a partner. We could hire the finest tutors for Tom. Or we could send him to the finest schools. I am quite rich, you know."

Mary set the tub of elderberries to the side. "You would woo me with promises for my brother?"

Sudbury chuckled. "Only because I know you too well. I admire your fierce loyalty to Tom and the love you bear for him. But London

253

holds opportunities for you as well, Mary. You can continue with your healing and your cookery, continue making discoveries that will help people. I can introduce you to those who have similar knowledge and can teach you, guide you in your studies. I am sure Mrs. Chamberlen would welcome you and Tom at Chamberlen House."

Her first instinct was to say no, to stay safe in Bicknacre, to cling to her recipes and her duties. But her heart pounded, and anticipation and ambition roiled her belly. Why choose the drudgery and suspicion in Bicknacre over the exhilaration of London? She remembered the giddiness she felt in the streets of the city, the way her mind raced when discussing ideas with Sudbury and Bradford. She recalled her fascination with the hustle and bustle of St. Paul's—what other wonders might await her?

She felt the thrill of the unknown, the intoxication of the possible, and not just of what she might experience but what she might become. What unexplored abilities and powers could she discover? What if she allowed herself to dare?

Mary looked into Robert's face. His eyes were guarded, and she could see a blush rising below his scars.

"You make an appealing offer, and yet something is not quite right."

Sudbury's face fell. "I understand," he said. "It would be hard to live with this face."

He looked up in surprise at the disgusted snort from Mary.

"Honestly, Robert Sudbury, you must be the vainest man I've ever met."

"Likely, but what do you mean, Mary?"

"You have said nothing of affection."

Sudbury sucked in his breath. "Is that something you want from me?" He ran his hand through his hair. "You are brilliant and beautiful, and I would do anything to keep you near me for as long as you'll allow."

Mary took a deep, trembling breath.

"Very well, that will do," she replied in a teasing voice. "I am no poet. I will need more time to discover how I feel and put it into words. But yes. Yes, I want to come to London with you."

As she said it, she felt her world tilt. This was what she had been craving. This felt right.

Sudbury grabbed both her hands and squeezed. "Shall we tell everyone?"

"Not yet," Mary said. "I can't give you a decision until I know what Tom wants. I can't take him away from the village unless he wants to go. I can't separate him from all he has ever known."

The next day bloomed with what now felt like precious normalcy. Mary had returned to her cookery, mixing a poultice of ox dung and mallow to apply to the scalp to slow balding. Tom sat on the floor, practicing his letters, Greedyguts watching him from the door.

Mary had not slept all night, thinking about Sudbury's proposal.

She thought about the buzzing excitement of London, the way she felt alive and alit walking the streets of the city, how the crowds at St. Paul's had pulled her in with their endless variety and fascination.

Mary set down her wooden spoon. "Tom?"

"Mmmm," Tom answered, distracted.

"Do you like living in Bicknacre?"

Tom looked up at Mary. "No. I hate it."

Mary was shocked. "Why?"

"Nobody helped us when we were in jail, Mary. Only Mr. Sudbury and Mr. and Mrs. Woods and Mrs. Chamberlen. None of the people you help, nobody from church. They just . . . they just let that witch-finder hurt us."

Mary pulled Tom onto her lap.

"Well, my dear, I might have a plan for us . . ."

Three weeks later, Mary had cleared out her cottage and sent everything she cared to keep to London. She and Tom would keep the small cottage, she decided, so they could return to visit their friends. Reluctant to leave it standing empty, however, she offered Bridget the use of it. They would make their home in London at Chamberlen House while Sudbury stayed with Mr. Bradford. Mrs. Chamberlen was thrilled she would have their company, and in return, Mary could care for her as her cancer progressed.

As she walked through the village one last time with Tom and Robert, Mary stopped at the gallows on which she had seen Mr. Grandley's pig dangling. It was bare now, stark and ominous. No ghastly flesh hung from the rope; no smell of death attacked the nose. No crowds pushed to see the spectacle. Only wooden beams, a raised floor, and some rough-hewn steps. And yet it terrified Mary.

She shuddered.

Tom grabbed her hand and Sudbury resettled her shawl on her shoulders. She took a deep breath and walked toward the coach that would take them to London, to life and light and learning. Bicknacre would always be her home—where she had loved her parents, her brother, her baby, and Jack; where Mr. and Mrs. Woods had shown her what neighbors could do and be; where the Osbornes had taught her what true charity could look like; and where Bridget had taught her the dangers of misjudging others and the importance of second chances.

And it was where she had learned so much from Agnes: improving her craft and honing her skills, certainly, but also about the terrible beauty of being human and the awful risks of love.

She would put her lessons to good use.

ACKNOWLEDGMENTS

Writing a book is hard. Knowing what to do with that book is even harder.

I've been so very fortunate to have terrific guides to help me wander the strange, labyrinthine paths of putting a book out into the world.

Alicia Brooks of JVNLA has been an agent extraordinaire, providing guidance, assurance, encouragement, and the benefit of her deep and broad experience. Thank you so much for your faith in this book, Alicia!

At Lake Union, Erin Adair-Hodges and Jodi Warshaw have been spectacular editors. They worked their own kind of empathetic magic, somehow balancing enthusiastic reading with razor-sharp insight and editing. My thanks also to Kelley Frodel, Valerie Paquin, and Nicole Brugger-Dethmers: I am in awe of your eagle eyes and phenomenal attention to detail. To production manager Kyra Wojdyla: thank you for your marvelous organizational skills and stellar communication. Cassie Gonzalez: thank you for the gorgeous, evocative cover that perfectly captures the spirit of the book. (Greedyguts thanks you for the portrait, as well.) You all are wizards of the word and image, and I'm so grateful to the entire team at Lake Union.

I never would have discovered the wild, wonderful world of historical recipes without Dr. Lisa Smith, who invited me to contribute to the academic blog *The Recipes Project*. I owe her and the other editors at the time—Dr. Amanda Herbert, Dr. Elaine Leong, and Dr. Laurence Totelin—a huge debt of gratitude for welcoming me into that brilliant community.

With great love to my whole family: thank you. To Tim: Your love, patience, and sage advice have kept me going these many years. You are the very best person I know. To Lucy and Miriam: You two inspire, enlighten, and entertain me every day. I'm so lucky to be your mom.

To Teresa Stover, my first and best beta reader: I can't thank you enough, T, for the insights, the cheering on, the shoulder to cry on, and the endless cups of coffee. Your friendship is a gift.

To all of my dear friends: You've heard more about early modern healing recipes than any person should be forced to bear. I can't tell you how much your friendship means to me.

While I'm fascinated by early modern medicines and healing traditions, I owe my life and my children's lives to modern-day medicine. To all those who heal—and particularly to Dr. Tim Roberts, Dr. Megan Frost, Dr. Sandra Taylor, and Dr. Nathan Selden—thank you from the bottom of my heart.

And finally, thanks to you, readers, for spending time in Mary Fawcett's world.

AUTHOR'S NOTE

Dear reader,

Oh, I've been eager to write this note to you! Through the months and years I've been writing this book, the collective "you" have been whispering in my ear, asking questions. Here is my attempt to answer some of them.

Are these recipes real?

The recipes are real, though I have modernized some of the spelling and syntax. As you can see in Full Text and Sources for the Recipes, most are in digitized form at the Folger Shakespeare Library in a manuscript titled *A Book of Such Medicines as Have Been Approved by the Speciall Practize of Mrs Corlyon*. You can find information on accessing these recipes in the sources. Do yourself a favor and check out the collections. These recipes are wonderful and wild (to modern eyes), and, though most of them come from recipe collections of the gentry and nobility, they offer a unique insight into the daily lives and ways of thinking in seventeenth-century England. It's like a form of tourism—time travel you can experience from the comfort of your couch.

A wonderful crowdsourced collaboration made up of students, volunteers, and docents called "Shakespeare's World" has transcribed the sometimes difficult handwriting into text. (Mrs. Corlyon has some of the nicest handwriting I've seen in these recipe books, but even so, it can be rough going!) More information about the project can be found at www.zooniverse.org/projects/zooniverse/shakespeares-world.

Mary Fawcett

Mary Fawcett is my own creation, and I am inordinately fond of her. When I told others about Mary's skill set and recipes, some asked whether such things were possible—could Mary have read and written the recipes she used? It's a valid question—literacy was certainly not as widespread in seventeenth-century England as it would be in later centuries. The literacy rate is often cited as around 30 percent for adult men (around 50 percent for men in the middling class, such as successful farmers) and 10 percent for adult women. Some historians (see, for example, Mark Hailwood) have been revisiting that research, based as it was on studies of signatures conducted in the 1970s by David Cressy. The actual rate was likely higher. My interpretation is that it wouldn't be outlandish to encounter an intelligent woman, from a line of prosperous farmers and merchants, who'd been taught to keep her family's treasured records and recipes.

Who was Matthew Hopkins, and was he really that terrible?

Matthew Hopkins, the self-styled "Witchfinder General" who terrorizes Agnes and Mary, is a character based on the real Hopkins, a lawyer from Essex. He is said to have accused over 230 people of witchcraft and to have been responsible for the execution of over one hundred souls. When he died in 1647, rumors swirled that he himself had been tried as a witch, found guilty, and executed. The historical record is less devoted to poetic justice, however—he very likely died of tuberculosis. Those rumors did, however, inspire the final moments of Hopkins's life as set out in this novel.

What is the philosopher's stone?

The quest to find the philosopher's stone has obsessed alchemists for centuries and can be traced to ancient Greece, but the ideas of what constitutes the stone and the power it wields have never been static. The modern imagination associates the stone with turning lead into gold, but natural philosophers have had various opinions of its capabilities: some (such as John Dee) thought it allowed the philosopher to speak to angels, some that it had limitless capacity to heal or even bring people back to life. Some thought it was not one stone, but three, each with its own properties. As one can imagine with any object with such a mythic and storied history, the accretion of theories around the philosopher's stone has shifted with the culture, history, and religion of those pursuing it.

Some other notes:

The story of Verity Martin is inspired by the real-life story of Anne Gunter, a young woman who in 1604 fell ill and blamed her sickness on witchcraft. The historical Anne's story is even stranger than the fictional Verity's, and it's told beautifully by historian of witchcraft James Sharpe in *The Bewitching of Anne Gunter: A Horrible and True Story of Football, Witchcraft, Murder, and the King of England.*

FULL TEXT AND SOURCES FOR THE RECIPES IN *THE VILLAGE HEALER'S BOOK OF CURES*

Author's Note: I've taken the liberty of modernizing some of the language when I felt that the original would be confusing.

Chapter 1:

The way how to distill a pig, good for those that are weak and faint and yet not sick

Take a pig of twelve days old or thereabouts being scalded and washed, and take the four quarters and the feet thereof and wash them in a pint of white wine, one after another, and let them soak a little in the wine, then dry them with a dry cloth, and rub them over with a spoonful of salt. Then put them into a pewter pot or a pottle and lay half a handful of sage under them in the pot, then put thereto a pint of white wine, as much of fair water, an ounce of cinnamon, being broken in small pieces, 2 spoonfuls of wine vinegar, and as much sugar as a good apple. Put all these together into your pot and lay half a handful of sage high upon the top of all. Then stop up your pot close, as in the distillations going before, and so set it in a kettle of seething water, up to the neck and let it boil continually the space of 14 hours, and as the water wasteth, fill it up again with hot water, and when it hath boiled so long, pour it into a strainer and let it run without wringing, until it be run dry, then keep it, and give the party thereof warmed 5 or 6 spoonfuls at a time, and continue it as long as they list, and they shall find ease thereby.

Mrs Corlyon, p. 141

Chapter 2

A medicine for those that have lost their speech, either by sickness, fear, or otherwise

Take a primrose root, scrape it clean, then take a slice of the inner part of it, of a good thickness, and put it under the party's tongue, then anoint the noddle of his head, the nape of his neck and about his ears, and jaws, with the ointment for the palsy (you shall find it hereafter in this book), chafe it well, and lap a cloth about it, being but warmed, at the fire, and so lap it up close with sufficient cloths to keep it warm: dress him thus once in 12 hours and continue it as you shall see occasion: too much heat of the fire is hurtful to those that have the palsy, but warm is good.

Mrs Corlyon, pp. 41–42

Chapter 3

A special good drink for those that be given to melancholy and weeping

Take a quart of claret wine, put it into an earthen pipkin, add thereto half a pound of sugar, and so set it upon a very soft fire, and when it doth boil, and is clean skimmed, put thereto a quart of rosemary flowers, being clean picked, and half an ounce of cinnamon and so let them simmer softly together for the space of an hour, then take it off, and when it is cold, put it into a glass altogether, and drink thereof, with a little claret wine after meat, and when you go to bed. Note that if you do make it of dried flowers, a pint will serve, to a quart of wine.

Mrs Corlyon, p. 102

Chapter 4

A medicine, to cleanse the brain of corrupt matter, and to help those that have a stinking air at their noses, and to cleanse the lungs of such gross humors, as are distilled down from the putrefied head

Take a good quantity of rosemary leaves, and chew them lightly in your mouth, that the air may ascend into your head, and as you do this hold down your head and void the humors, out of your mouth, as they do fall: do this for the space of half an hour at a time, changing the leaves, as you shall see occasion, do this in the morning fasting, and two hours before you go to supper, and at every time, presently after you have taken this, eat the quantity of two walnuts of this receipt following. Take a good quantity of pennyroyal, shred it very small then mingle it with the best hard honey, and beat them together, until they be like a conserve, then keep it for your use, and eat of it, as is aforesaid, do this as you shall feel occasion. And when you have made an end with these, then you must have tents to up into your nose to open the conduits, and to draw down the corrupt matter, that offendeth you: make your tents of fine linen cloth, and small at the upper end, wet these tents in the juice of primrose leaves, and a little clarified butter, to make them to slip. Put these up into your nose, and let them stay there a pretty while, then take them out, and wet them again in the juice only, and put them in as before, this do for the space of half an hour at a time, use this for a good space, and it will help you.

Mrs Corlyon, p. 20

Chapter 5

To deliver a woman of a dead child

Take leek blades and scald them in hot water and bind them to her navel and she shall be delivered. Take them soon away, or they will cause her to cast all in her belly.

Medicinal and Cookery Recipes of Mary Baumfylde and Others, n.p.

Chapter 6

A recipe for puppy water

Take one young fat puppy and put him into a flat still, quartered, guts and all ye skin upon him, then put in a quart of new buttermilk, two quarts of white wine, four lemons purely pared and then sliced, a good handful of fumitory and agrimony, and three penny worth of camphire, a pint of fasting spittle which you must gather into a bottle beforehand, a handful of plantain leaves, six penny worth of ye best *venice turpentine* prepared with red rose water. Let all these be stilled in a very gentle fire under ye still and wet napkins continually upon ye head of your still. Let your water drop upon a little white sugar candy, as much as a nut is enough for a quart of water. Eighteen good pippins must be sliced in with ye puppy.

Mary Doggett's *Book of Receipts*, n.p.

Chapter 7

The admirable oil the virtues whereof are these. It maketh sound and healeth all wounds in short time, the sinnows being cut, it is good for any burning with fire, it easeth the passion of the stomach. It provoketh urine, it alayeth the pain of the bladder and lower parts of the belly and thighs, it is good for the morning in children for gouts and deafness

Take eight wine pints of old oil, two like pints of good white wine, eight handfuls of the buds of Saint-John's-wort, bruise it in a mortar and put them all in a glass stopped very close that no air get in, setting it in the sun two days. Then boil it in a cauldron of water so great that your glass may easily go into it and stuff it well with straw that it stir not in boiling. After it hath boiled half an hour, strain it and put to it new fresh buds of Saint-John's-wort as before. This must be done three or four times after so many boilings. After the last boiling strain it very hard and measure it, putting to every wine pint twelve ounces of the best venice turpentine, six ounces of the oil of almonds, dittander gentian, tormentil, *calamus aromaticus, carduus benedictus* of each four drams, red earthworms four washed in good white wine and slit, you must beat all the rest in a mortar but not the worms. Then put all together into the oil, adding to every pint three penny worth of English saffron whole, then put there too likewise two great handfuls of fresh buds of Saint-John's-wort bruised, so being mixed altogether then must you set it into the sun for the space of ten days or into an oven as soon as the bread is drawn. Then strain it into glasses well closed up and so keep it. The older it is the better it is.

Mrs Corlyon, pp. 258–259

Chapter 8

A receipt for the cure of the falling sickness

Take 3 ounces of dead men's skull which you may have at the apothecary's, 4 ounces of mistletoe of the oak, 4 ounces of red coral, 4 ounces of wood betony, let all these be wiped dry and clean, then dry them and beat them to fine powder and mix them together. This is to be given morning and evening first and last in 1 spoonful of posset ale during the time the fits do last and while it is upon them and when the fit begins to leave them and against every change and full of the moon for 2 or 3 days if they be young children by God's blessing it will cure. You must give at a time but as much as will lie upon a sixpence and take a little warm posset ale after it and give a little sugar to season the mouth after it and let them fast 2 hours after it instead of mixing it with posset, mix it with conserve of roses or clove, gillyflowers the bigness of a nutmeg and so drink 5 or 6 spoonfuls of black cherry water after it.

The Receipt Book of Catherine Bacon, p. 120

Chapter 9

A broth for those that are grieved with melancholy

Take the knuckles of mutton and chop them small and put them into a pipkin with three pints of water and set them on the fire, and let them boil until such time as the broth doth smell of the meat, and always as the scum doth arise take it off, and then put into it a chicken whole with all the appurtenances saving the small puddings, and then let it boil again, and scum it clean: put into it half a dozen leaves of bugle, so much of borage and of thyme, half a dozen branches of tamarisk and as much sidrake as you may take up between your three fingers, and 50 great raisins of the sun the stones being taken out, and a crust of a manchet and so let it boil softly, till it come to the quantity of a pint, and season it with a little salt, then take up the chicken and the raisins with the herbs and stamp them in a mortar, and strain it with the same broth, and so put it up in a pot, and drink it in the morning and at four of the clock in the afternoon something warm.

Mrs Corlyon, p. 148

Chapter 10

A medicine or syrup to open the pipes to comfort the heart and to expel melancholy

Take a quart of honey, and put it into a wide-mouthed glass, add thereto so many of the flowers of rosemary as you can moisten therein by stirring them well together, then set it in the sun two or three days, and as the honey waxeth thin with the heat of the sun, so stuff it full with the flowers, this do as there ariseth any moisture to cover your flowers, and when your honey being thoroughly melted in the sun in this sort, will contain no more flowers, then being very well stirred together, set it in the sun to distill together, the space of four months, and it will be like a conserve, you must turn your glass oftentimes that all may take the sun alike. And when you have thus done, keep it for your use. And when it is a quarter of a year old, then take thereof every morning, the quantity of a walnut, and you shall find the operation thereof to be very effectual.

Mrs Corlyon, p. 175

Chapter 11

To make a broth for those that be weak with sickness

Take a good capon of two years old, being well fleshed but not very fat, dress him as you would do to boil, leaving the head and the legs at the body. Then fill the belly full of currants, blend with an ounce of mace, and so sew up the belly. You must have a pipkin on the fire with a gallon of water, and when it doeth seethe, put in your capon with the breast downward, and when it is clean skimmed, let it simmer upon a very soft fire the space of two hours, then put thereto a branch of rosemary, two borage roots, being sliced, and a good crust of manchet and so let it boil very leisurely the space of three hours more until the broth be consumed to a quart, or thereabout, but stir not your broth in any wise, for breaking the capon, then season your broth with salt, and a little bruised pepper, and having thus done, take it from the fire, and pour your broth as clean as you can from the capon, into such a thing as you do mean to keep it in, and when it is cold, it will be like a yellow jelly, then you may give it warmed to the party, as you shall see cause, but warm no more thereof, at once, then you do mean to spend at that time, you may bestow your capon at your pleasure.

Mrs Corlyon, pp. 133–134

Chapter 12

A medicine to preserve a breast that is sore from breaking and to assuage any swelling or anguish, whether it come of bruise or otherwise, if it be taken in time

Take the ointment called papillon and anoint the place therewith: take of rosin wax and deer's suet of each of these a like quantity, and one spoonful of the oil of linseed. Boil these together, then take a piece of new lockram, as big as will cover the place, and dip it in the liquor and lay it upon the place somewhat warm. Dress it thus in the day three times, and it will assuage it, but if it does come amongst the salves, and spread it upon the flesh side of tawed sheep's leather, and apply it to the place, till it do all of itself.

Chapter 13

The way how to make rosa solis [for courage and cheer]

Take half a peck of the herb called rosa solis being gathered before the sun do arise, in the latter end of June, or the beginning of July. Pick them and lay them upon a board to dry all a day. Then take a quarter pound of raisins of the sun, the stones being taken out, six dates, and twelve figs. Shred all these together, somewhat small, and put them into a great mouthed glass, then take of licorice, and anise seeds of each one ounce, of cinnamon half an ounce, a spoonful of cloves, three nutmegs, of coriander seeds, and of caraway seeds, of each of these half an ounce. Bruise all these, and put them into your glass, also, then put in your herbs, and two pounds of sugar, of the best, being finely beaten, and put thereto a pottle of good aquavit. Then stir them well together, and when you have thus done, stop your glass very close, then set it in the sun for the space of 7 or 8 weeks, often turning your glass about in the sun, but let it stand where the rain may not come to it, and shake it oftentimes together, and when it hath stood so long, strain it, and put your water up into a double glass, and so keep it for your use, and if you please when you have strained it, you may put thereto, a leaf of gold, and a grain or two of musk.

Chapter 14

To make a seed cake

Take the whites of 8 eggs, beat them very well, then put the yolks to them and beat them very well together, then put to it a pound of sugar, beat and sifted very fine, and beat it for half an hour, then make it a little warm over the fire, and after that put in 3 quarters of a pound of flour, very well dried, a quarter of an ounce of caraway seeds, stir it well together and put it into the pan, it will take 3 quarters of an hour to bake it.

Catharine Cotton's *Recipe Book*

(This recipe was featured in the *Cooking in the Archives* blog by Marissa Nicosia and Alyssa Connell on March 18, 2016.)

Chapter 15

To make an ointment of swallows good for the shrinking of sinews or for a strain

Take of lavender cotton, of hyssop, and of the runnings out of strawberries, of each of these a great handful, chop them small, and stamp them with a pound of fresh butter, that hath neither been washed nor salted, and stamp therewith eight young swallows out of the nest, putting them in by one and one, feathers, guts, and all, and so stamp them until they be very small, then boil altogether upon a soft fire until it do look very green, then strain it, and put it up into a pot, and keep it for your use.

Mrs Corlyon, p. 213

Chapter 16

A medicine for the stone

Take the blood of a goat dried and made into fine powder, put a good quantity thereof into a draft of ale and drink of it.

Mrs Corlyon, p. 89

Chapter 17

A broth to keep the back from slimy causes and from the breeding of the stone

Take a knuckle of veal and a young cock or pullet, lay them in water to soak out all the blood an hour or two, and set them on the fire in a gallon and a half of water, and so fair scum it, then take two ounces of french barley and wash it in a little warm water, and seethe it by itself in two waters until the redness be one, then let the water drain from it, and cast the barley into the broth where the flesh is, then take an ounce of the four great cold seeds and bruise them grossly in a mortar, and put them into the broth and therewith plums of Sebastion, and 40 raisins of the sun, the stones being taken out. Then take half an ounce of asparagus roots the pit being taken out, and as much of kneeholm roots otherwise called butcher's broom, of parsley roots, and fennel roots a like quantity the pit being taken out, of lettuce and purslane of each half a handful, of borage and bugloss leaves and flowers half an ounce. You must let all these seethe together till the flesh be come from the bones and the broth like a thin jelly, then take the clearest of it, and strain it through an hippocras bag or thick strainer till it be clear, and so put it up into an earthen pot, and it will last four days. When you will use it, you must take three or four spoonfuls of this broth and put to it a spoonful and a half of the syrup of marshmallows, and the juice of a lemon and set it on the fire, and heat it, and drink it when it is blood warm. The four great cold seeds are these: cowcumbers, millions, pompions, gourdes. The four lesser cold seeds are these: lettuce, purslane, endive, succory.

Mrs Corlyon, pp. 147–148

Chapter 18

A medicine for such as make water like clear blood

Take a good handful of betony boiled in new milk of a cow that hath not been at bull, and drink it warm every morning and evening.

Mrs Corlyon, p. 242

Chapter 19

To make a syrup cordial good for such as have taken thought

Take half a pint of the juice of borage, as much of the juice of bugloss, the like quantity of the juice of balm, put all these juices together, and seethe them in a skillet, and the green will rise up thick, like a posset curdle, then clear it with the whites of two eggs, well beaten, and scum it clean, put it into a clean basin, and set it upon a chafing dish of coals. Put thereto half a pint of red rose water, with the weight of four pence of dried violet flowers, add the like quantity of dried rosemary flowers, with as much of cowslip flowers being dried, as much of primrose flowers, and likewise of the clove gillyflowers, well dried, with three blades of saffron. Thus let it boil upon the coals until it be consumed to a good pint. Then strain it through a piece of white cotton, and put in a pound of white sugar, and scum it with the white of an egg beaten with red rose water, and boil it to syrup height. When it is almost boiled, take a grain of musk, well mixed with two spoonfuls of rose water, and put it therein, you must take a spoonful thereof at once.

Mrs Corlyon, pp. 172–173

Chapter 20

To make a water good for the passion of the heart and for those that have taken thought and it is to be made only in the month of May

Take four great handfuls of rosemary flowers, buds and all, and of sage, of elecampane roots, being scraped and sliced, and of thyme that is blown, of each of these two good handfuls, and of primrose flowers, and cowslip flowers a platterful, and of violet flowers, bugloss flowers, and borage flowers, the like quantity; of dried red rose leaves two handfuls, and put thereto as much of balm, as there is of all the rest. Stamp all these well together, and put them into a gallon of good claret wine, adding thereto a pound of anise seeds, as much of licorice, four good nutmegs, and half an ounce of cloves, all being beaten small. Stir all these together in your wine, and so let it stand 24 hours, then distill it in a stilletor of glass, or in a common stilletor, then put the water into a glass, and keep it for your use, and use it as you do find occasion. It will remain good three years being well kept and close stopped.

Mrs Corlyon, p. 242

Chapter 21

To make a salve called Gratia Dei

Take half a pound of rosin, so much of sheep's tallow, set them upon the fire, with a quart of fayre water, and when it is melted, put

into it of barrel soap, half a quarter of a pound, then let it boil well
the space of half a quarter of an hour, and strain it into a vessel of cold
water, letting it stand one day and a night, then work it up in rolls and
if you will have the flesh to grow in the wound, boil in it three good
handfuls of alehoof or alehoof chopped and stamped, and boil it till it
looks green. The soap must be put in after all the herbs.

Mrs Corlyon, p. 190

Sources

Bacon, Catherine. *The Receipt Book of Catherine Bacon* [MS], ca. 1680–
1739. Folger Shakespeare Library. Call number V.a.621.

Baumfylde, Mary. *Medicinal and Cookery Recipes of Mary Baumfylde and
Others* [MS], ca. 1626, 1702–1758. Folger Shakespeare Library.
Call number V.a.456.

Corlyon. *A Book of Such Medicines as Have Been Approved by the Speciall
Practize of Mrs Corlyon* [MS], ca. 1606. Folger Shakespeare Library.
Call number V.a.388.

Cotton, Catharine. *Recipe Book* [MS], ca. 1698. Kislak Center for
Special Collections, Rare Books and Manuscripts, University of
Pennsylvania. MS Codex 214.

Doggett, Mary. *Book of Receipts* [MS], ca. 1682. British Library. Add
MS 27466.

ABOUT THE AUTHOR

Jennifer Sherman Roberts holds a PhD in Renaissance literature from the University of Minnesota. She became interested in early modern recipes and recipe books as she researched the medicinal properties of folk cures. She has written about early modern recipes on the academic blog *The Recipes Project*, and she has worked with Oregon Humanities facilitating conversation projects about the historical roots and cultural implications of the recipe genre. She is also a fierce library advocate, occasional knitter, and aspiring mead maker who lives in southern Oregon, where the mountains are tall, the lakes crystal clear, and the beer hoppy. For more information, visit www.jenshermanroberts.com.